DIVERSION

DIVERSION

A PROBATION CASE FILES MYSTERY

CINDY GOYETTE

Author Photo Credit: Jon DEmilio

First edition

ISBN: 979-8-89820-177-7

Cover art by Michael Verdun

This book was professionally typeset on Reedsy.
Find out more at reedsy.com

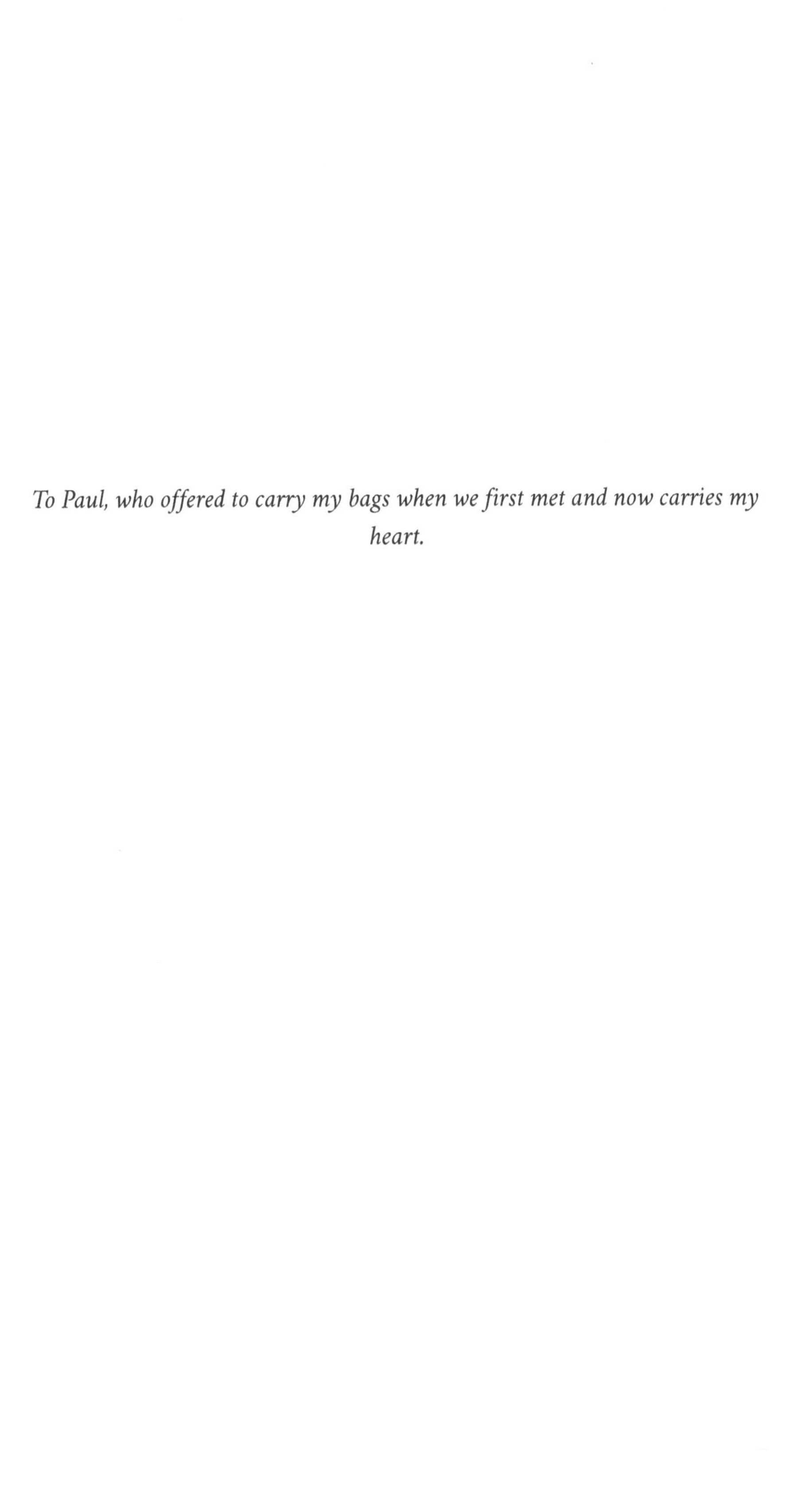

To Paul, who offered to carry my bags when we first met and now carries my heart.

Praise for Diversion

"A breakneck adrenaline rush of wilderness adventure, emotional angst, and high personal stakes. Whether you're a fan of the Probation Case Files Mysteries or jumping in for the first time, Cindy Goyette's *Diversion* is certain to entertain!"—**Tori Eldridge**, bestselling author of *Kaua'I Storm*

"Casey Carson is a hands-on probation officer with a lot on her hands in Cindy Goyette's engrossing novel, *Diversion*: Two men's affections, shepherding troubled teens on a wilderness hike gone wrong, and an escaped killer on the loose closing in. A lot of balls in the air that Goyette handles masterfully, all while torquing up the tension."—**Matt Coyle**, author of the award-winning Rick Cahill crime series

"With nonstop action, continually mounting stakes, and a fearless heroine, Cindy Goyette's *Diversion* doesn't let go and will have you turning its pages well past bedtime—and not regretting it one bit in the morning."—**Audrey Lee**, Edgar and Anthony-nominated author of *The Mechanics of Memory* and *Never to Be Told*

Prologue

The girl held her breath, hoping her pounding heart wouldn't give her away. She'd squeezed herself under her parents' four-poster bed, between totes of out-of-season clothes. It had been her favorite place to hide when she was little…but she was almost full-grown now. A stupid choice. Wouldn't it be the first place they looked?

Fear wouldn't let her chance a move.

The roar in her head made it difficult to hear what was happening in the other room. Still, she listened.

She knew one thing. Her parents were dead. She'd heard their pleas, their screams. Then gunshots.

Silence after that.

She fought back her tears. Swallowed hard. Held her breath.

Now, the killer was rummaging through the house. Looking for something. Looking for her.

Heavy footsteps sounded in the hall and then stopped at the bedroom doorway.

She clamped her hand over her mouth. Tears dripped down her cheeks, gathering at the cleft of her chin before landing soundlessly on the carpeted floor.

Scuffed black boots walked across the room and came to a stop at the foot of the bed. So close, she could reach out and touch them.

She squeezed her eyes shut, unable to face her fate as it unfolded. She was next.

But a cell phone chimed, and the boots turned. The footsteps moved away and toward the door.

She opened her eyes and risked a small breath.

In her hand, she gripped the key her father had passed to her just before he'd told her to hide.

Chapter One

Six months later

I stuffed crackers in my mouth and washed them down with a Diet Coke before leaving my desk and heading for the probation department's training room. It was early morning, and I felt like I had a killer hangover. Strange, because I'd had nothing to drink in the last few days. I'd thought about calling in sick, but I'd never done that before, and I didn't want to ruin my perfect record. Even if no one else was keeping track.

Plus, this training was mandatory. I'd put it off until the last class offering, and I needed to get it done.

Most of the seats in the cramped room were already taken. I didn't have a record of being on time, so I didn't sweat it.

"Casey," my coworker Claire called from across the room. "I saved you a seat."

I dropped into the chair next to her, took another drink, and placed my Big Gulp on the table. "I can't take another day of this," I said, under my breath.

"Sorry to hear that," the trainer said, reaching around me and placing a binder in my lap. "Just for that, you get to go first."

I cringed. "Sorry. Didn't know you were standing there."

"Obviously not." The trainer walked over to the dry-erase board, picked up a marker, and opened the cap with a flourish. I didn't know her well, but she was on the fast track to becoming a supervisor. I also didn't know she hated me until now. "So, Casey, give us your greatest weakness."

Right now, it was my stomach. The leftover burrito I'd eaten for dinner last night must have been spoiled, but that wasn't what she meant. I hated this question. The goal was to name something that you could turn into a strength. Nothing came to mind.

Hands shot up around the room. Apparently, not the case for those around me.

"Impatient," someone yelled.

"Opinionated!"

"Sarcastic!"

"Workaholic!"

The trainer couldn't write fast enough.

"Okay, that's plenty," I said. I loved my job, but clearly had to work on my reputation.

The list was moving into a second column when my work cell vibrated in my pocket. I pulled it out. Betz, my ex-husband. Well, he was more than that, but I'd pumped the brakes on reconciling while I figured some things out. Still, taking his call was a good excuse to escape the room and the assassination of my character, my peers were treating like a game show. "Gotta take this." I got to my feet and hurried from the room. "It's a detective."

"Evasive," someone added to the list before I silenced them by closing the door. I answered as I walked down the hall. "What's up?"

"Sorry to interrupt your day," Betz said. I could picture him rubbing the back of his neck. Didn't matter what he was calling about, most times when we talked, he rubbed his neck, shook his head, and I'm pretty sure his blood pressure rose. And yet, he wanted us to get back together. If we reconciled, he'd probably stroke out at the young age of thirty-five from the stress I caused him. Still, he loved me.

"No problem," I said. "You're saving me from a painful day of training. Please tell me you have something that can get me out of finishing the class."

"You supervise Martin Phillips?"

"I do."

"He's a suspect in a double murder that happened six months ago. Think it's over drug money. We want to take him into custody, but we don't want to spook him since he's armed and dangerous. Think you can trick him into showing himself?"

My adrenaline kicked in, stomach problems vanishing. A double murder was nothing to sneeze at. And if it had happened months ago, before he was on probation, there was nothing I could have done to stop it. Now we had to get my client off the street. "I can text him. Tell him I need to do a field visit, and I need him to be home."

Typically, we didn't warn our clients we were coming. But sometimes, if we had enough failed attempts, we'd set something up. Anyway, Phillips was fairly new on supervision. He didn't know the drill. But he knew we had to do regular home visits, and he was due. He'd probably fall for it.

"That should work," Betz said. "Gear up, and I'll meet you at the employee entrance in ten."

I disconnected the call and took the stairs two at a time to my cubicle. I loved playing with cops. Although I never wanted to be one. Too much blood and guts for me.

Chapter Two

I wasn't armed, not at work at least. Betz had given me a gun to protect myself, but I'd yet to complete the training required to carry one at work. Gearing up meant clamping my pepper spray, radio, and handcuffs to my belt and donning my bulletproof vest.

I hated guns, especially after my mom met her fate at the hands of someone carrying one. And the one time I'd had to shoot someone still caused me nightmares. But recent events—namely Phoenix's notorious Diablo gang wanting me dead—had me rethinking my revulsion. I'd signed up for the training required to carry and was waiting for the date to roll around. In the meantime, Betz had taken me to the range a few times, but I kept the weapon he'd given me locked in a safe at home.

I made it downstairs and to the employee exit door at the rear of the building before Betz's arrival. As an afterthought, I sent my supervisor, Alma, a text. *Had to duck out of training. One of my clients is a murder suspect, and I'm accompanying the police, hoping to take him into custody.*

She'd have questions. Maybe even tell me not to go. I shut my phone off to avoid adding "insubordinate" to my list of shortcomings.

A few minutes later, the Interceptor pulled up. Betz sat in the driver's seat and his frequent partner, Anita Moody, rode shotgun. That meant I needed to cram myself into the backseat. Whoever designed these vehicles had never been arrested. I was only five-six, yet when I sat down in the small space, my knees brushed my earlobes. Unlike the usual occupants, my hands weren't cuffed behind my back. I couldn't imagine how uncomfortable that would be.

"Hey, Casey, good to see you," Moody said.

"You too." I liked Anita. She didn't take any crap, not even from Betz. We used to socialize, but I guess you could say I lost her in the divorce. "A double murder, really? You sure it was Phillips? And that he was the shooter?"

"Security footage from the house across the street shows the suspects leaving the victims' home shortly after gunshots were heard. It was Phillips and another man we've yet to identify. Not sure which one pulled the trigger."

Moody passed her phone through the cage that separated us, and I watched the video. "Yeah, that's him."

"I know," Betz said. "I'm familiar with Phillips. I was involved in the arrest that got him probation."

I vaguely remembered seeing Betz's name in the police report when I'd first received the file.

We stopped at a Circle K store, pulling up next to an identical SUV. Two cops occupied the vehicle. Betz rolled down his window. "He home?"

The driver didn't introduce himself, and I didn't recognize him. Most of the cops I dealt with were cool, but some failed to recognize our status as sworn officers, although our authority applied only to probationers. They often asked us to help connect them with our clients, but considered us a step lower than them on the law enforcement ladder. "We've had eyes on his duplex. No activity for hours. Don't think so," the nameless cop said.

I handed Moody her phone back. "Want me to text him? Tell him I'm coming by?"

"Do it," Betz said.

I pulled up Phillip's number and wrote a quick message, opting for a casual tone so he wouldn't know we were on to him. *Hey, Martin, Casey, your PO, here. I'm in the field and need to verify your address. You home?*

We waited. Moody got out to use the store restroom and came back with a tray of coffees and a can of Diet Coke. She pushed one through the cage to me. I was touched by her remembering my addiction.

Because it was a police car, I couldn't open the door to let myself out, and I struggled to get comfortable. "You okay back there?" Betz asked.

"I'm a sardine."

He laughed, got out, and opened the door. I unfolded myself, slid off the seat, and stretched. Betz met me at the hood of the car while we waited for Phillips to respond. "Thanks for loaning me the backpack for my trip," I said. "It'll come in handy."

He took a sip of coffee. "You're really heading to the mountains? Don't you have better things to do with your vacation time than take on a temp job?"

I sighed. "I know. I'd rather go to the beach, but I could use the money. Mostly, I want to support Hope." Hope was my cousin. She'd recently lost her job as a PO after she made some poor decisions that earned her a criminal record. After completing the exams to become a certified counselor, her new gig was supposed to be her path back to normal.

It was a diversion program for teenagers. Supposed to show kids there are natural highs better than what drugs or alcohol could provide, and teach them to have fun in more wholesome ways.

The program featured activities like whitewater rafting, rock climbing, and the wilderness adventure I'd been recruited for. The company hired off-duty POs to keep the delinquents in line.

"You really need the money that badly?" Betz asked. "You don't even like kids."

"Who says?" I was quick to answer. But neither Hope nor I were used to dealing with troubled teens. They were a completely different species from the adults we supervised as POs.

Betz laughed. "If you say so. When do you leave?"

"Tomorrow." It was just ten days. And maybe some fresh air would clear my head. There was a lot going on in there. Mostly Betz's proposal that we get back together, and my pull toward Marcus, Betz's polar opposite. "Anyway, the sale of my house has gone through, and I've been staying with my dad and his girlfriend. I can't take much more of that. With this side job, I'll have enough for a down payment so I can get my own place."

"I'm glad you haven't been staying there. Diablo has that address."

And in that house, I startled every time I heard a noise, thinking they had come for me. "Yeah, I need to make their finding me as difficult as possible."

My phone buzzed in my hand. I glanced down at the text from Phillips. *Can't it wait?*

I rolled my eyes. I used to try not to do that, but what was the use? My eyes had a mind of their own. *We have contact standards. Your home visit's overdue. I'd appreciate it if I could get it done. Shouldn't take more than a few minutes.*

I waited a beat.

Okay, I'll be home in ten.

"He took the bait," I said to Betz. "We have ten minutes."

Betz took a last drink from his cup and tossed it in the trash. Then he tapped his palms on the hoods of both cars, making the occupants jump. "Showtime," he said.

Unmarked cars were surveilling each end of Phillip's street. We waited around the corner. My heart pounded in anticipation, even though I knew my role from here on out was as a bystander. I said a silent prayer that nothing would go wrong.

A voice came over the radio. "He just turned onto the street."

Betz put the Interceptor into drive and punched the gas.

Phillips drove a dented white Buick. When he pulled into his driveway, two police SUVs drove into the front yard, boxing him in. The unmarked cars stopped on the street behind us. Moody and Betz bailed from the vehicle, rushing the driver's side of the Buick before Phillips could finish exiting the car.

"On your knees!" Betz shouted, grabbing Phillips by the arm and tossing him onto the driveway.

The other cops cleared Phillip's car while, in a fluid movement, Betz twisted his detainee's arm behind his back. But Phillips didn't want to go to jail. With his free hand, he took a swing at Betz, who dodged the punch. Phillips broke free. He had only gotten two steps away before cops swarmed him, taking him to the ground. It was hard to follow what came next in the confusion, but somehow Betz secured him with handcuffs.

Dragging the man to his feet, Betz pulled a handgun from the waistband of Phillips' jeans and handed it to Moody.

I silently ticked off the probation violations I'd allege. Failing to obey all laws and weapons possession for starters. Those should hold him in custody even if the new charges didn't stick.

Chapter Three

Betz dropped me back at the office. After stepping out of the SUV, he stood with me outside the employee entrance. Moody remained in the front seat, listening, making conversation awkward. Betz and I hadn't spoken often since I'd asked for time to consider what path our relationship would take. Friends, sure. That was a given. Could it be more than that?

He ran a hand through his hair, and I felt responsible for the awkward space between us.

"Teenagers," Betz said, like I'd be handling rabid bats.

"It will be fine," I said.

"You have bear spray?"

"Does that work on juvenile delinquents?"

"I mean, can you protect yourself?" he said with a shake of his head.

"Got an assault rifle, a couple of grenades."

He laughed. "Smartass. You're not used to roughing it."

"I hang out in the hood almost every day. If that's not roughing it, I don't know what is."

"Anyway," he said. "Be safe. How about dinner when you get back?"

Since I hoped to come to a decision on this trip, we'd definitely have something to talk about. "Sounds good."

He stepped forward and gave me a stiff hug. We both had vests on, and it was like two turtles embracing.

Turning my back on him, I entered the building.

* * *

Preparing to go on vacation always made me question whether it was worth it. Claire had agreed to cover my caseload. Although I had nothing scheduled, stuff always came up, and I'd no doubt come back to a mountain of work.

I contacted the jail and placed a hold on Martin Phillips for probation violations. I hoped the report to the court could wait until I returned. Just in case, I shared my intention to make a revocation recommendation with Claire and my supervisor.

After making sure I'd marked myself "out of office" everywhere required, it was almost eight o'clock.

When I pulled into my dad's driveway, Marcus waited at the curb. Leaning against his motorcycle, he looked lean and healthy. After a head injury, he'd fought his way back to recovery, earning him my respect. It was hard not to be taken in by his beauty. Something he downplayed by letting his hair and stubble grow scruffy. He wore scuffed boots and tattered, worn jeans. He didn't seem to realize it only made him more appealing to me.

"Hey, Sunshine," he said as I got out of my Wrangler.

"Hi," I said.

Draping an arm over my shoulder, he steered me to a bench on the front porch. "Wanted to see you before you left town."

"It's only ten days," I said. But I was happy to see him. He, like Betz, had been mostly keeping his distance while I figured things out. We'd exchanged occasional texts, but I hadn't laid eyes on him in almost a month. I'd let him know that I'd drop everything if he needed me to nurse him back to health after what Diablo did to him, but he never took me up on it. He'd told me to do what I had to do and take the time I needed to decide if we could be more than friends. Looking at him now, I realized I wouldn't have been able to clear my head if he had been around every day. It would be like placing a stiff drink in front of an alcoholic and asking them not to take a sip. I didn't have that kind of willpower. With Marcus, it was all or nothing.

Who knows what I would have done if my dad and his girlfriend, Millie, weren't on the other side of the door. But they were, so I restrained myself.

"Flagstaff," he said. "I looked it up. Lots of trees."

I laughed. "The mountains. We'll hike to camp. Cut off from the world for ten days."

"No Diet Coke?"

"It's not jail. I can bring necessities."

"But you have to carry it."

I shrugged. "Worth it."

"Dinner when you get back?"

The image of me, Marcus, and Betz having dinner together flashed through my mind. It was almost comical. "Sure thing."

I could hear Felony, my cocker spaniel-mix, whining at the door.

Marcus cocked his head. "Someone knows you're out here."

"He's losing his mind. And I have to pack."

"I'll let you get to it," he said. He placed his hand on my knee and gave it a squeeze. "Don't do anything too crazy in the wild."

He leaned over and kissed me. His lips were soft against mine. He pulled away sooner than I wanted him to. Not that I blamed him. I was sending mixed signals.

"See you, sunshine," he said. And then he walked away.

Chapter Four

The next morning came too soon.

I'd been in freak-out mode for hours.

Please tell me this isn't happening...

Not here. Not in a state park bathroom. A bare-bones facility with no mirrors and metal toilet seats that froze your butt when you sat down. Yet, here I was, peeing on a stick in the mountains just outside of Flagstaff.

I'd woken in a cold sweat that morning as it hit me. It wasn't a bad burrito. Not a hangover. My period was weeks late. I was on birth control, sure. I wasn't totally irresponsible. I'd been on the pill since I was seventeen. But everyone knew there was a one-in-a-bazillion chance it wouldn't work. Leave it to me to be an outlier.

My father had promised to drive Hope and me to the bus that would take us to Flagstaff. I'd asked him to take a quick detour and stop at a pharmacy. I ran inside while they waited in the car, claiming I needed to buy a last-minute item, keeping from them that that item was a pregnancy test.

Afterward, my dad had dropped me, Hope, and Felony at the bus, where we'd catch the ride that brought us and the other campers to the start of the trail.

This wasn't how I'd pictured this moment in my life. Not that I'd really thought about it. Because…. Hello? I wasn't ready. Maybe someday in the future. But not now. Not when everything in my life was uncertain.

I'd assumed if this time ever came, it would be because I'd planned it. It would be something I desperately wanted.

But this wasn't the time or place to lose my shit. Nine people and a dog were outside waiting for me. Waiting to get this show on the road.

The instructions on the box said it would take three minutes for the results to show.

It had taken me ten just to get the nerve to open the packaging.

My travel companions probably wondered what was taking me so long.

Let them picture the worst.

I wasn't ready for this. Could I even handle the results? I didn't want the information to be a reason to choose between Marcus and Betz. Or to decide I was better off alone. Could I even pull myself together and start the hike to camp knowing?

The result wouldn't change if I waited. I could check later.

Stuffing the stick in the side pocket of my hiking pants, I rinsed my hands under a trickle of cold water. I would have checked my reflection and made sure I had my game face on, but again, no mirrors.

Smoothing my hair, I said a silent prayer and stepped out into the parking lot, forcing myself to face the day.

* * *

Outside, the bus idled—the driver obviously eager to leave us behind and get back to his life. Felony wagged his tail the moment he saw me. Hope held his leash, which went taut as he tugged his way toward me like I'd just returned from seven weeks at sea. His wiggle butt and excited yip almost quashed my sour mood. But I was no quitter.

I retrieved the enormous backpack Betz had loaned me and hefted it onto my shoulders. It was full of necessities, including a twelve-pack of Diet Coke and the container of chocolate chip cookies my sister Kate had lovingly baked for me. She'd strongly suggested I share them. We'd see about that.

Hope looked like a model for REI. Dressed in high-end hiking clothes and brand-new boots that matched her pack, she checked her watch. Nervous energy buzzed off her. I needed to keep it together for her sake. She saw a path forward for the first time since her legal troubles began.

I tried to keep my mind off the test I'd just taken. And the two men vying for my affection. After last night's kiss, I couldn't stop myself from thinking about Marcus. My nerves tingled at the memory. He had a way about him that made my heart flutter, and my common sense dissolve. Thus, the stick in my pocket.

We'd only had sex once, but I thought about it every day. And Betz and me? Well, we hadn't slept together in years. But we had a history. No one knew me like he did.

I hoped a little time away from them might give me the opportunity to put things into perspective.

Not that Betz had given me the space I'd asked for. Arresting murderers was one thing. But the countless texts he had sent me since they took Phillips into custody had nothing to do with the arrest. He warned me of a pending heat wave, claiming it would trick snakes, bears, and other creepy critters out of hibernation. Not comforting. He knew how I felt about snakes.

I didn't mind the outdoors. Especially if it was on the other side of a sliding glass door and I had access to a bathroom, a comfy bed, and a well-stocked fridge. I didn't dislike nature; Felony and I ran outside most mornings.

But, as Kate had so kindly pointed out, my runs were in a suburban neighborhood. The scariest thing I might encounter was a bunch of middle schoolers waiting for the bus.

Not that they didn't give me pause—kids could be scary—but camping with juvenile delinquents was a whole other level.

And the five kids on this trip had more issues than the run-of-the-mill teen. I knew. I'd read their files. As a PO, I was used to working with addicts. But my clients were adults. Kids were a lot more complicated.

I was tired of complicated.

But I'd committed. I was going on this trek through the woods. A nine-mile hike, Grizzly, our bear-sized naturalist, had announced. Not to worry. He knew these woods like the back of his sun-weathered hand. He had the satellite radio and First Aid Kit, not to mention the knowledge about all things wilderness that were supposed to keep us safe. And probably the bear spray Betz had asked me about.

Hope, Grizzly (okay, his name was Rick Santos, but that didn't work for me), and I weren't the only staff. Gary, an obnoxious PO, and Izzy, a purple-haired, nose-ring-wearing counselor, were also along. I'd met Izzy for the first time when she'd boarded the bus and hadn't yet formed an opinion of her. Five kids completed the group. Even-steven.

Rico, with slouched shoulders and a look that said he'd punch you in the face and steal your lunch money, had come with a warning label on his file: anger management issues. Nothing to worry about, the notes said. Just a recommendation to watch him closely and redirect him before he blew his cool. I'd felt for the kid when his ride had dropped him off that morning. A banged-up hatchback barely stopped as someone dumped Rico on the side of the road like an unwanted puppy. After tossing out his backpack, the car sped away. No wonder the kid had issues.

If Gary had had the final say, he would have left Rico behind after a search of his bag turned up contraband. Gary had held up a can of shaving cream like a prize, suspicious because the kid had a face as smooth as a nectarine. Unscrewing the false base, Gary revealed a secret compartment.

"Not very imaginative," he said with a smirk. "These false-bottom containers have been around for a while."

Rico shrugged. "Worth a try."

With a tap of the canister, a handful of joints fell into Gary's hand. "Worth some jail time," he shot back. "Take a seat."

It took a few minutes to convince Gary not to turn the ruffian over to the police. With Hope's backing, he finally relented. If we started kicking kids out of the program before we even got started, it wouldn't look good. We knew going in that we weren't working with angels, and the mission of the program was to find success through behavior change. That would take work, and Gary should have known that. The slogan was embroidered on his ball cap, for goodness' sakes. "Fine," he'd relented. "But Rico is your problem."

Fucking great.

* * *

The bus made a giant whooshing noise when it pulled away and disappeared out of the parking lot.

This was really happening.

"The trail starts here." Grizzly pointed to a small path that disappeared into a lush forest. "Nine miles, which should take up a good chunk of the day. The hike is rated as moderate, so nothing we can't handle. There are some steep parts, though. We'll stop for breaks as needed. I expect everyone to stick together. And watch out for wildlife. A mountain lion attacked a hiker a few days ago."

Not on Betz's list of things that might kill me. Probably what the waiver the agency had us sign was about. Thinking it was a formality, I'd signed the form without reading it. Was it too late to call the bus back?

I glanced down at Felony. He cocked his head, obviously worried, too.

We started off single file. Grizzly, then Gary, followed by Izzy, and behind them the five kids, Rico, Hana, the twins, Tristen, and Mika, with the tall, stone-faced Yuki in front of Hope and me. Footsteps and distant bird noises were all I could hear over my ragged breathing. My regular runs left me in decent shape, but I instantly felt fatigued, and I wondered again if I was coming down with something. My mind took a hard turn to the stick in my pocket. Would that something cause me to gain thirty pounds and not make an appearance until next summer? Ugh.

Swallowed by trees, we came upon an incline, making it even more difficult to breathe. But I wasn't about to admit that to anyone. It would ruin my street cred.

Hope was the first to cave. "Holey Moley," she said, leaning against a tree. "I'm out of shape."

"It's the altitude," Grizzly said from behind us. "You should adjust in a day or two."

"A day or two?" I parroted. "You mean after we've reached our destination?"

Grizzly chuckled. He seemed unfazed by it. I wanted to smack him, but I didn't have the stamina. Plus, I was supposed to be a role model for the kids.

Hana, the youngest of the group at fifteen, brought an inhaler out of her pocket and took a hit. She looked sweet in pigtails and a white puffy vest. But I knew from her file she had a habit of stealing benzos from her foster parents' medicine cabinet. If they hid them from her, she'd hit the bathrooms of her friends' parents. It surprised me how many households had narcotics lying around. It had never occurred to me when I was a teen to raid people's medication stash. I was no angel. As a teen, my friends and I drank from our parents' liquor cabinets, but I never felt the urge to take pills.

I tried to keep in mind that these kids had parents. They were once somebody's baby. Their moms and dads probably held high hopes and dreams for their little bundles of joy when they agonized over picking out a name, never imagining their kids would become involved in the criminal justice system. But as I got a glimpse of some of the parents, I remembered the apple rarely falls far from the tree.

Everyone seemed exhausted from the climb, and we moved slowly, stopping every fifty yards or so to catch our breath. At this rate, we'd be lucky to make it by nightfall. With everyone so breathless, conversation wasn't an option, which was fine by me.

The stick in my pocket felt like it weighed twenty pounds. Like a torn fingernail that drives you nuts until you can get your hands on some clippers, I couldn't stop thinking about it. I should have waited until I got back home to take the test. But I knew myself. I needed to be able to look when I was ready.

I tried to focus on positive things, like the surrounding wilderness. But with the dense forest, I could only see a wall of green and Hope's backpack as she moved a few feet in front of me. Thick underbrush flanking both sides of the narrow path obscured whatever beauty might lie beyond the trees.

And I couldn't shake the feeling that something was off. I wasn't sure if it was an unseen foe waiting in the bushes or someone in the group. But my gut flashed a warning sign.

Above us, the sky was cloudless, the morning sun already unrelenting as it beat down through the treetops. When we finally arrived at a clearing, we stopped, and I shed my hoodie, tying it around my waist. Most of the others peeled off layers as well.

After squirting water into Felony's mouth, I checked my watch, expecting we'd at least traveled two miles. But it showed we'd only hiked half a mile. I tapped the device. "This damn thing isn't working."

Grizzly shrugged. "Guess you didn't train for this."

I stuck my tongue out at him, and Hana laughed. It was the first emotion I'd seen from her.

Hope collapsed onto a rock and gulped water from her hydration pack. "Casey runs all the time. I'm the one who's gonna die."

Grizzly snapped photos, even though everyone looked miserable. They probably wouldn't make it into the agency brochure.

I sipped water, reminding myself to keep some in reserve so I had enough to sustain me and Felony throughout the day. As my heart rate returned to normal, I took in our surroundings. Patches of pine trees flanked hillsides between some bare spots where logging had altered the landscape. It was breathtaking, although the word seemed to fit in more ways than one.

The kids didn't need as much time to recover. In a flash, they went from dragging their feet to playful.

My thirty-one years felt like ninety.

Rico kicked a rock, and it ricocheted off Yuki Saito's shin. Yuki was tall and reedy, with a little fuzz on his angular face. He was on probation for his part in a shoplifting ring. He yelped when the rock hit him, then puffed out his chest and shoved Rico a few feet back.

The joyful mood evaporated as quickly as it had started. Rico went red-faced and tucked his fists into tight balls, which he banged against his thighs. Even from ten feet away, his pupils looked like giant saucers.

Here we go.

We should have let him keep the weed to mellow him out.

Yuki laughed at Rico's posturing. "You ain't got the guts."

I pushed to my feet, ignoring my screaming quads. "Hey, Rico, come here."

He glared at me. Didn't budge.

"Yeah, Rico," Yuki mocked. "Go cry to the lady."

Lady?

Rico geared up and took a swing at Yuki, who sidestepped the attack. As Rico reloaded, I reached out and wrapped my arms around his bicep, surprised how strong the little guy was. But my weight pulled down his arm before his second attempt to connect his fist to Yuki's jaw.

"Stop," I yelled, still hanging on. "Do you really want to wash out before we even get started?"

Rico shook me off and stalked away. I turned to Yuki. "Pull another stunt like that, and I'll escort you back to the parking lot myself. Your mom can come and get you, and you can explain to your PO why you washed out of the program."

He hung his head. "Yes, Ma'am."

Lady? Ma'am? I felt a midlife crisis coming on.

I watched him storm off in the opposite direction of Rico. I'd have to keep an eye on them. I hoped that little scuffle wasn't a bad omen of things to come.

Gary walked toward me, securing his backpack onto his shoulders.

"Thanks for the help," I said. Maybe my coworkers were right about the sarcasm thing.

Gary snorted. "You should have let me leave Rico behind when I found the weed."

It would have looked bad after my lecture to get into it with Gary, as tempting as it was, so I swallowed my anger. Adulting sucked.

"Ready?" Grizzly called out.

Grunts and moans filled the air. With the enthusiasm of a group of sloths, we were once again underway. Somehow, I got last place in the single-file hiker progression again. I took nervous glances over my shoulder, thinking I'd be easy pickings for the rogue mountain lion who'd attacked a hiker.

The sensation that someone watched us from the thicket forced a chill down my spine. But when I stared into the brush, I found no one.

I shortened Felony's leash and continued on. Another steep incline and I was too tired to care.

Chapter Five

After what felt like an eternity, we stopped for lunch. Grizzly knew the trails and led us through twists and switchbacks, pushing us until we reached the perfect spot for a break. We'd endured miles of thick woods before coming to the clearing perched on a ridge. A sheer drop-off seemed a mile high and gave an awe-inspiring view of the valley below. Nothing but a sea of treetops. If you looked carefully, you could spot the trail snaking through the forest that had taken us most of the day to climb. I marveled at how far we'd come and at the fact that all of us were still on our feet.

It was hard not to feel insignificant so high up and far away from civilization. There were no signs that roads, houses, or even people outside of our group existed.

World War three could have broken out, and we wouldn't have known.

The remoteness of the location both strangled me with fear and exhilarated me. We were on our own. Problems back home seemed insignificant. Except for the secret I carried in my pocket, nothing seemed important. I still hadn't gathered the nerve to check the results.

I tried not to dwell on that and forced myself to remain in the moment.

Finding a spot with a view, yet far enough back that I didn't feel like I was about to plummet to my death, I dropped my pack to the ground. I pushed gruesome thoughts about how easy it would be to commit murder in a place like this and tried to look at nature's wonders like a normal person, and not from the jaded perspective of someone in law enforcement.

With a tap of my palm to my thigh, I coaxed Felony to lie down on the flat rock before I settled next to him. My back was to the other hikers, so I could drink in the view. Soaking in our surroundings, I was suddenly grateful I'd come. The rugged beauty, the bond with nature, had been missing from my life. It was easy to remain on the tiny speck of earth one inhabited, and I'd been guilty of that. I made a silent promise to broaden my horizons.

In my peripheral vision, I caught the twins, Mika and Tristen Lowe, settling on a rock several feet away. They were cute kids with decent parents who had paid out of pocket for this adventure, in contrast to the other kids who'd been court-ordered into subsidized treatment. Their records were unblemished, but their parents had found a little marijuana in the house and went into full panic mode. Sending them on this trip seemed like an overreaction. If it were up to me, I'd have told them to keep their money. I knew from the trainings I'd attended that putting low-risk offenders with high-risk ones wasn't a smart move. One would hope the good ones would rub off on the bad, but it mostly happened the other way around.

As usual, no one had asked for my opinion.

Someone settling on the rock beside me shattered my solitude. Felony was the first to say hello. He was an attention seeker, for sure. I broke my gaze from the view and turned to face Hana, who sat cross-legged by my side. Pink knees peeked out from beneath frayed jeans. "Hey," I said.

She absently fluffed Felony's ears as he snuggled against her. "It's amazing," she said, taking in the view. "I've only seen this in the movies."

I was ashamed to admit that being this deep in the woods was my first experience, too. The trail was only a three-hour drive from Phoenix. It should have been in my exercise rotation. Maybe something Betz and I could do on a Saturday. Or Marcus…

"I feel so safe here," she said. "Like no one can find me."

Heavy words for someone so young. "Is someone looking for you?"

She shrugged. "Could be. Gives me nightmares."

A jealous ex? A stalker? "Who?"

Hana toyed with the tear in her jeans, her gaze fixed on the horizon. "Don't really want to talk about it."

Guess it was all perspective. I found the distance from civilization exhilarating, if not overwhelming. Yet, it was comforting to her. What had made her feel that way? I feared mountain lions, bears, and snakes. But animals killed for survival, not because they were evil. Not like the Diablo gang members and their never-ending quest for revenge. Hana was right. Humans were more frightening.

"Well," I said. "No one will find you here. If Grizzly doesn't kill us by making us hike a thousand miles, we should be perfectly safe."

She laughed. "You called him Grizzly."

I held a finger to my lips. "Oops. I have a habit of making up names for people. Let it be our little secret."

She gave me the side-eye. "Do you have a name for me?"

Bambi came to mind. She was young and timid, like a doe. And her eyes seemed too large for her head. Baby animal or cartoon-like. But I wouldn't share that with her. "Just Hana. Your name suits you just fine."

"I'm named after my grandma."

"That's special. A tribute to her."

"Not that I remember her much."

"Whether or not you're aware of it, she's being honored every time someone says your name."

We sat with that for a moment, and I thought about naming my child, if I was having one. If I could honor my mother… I pushed the thought away. Best to stay in the moment.

Hana took out a plastic container that held a peanut butter sandwich and an apple. I almost drooled. Felony actually did. Hana tore off a piece of crust and passed it to him. All I'd packed were a few granola bars and Kate's cookies. And kibble. The kid's foster mom took better care of Hana than I did of myself. I'd make a lousy mom.

With my phone, I snapped photos of the scenery.

Switching my cell off airplane mode, I checked for service, surprised to see I had one bar. Enough for two text messages to slip through before the bar disappeared. I jumped to my feet and held my phone over my head, searching, but I'd lost service.

The first message was from Marcus. *Enjoy your trip with the hoodlums.*

Give Felony a belly rub for me and stay safe.

I smiled at the thought of him. I felt Hana's eyes on me, and my face flushed red, as if she could read my private thoughts.

The next message was from Betz. *Found this article. Thought you should read it.* Attached was a link with advice on how to react to a bear attack, but without service, I couldn't open it.

Like being mauled to death wasn't already in my head. Betz always looked out for me. I was appreciative and annoyed at the same time. Rolling my eyes, I shut my phone off and stuffed it in my pocket.

Standing on a rock, Grizzly clapped his hands and commanded our attention. "Only a few miles to go. Let's get going so we arrive before nightfall."

I looked skyward. Clouds had rolled in, settling like a fluffy blanket over the forest and giving us a welcome break from the unrelenting sun. Unfortunately, it also trapped the humidity, and the air felt too thick to breathe in. My feet ached, and I looked forward to finishing the trip and kicking off my boots. But we had to carry on, as we still had a few more hours of hiking ahead of us. My quads protested as I followed the procession, picking up the trail.

Piece of cake, I told myself. Only a few more miles. But I wasn't that stupid.

The wind had picked up, and when we moved deeper into the shaded trail, the temperature seemed to drop several degrees. I put my hoodie back on, zipped it up, and followed the group further into the woods.

Chapter Six

Betz

Betz had a standing breakfast date with his sister, Jasmine. Serving as his lieutenant wasn't that different from being his sister. She was always in charge. Several years older than him, she'd stepped in when their mother was deep in her addiction, which was more often than not. Although they had different fathers, both men were cut from the same cloth and treated jail like it had a revolving door. An aversion to that lifestyle had led them both to become law enforcement officers.

When Jasmine had moved out of the home she'd shared with her girlfriend, Betz had invited her to stay in his guestroom. It was supposed to be a temporary arrangement, but she'd gotten comfortable. Too comfortable.

He had to wonder if she was part of the reason Casey held him at bay. Jasmine was overprotective, and she'd long ago decided that Casey was a heartbreaker. True. But it took two to tango, and he wasn't blameless. If only he could convince his sister of that.

But Casey felt her disdain and avoided her whenever possible.

Dressed in a sharp navy suit with a pale-yellow blouse, Jasmine strutted across the restaurant, confidence wafting off of her like too-strong perfume. At the table, she slid into the seat across from him.

"I've been on the phone with the Sheriff's office all morning," she said.

Betz took a bite of eggs. He'd ordered the special for himself and a bowl of steel-cut oatmeal for Jasmine. She was a health nut. Another reason he wanted her to move out. She stocked the kitchen with low-carb food and made him feel guilty if he ate a cookie.

"Yeah," he said. "What's going on?"

"Actually, it's about one of your cases."

Betz dropped his fork on his plate, and it made a clattering sound that had people at other tables looking up from their phones. "Which one?"

"Martin Phillips."

Betz brushed his napkin over his mouth, wadded it up, and threw it on his plate. "Please tell me someone tracked down his accomplice."

Jasmine blew on the cereal on her spoon even though, since she was late, it couldn't be hot. "I wish. It's not good news. He escaped."

"From jail?" Of course, it was from jail. But he couldn't wrap his mind around it.

"Happened when they were transferring him from court back to jail. They're still looking into what went wrong."

Betz pulled a twenty from his wallet and threw it on the table. "On it," he said. "Talk to you later."

And he headed toward the door.

Chapter Seven

"I don't know, but I've been told," Grizzly bellowed Marine-like as we trudged single file along a path that was only about a foot and a half wide.

"Hike the trail or go to jail," Gary sang out with a hearty laugh.

Izzy took a turn. "Up we go, no time to rest."

"Hiking these hills is quite the test," Grizzly finished.

He started the chant over, and even the twins chimed in. It lifted the somber mood, and I almost forgot how uncomfortable I was.

But then Yuki tripped, stumbling into Rico, who tumbled against Izzy. All three went down like scattered marbles. Everyone else stopped and seemed to hold a collective breath. Rico jumped to his feet and danced like a boxer while Yuki stood up slowly, like a vampire exiting his coffin. He towered over Rico, but that didn't stop the boy from shoving Yuki in the chest. "You did that on purpose."

Yuki threw his pack on the ground, cracked his neck, and pushed Rico back a few steps. "Did not, dumbass."

I caught Hope's eye as I rushed forward, ready to referee once again. But Grizzly beat me to it, dropping his backpack as he approached the two boys. "Take a breath," he ordered.

"Screw you." Rico was red-faced, anger steaming off him. He looked around, paced, then leaned down and picked a discarded backpack off the ground. Hoisting it over his head, he gave a manic laugh, then heaved it off the cliff.

We all watched it bounce off jagged rocks before it rolled the rest of the way down the mountain, eventually splashing into the fast-moving river below us.

"Brilliant," Yuki mocked.

Grizzly's hands went to his head, and he scrunched fistfuls of hair while side-stepping along the cliff, following the bobbing backpack on its journey down the river.

For a moment, I thought he was going to throw Rico in after it. Rico must have had the same thought, because he took several steps back, ducking out of reach.

I looked back to the river, spying the pack just in time to see the water rush it around a bend and out of sight.

"Now you've done it, you self-centered brat," Grizzly growled. Spittle flew out of his mouth like a rabid dog. "Our satellite phones were in there. Not to mention all of my supplies."

The flush drained from Rico's face, leaving it paper white. "Sorry. I thought it was Yuki's pack."

"You mean," Hope said. "We have no way of contacting anyone? To let them know we've arrived safely? Or to get help if we need it?"

Gary held up both hands. "Everyone, calm down. The newer cell phones have satellite capabilities. Unfortunately, mine doesn't. But someone must have a newer phone."

"How new?" Hope asked.

"Most models that came out in the last few years have the capability," Gary said.

Everyone pulled out their phones and shook their heads. No one in this group was flush with cash. Most of the kids' tuitions were subsidized. The rest of us needed the money or we wouldn't be here working a shit job.

"I do," Yuki said. "Mine's brand new. But it's not charged."

And probably stolen.

Grizzly wiped his hands on his pants and faked a punch Rico's way. Rico startled and took refuge behind a tree.

With a shuddering sigh, Grizzly struggled to compose himself. "So, no way to communicate with anyone, which we're supposed to do. We have to turn back."

Izzy glanced about nervously. "But it's almost dark. We can't hike another nine miles. Not at night."

Grizzly took a moment, walking in a tight circle and mumbling to himself.

"Good job, asshole," Yuki prodded Rico.

"Fuck you," Rico shot back from his hiding place. "If you hadn't knocked me down, this wouldn't have happened."

"Stop it," I said. "Everyone, just stop. We have no choice but to continue to camp. We can head back in the morning."

There were grumbles all around, but we started moving again. Everyone seemed to be lost in their own thoughts. I fought the urge to make both Rico and Yuki do a high dive to retrieve our only means of communication.

I was supposed to be the mature one.

Chapter Eight

The trail twisted deeper into the forest and then along a ridge, and I wondered if the promise of reaching camp in a day was a cruel joke. My watch had died a while ago, and I had no idea how close we were to the nine miles we'd been told it would take to reach our destination. I could have asked someone else, but figured I was probably better off not knowing.

Just as I was about to whine about it, we entered a clearing, and the camp came into view. The AI-generated brochure I'd seen when signing the contract bore a vague resemblance to the shabby camp before us. The layout was familiar, though, as I'd seen a map on the company website.

There were two cabins, one for men and one for women. Two outhouses stood on the perimeter of the camp. I was happy to see them as it was better than peeing in the bushes as we'd done on the way up the mountain. But it wasn't the spa-like bathroom I longed for. I wouldn't be getting up in the middle of the night to use them, that was for sure. I knew the last building housed a kitchen and a small dining hall.

"Anybody got service?" Gary asked, checking his phone.

We all tried our cells and shook our heads.

My stomach growled, thinking of Kate's cookies in my bag. The granola bar I'd eaten earlier had left me hours ago.

Thick woods encircled the camp, casting shadows. Foreboding in the fading light. Anyone or anything could watch us from the foliage, and we'd never see them. Too exhausted to worry about it, I dropped my pack on a splintered picnic table and stretched, then retrieved my first Diet Coke of the day. A record for me.

Popping the cookie container open, I laid it on the table for whoever wanted one. The treat drew my hiking mates in like bees to a lavender bush. Thank you, Kate.

Quiet while we ate, I snagged two before only cookie dust remained at the bottom of the container. Feeling slightly better, I wandered to the women's cabin. Squinting in the fading light, I saw six single cots lined up like I'd seen in hurricane evacuation shelters on TV. Each bed had a rolled-up sleeping bag at its foot. No pillows.

The damp cold and the smell of mildew had me looking forward to the hike back down the mountain. Was one night long enough for mold poisoning to set in? It was dusk; we weren't going anywhere tonight. I needed to make the best of it.

My feet wept. I hobbled over to the farthest bed and dropped my pack onto it. Sitting down, I untied my boots and eased them off. They were so tight I wondered if I'd ever get them back on.

Wiggling my toes, I tried to get the blood flowing. My feet expanded like mattress toppers set free from shrink wrap.

One by one, the others came in behind me. Hana took the bed next to mine, Hope the next one, then Mika, with Izzy occupying the one closest to the door. The girls had yet to say a word to each other.

Silently, we made up our beds. Afraid a snake had sought the warmth of my cover, I shook out my sleeping bag before laying it on the cot. No one seemed to have the energy to form a sentence.

Grizzly stuck his head through the door. "Hey, ladies, dinner's ready. We got a fire going. Come join us."

I glanced at my boots, which now seemed two sizes too small. Luckily, I'd crammed a pair of running shoes into my bag at the last minute. I slipped them on, leaving the laces undone and fluffing the tongue so I had more room. Gingerly, I made my way across the uneven ground covered with stones and sticks to the campfire. Tree stumps positioned around the blaze served as benches. I placed a bowl of kibble and another of water for Felony next to one stump and then accepted the bowl of beef stew Gary passed me before taking a seat next to Hope.

"This is awful," she whispered, grimacing.

I took a tentative bite. It obviously came from a can, but as a single woman and not much of a cook, I was used to worse. And the cookies I'd devoured earlier had done little to fill the hole in my stomach. I finished the meal in minutes and chased it with the rest of my Diet Coke.

Hope stared at me in disbelief and offered me her bowl. "You want mine?"

"You'd better choke it down. We have a big day tomorrow."

"I was thinking about that," Gary said. "Maybe just two of us should go. We can restock our supplies and come back."

Grizzly finished his stew and placed the bowl between his feet. "That will take two days. One up and one down. Don't think we should risk something going wrong in that time. We need to stick together. We'll head out early tomorrow," he said, deciding for us. I wasn't sure of the hierarchy as to who was in charge, but Grizzly easily stepped into the role, and I wasn't about to challenge him for it. "Chalk this up to a trial run. We'll get it right next time."

"And screen the applicants more carefully," Gary said, shooting a hard stare Rico's way.

Rico didn't look so good, and he didn't respond. He'd barely touched his dinner. Had the hike done him in, or was he remorseful for his behavior? From what I'd seen thus far, he didn't seem like the type to take a whole lot of responsibility for his actions.

For me, there wouldn't be a next time. I'd come back to the mountain, sure. But it'd be with people I trusted.

We sat in silence. I couldn't tell if everyone was exhausted, or if they were depleted by the thought of another long hike so soon. I was in decent shape, and I wanted to spend the next twenty-four hours in the fetal position. The slump of everyone's shoulders told me some felt worse than me.

Hope cleared her throat. "How about an exercise that will help us get to know each other better?"

Groans filled the air.

I knew she was trying her counselor hat on for size, but I hated these kinds of activities. They felt forced and unnatural. Plus, I flashed back to my coworkers and how they'd gleefully pointed out my flaws.

"Come on," Hope said. "It'll be fun. Let's start by sharing our first memories. What's the first thing you remember?"

Everyone looked at the ground.

"Anyone?"

I wanted to help her, but I couldn't think of a damn thing.

Hope sighed. "Okay, I'll go first. The first thing I remember is cotton candy. Casey's parents took us to a carnival." She looked at me, and I shrugged. Not ringing a bell. She went on. "I must have been about four, and I got this giant stick of cotton candy the size of my head. Before long, my hands and face were a sticky mess. I was trying to finish it in the back seat of the car on our way home. Uncle Albert pulled over, reached over the seat, and grabbed it out of my hands before throwing it out the window, complaining that I was getting sugar everywhere. I cried all the way home."

"Touching," Gary said with a smirk.

I shot him a death glare. "I could see my dad doing that."

Hope patted my knee. "You were there; don't you remember?"

I would have been three. "Sorry, no."

"Who wants to go next?" Hope asked.

When no one answered, Hope gave a nervous laugh. Rough crowd.

Izzy raised her hand. "I'll go. You know how, when you were a kid, and you wanted to kill your friend?"

The rest of us exchanged nervous glances. "No," Yuki said. "Nobody knows that. Nobody who doesn't become a serial killer."

"Come on," Izzy said with a nervous laugh. Her nose ring caught the light of the fire and made her face glow. "I didn't say I did it. Just that I had the thought."

Grizzly laughed. "Yeah, not normal."

Izzy didn't let it deter her. "She was always bragging. Her bedroom was nicer, her clothes were more expensive. She had all the best toys. I was sick of it. So, I dug a hole in the path we took to the playground. I planned to lead her to it, and when she fell in, I'd bury her."

"This doesn't seem appropriate," Hope said. "Not a good thing to put in people's heads."

Apparently, Izzy hadn't taken the same counseling classes as Hope. Rico was probably taking notes so he could finish Yuki off.

Izzy clasped her hands together and leaned forward. "Like I said, I didn't do it. She was sick and couldn't come out and play that day."

"Lucky for her," I said under my breath. Something wasn't right with this chick. Were drugs in play?

"But if she'd come," Gary said. "You would have done it."

Izzy tucked her hair behind her ear. "Probably not."

I wasn't convinced. If she'd carried that around with her for all these years and it still irked her, she probably needed therapy. And her friends should watch their backs.

I was glad we were heading home in the morning. I wondered what screening process the agency had for hiring counselors. Not to take anything away from Hope, but she had a felony conviction and was on probation. I was sorry I hadn't vetted the organization before I agreed to come. The money would be nice, sure, but mostly I wanted to support Hope. But the camp was rundown, Grizzly hadn't had a backup plan when Rico threw the satellite radios down the mountain, and Izzy was going to make the kids worse. I wanted to go home.

But Hope's exercise worked. We were getting to know each other better, even if that knowledge had me fearing for my safety. I stood and stretched. "On that note, I'm going to turn in. We should try to get some sleep before we head back."

"Yeah," Hope said. "Good idea. Me too."

As everyone took turns at the outhouses, I helped Grizzly bury the fire. When the others had gone to the cabins, I quickly used the facilities by the light of a lantern, then waited while Felony did his business before starting back to the woman's cabin. The night was still, and I picked my way over the uneven ground, careful where I stepped.

I froze when a crack sounded in the woods. Like a stick snapping. I scanned the treeline and waited. Felony stared hard toward the noise, the fur on the nape of his neck standing at attention. Whatever wildlife had caused the sound had to be heavy enough to break a fallen branch by stepping on it. Big enough that I didn't want to make its acquaintance.

Quickening my steps, I dragged Felony to the cabin, chancing a look over my shoulder. But the forest had gone quiet.

Shutting the door behind me, I tried to calm my thudding heart. Everyone else was already in bed, and I turned off the lantern so as not to disturb them. Feeling my way in the dark, I was unsure of each step. With the cloud cover and the lamp extinguished, the room was pitch black, darker than anyplace I'd ever been. I couldn't see a thing and whacked my shin on the frames of two cots on the way to mine.

My bed creaked when I lay down and again when Felony jumped up and snuggled against my side. The sleeping bag they provided smelled like wet wool. I placed one hand over my racing heart, and with the other, I felt for the pregnancy test stick in my pocket. I took some comfort in its being there. A key to my future I'd yet to check. As my mind ran through the possibilities, I wondered if I'd get any sleep.

Chapter Nine

Male voices outside the cabin window jolted me from a deep sleep.

"I'm so freaking sick. I think I'm gonna hurl."

"It's altitude sickness," Grizzly's gruff voice answered. "It will pass."

"When?"

"Could take a few days."

"You expect me to hike back down the mountain feeling like this? Not gonna happen."

Rico. He hadn't been remorseful for his actions. The kid was sick.

The voices faded as they moved away from the window, and I could no longer follow the conversation.

I struggled to sit up, my back stiff after a long night on the sagging cot. Beside me, Felony stretched. Blinking, I looked around the cabin. Mounds under sleeping bags were immobile. I was the first one up.

Unzipping my bag, I hung my feet over the bed and felt for my boots. Surprised they fit, I pulled them on without tying the laces and made a mad dash for the outhouse, stopping to let Felony relieve himself on the way. Afterward, I found Grizzly talking to Gary in front of the dormant firepit.

I stood before them, my arms crossed to keep warm. "What's for breakfast?"

Grizzly sipped from a metal coffee cup. He tossed me a granola bar. Since we were cutting our trip short, I didn't need to ration my Diet Coke, and I longed for one. But if I didn't want to be peeing in the bushes all the way down the mountain, I needed to show some restraint. Screw it. One wouldn't hurt. I ducked back inside the cabin and retrieved one from my bag, noting that no one inside had budged.

Grabbing a serving of kibble and a bowl, I rejoined the men outside. After serving Felony breakfast, I settled on a stump and took a long drink. I liked my Diet Coke ice-cold. It wasn't as satisfying as I'd hoped. But when the bubbles reached the back of my throat, I gave an audible moan.

"It will be easier going back," Gary said. "Since it's downhill."

"Depends on your knees," Grizzly said. "Once we get to where there's only one trail to choose from, some of us can go ahead. That way, the first group to make it to the parking lot can call for a ride. It will take the driver a while to get to us, and I don't want to spend the day waiting in the parking lot."

"Good thinking," Gary said. "I'll take the twins with me, and we'll go ahead."

Sure, take the easy kids. But I kept my mouth shut. Gary already made it clear he wanted nothing to do with Rico. Which reminded me of what he said earlier. "I take it Rico isn't feeling so good?"

"He's dragging," Grizzly said. "He'll have to suck it up. I—"

A high-pitched scream interrupted him. The three of us looked first to each other and then toward the woman's cabin, the source of the noise. Felony stood up, alert. I was the first to get to my feet and run that way.

Bursting through the door, I found Hana sitting on the edge of her cot. She had one boot on, which she yanked off and threw across the room. I ducked out of the way, letting Gary take the hit as the shoe nailed him in the chest. "What the hell?" he said, rubbing the sore spot.

"My foot," Hana cried. "Something bit me."

The commotion had awakened the others, and they milled about the cabin in dazed confusion.

Picking the boot off the floor, I gingerly peered inside. Nothing but a dark cavern. I shook it, then bent down and tapped it against the floor. A small scorpion scampered out. "Yikes." I dropped the shoe.

Felony darted toward the thing, but Grizzly stomped on it before he could reach it. Not wanting him to snarf up scorpion guts, I scooped the dog into my arms.

"What was that?" Hana asked, tears bubbling in her eyes as she rubbed her heel.

"Bark scorpion," Grizzly said.

Hana went wide-eyed. "Aren't those poisonous?"

Grizzly shrugged. "Hurts like the devil, but it shouldn't kill you."

Shouldn't? "Comforting," I said. Depositing Felony on Hana's cot, I sat next to her and rubbed her back.

"It really hurts." Tears welled in enormous, blinking eyes. "I can't...can't stand the pain."

"Should ease up in a few hours, or a day or two at the most," Grizzly said, rubbing his beard. "Of course, for a little thing like you, the ratio of venom to your body weight makes it worse."

Not helping.

Hana pulled off her sock. "My foot's on fire."

Gary crossed his arms, and in an authoritative voice said, "Everyone, check your shoes before putting them on."

"You think?" I blurted out before I could censure myself.

Gary shot me the stink eye. Grizzly tilted his head toward the door. "Casey, Gary, can I have a word?"

I patted Hana's back one more time. "Hope, can you sit with her? Get her some water? I'll be right back." I followed the men outside and to the firepit, where we'd be out of earshot.

"She can't hike today," Grizzly said. "Won't be able to put a shoe on for at least a day. Just too damn painful."

"You've been stung?" Gary asked.

"A few times," he said. "Only thing that hurt as much was passing a kidney stone."

Man's equivalent to childbirth. But I tried not to think about that.

"We could carry her," Gary said. "She can't weigh more than a hundred pounds."

"For nine miles?" Grizzly shook his head. "Not a good idea. Not with the terrain we have to cover."

"So, what do we do?" I asked.

Grizzly scratched his scraggy beard. "She needs to keep her foot elevated. If we had ice, that would help. Since my first aid kit is halfway to Mexico by now, I don't have any pain relievers to give her."

"Someone must have brought some." I headed back to the cabin.

Inside, everyone was checking their belongings to avoid becoming the next victim. Hana lay on her back, her knees drawn to her chest, as she rocked back and forth. Tears streaked her rosy cheeks.

"Anyone have ibuprofen or something like it?" I asked.

"I do." Hope got to her feet and laid her pack on her cot. Digging through it, she pulled out a bottle and tapped two pills into her hand.

Izzy rushed over and took them from her, then picked the bottle of water off the floor. She settled on the cot next to Hana. "Here you go," she said sweetly.

I went back outside. "She's in a lot of pain."

"Change of plans," Gary said. "Some of us will have to stay behind. I volunteer to hike back down with the twins."

"I'm going too," Grizzly said. "You take the wrong path, and you'll double your trip at best. Worst yet, you could get lost. Casey, you stay here with Hana and Rico. That will give him time to recover from his altitude sickness."

"What about the others?" Gary asked.

"We leave that up to them," Grizzly said.

After what had happened, I doubted anyone would want to stick around. I resented being given the babysitting assignment, but we couldn't leave the kids alone, and I was the obvious choice. That adulting thing again. I wasn't a fan.

Chapter Ten

Betz

Martin Phillips had been on the run for less than twelve hours after a well-coordinated escape from the Maricopa County Jail. Apparently, his girlfriend worked there as a corrections officer, and it was an inside job. She too, was missing. And they'd yet to identify Phillip's accomplice in the murders of Marilynn and Jacob Stevens.

Every minute that passed increased their chance of getting away. Mexico wasn't that far. Depending on the mode of transportation, neither was Canada.

While the Sheriff's office led the investigation, all police departments in the valley were on alert. They assumed the trio was armed and dangerous. With the death penalty on the table, they were also desperate.

Betz waited for Moody in the precinct parking lot. Phillip's face stared back at him from the laptop mounted on the dashboard of the Interceptor. The escapee was in his forties. His booking photo reminded Betz that Phillips hadn't gone quietly. Other than the black eye and bloody, swollen lip, he looked unassuming—an average middle-aged man. But Phillips wasn't average. He was a cold-blooded killer. He and his buddy had executed the Stevens by shooting them in the back of their heads as they knelt before them, pleading for their lives. All because of a drug deal gone bad.

At least that was the theory the prosecutors were working with.

Law enforcement knew the Stevens had screamed and begged for their lives because their teenage daughter overheard them. Phillips would have killed her, too, if he had known she was home. But the girl was supposed to be at school. He had no way of knowing she'd stayed home sick that day. Or that she was hiding under the bed and had heard everything.

Moody opened the passenger door of the SUV and settled in her seat. "Sorry to keep you waiting. I got a call."

Betz put the vehicle in gear. "Not a problem." He'd used the time to send Casey an article about bear attacks, instantly regretting it because she'd asked for some space after he'd told her he still had feelings for her. He needed to knock it off and restrain himself, or he was going to push her further away. But sometimes he couldn't help himself. She and trouble were on a first-name basis. If he could divert a disaster, why not try? "Was the call about Phillips?"

She nodded. "A witness called the tip line. She thinks she spotted him leaving her neighbor's house last night. Her address is off Sixteenth and Baseline."

"So, he's long gone?"

"She didn't think much of it until she saw the story of his escape on the morning news."

Betz headed south. "Let's check it out."

Chapter Eleven

Except for Hana and Izzy, everyone took a seat around the firepit. The mood was somber. Grizzly led the discussion while people passed around and ate granola bars. Once everyone had been updated on Hana's condition and the news that she, Rico, and I would stay behind, Grizzly asked who else wanted to wait it out.

Hope cast me a sideways glance. "I'll stay with Casey."

She'd better since she'd roped me into this.

"I'm hiking out," Yuki said.

Probably best to separate the boys, so I inwardly applauded his decision.

"That's everyone," Gary said. He'd already made it clear the twins were going with him.

"What about Izzy?"

Hope sighed. "She practically pushed me out of the way to take care of Hana. I think she'll stay."

Grizzly nodded. "Anyway, because it's downhill, we should make good time and arrive by mid-afternoon. We'll call for help as soon as we're in cell range so someone can start heading out to meet us. Then we'll send someone to rescue you. By then, Hana and Rico should be up for the hike. If not, the forest rangers can do their thing."

"Okay," I said, not liking the plan at all, but knowing it made sense. I was glad Hope would keep me company. I wasn't so sure about Izzy.

* * *

Within twenty minutes, everyone had packed and was ready to go. Izzy had disappeared. I checked the outhouses, and kitchen, but she was nowhere to be found. I feared she'd gone for a walk and had gotten lost, but there was nothing I could do about it. If I went looking for her, I risked getting lost too, and the last thing we needed was a Scooby Doo moment, where one by one, everyone disappeared.

"She's probably digging a hole to bury one of us," Yuki remarked when I shared my worries with the group.

Nervous laughter erupted before Grizzly regained control. "Whatever her reason, we have to get going."

I wasn't sure I wanted her on my team, but there was probably safety in numbers.

Hope and I watched the group descend into the woods, and a sense of foreboding settled in my gut. I tried to shake off the feeling, but this trip was doomed from the start, and I couldn't imagine things getting better anytime soon.

* * *

By mid-morning, the sun had already warmed the ground. I'd shed my hoodie and was still warm in my hiking pants and tank top. The pregnancy test sat like a weight in my pocket. If I could get some alone time, I might gather the courage to look at it. But I didn't want an audience when whatever emotions I might feel rushed out of me.

I settled at the picnic table with Hope, munching on granola bars and swigging Diet Coke. I wasn't so stingy with them since my supply no longer needed to last ten days.

"Do you think they'll come for us tonight or tomorrow?" Hope asked.

I shrugged. "Depends on whether there's another way to get to us or not. With all these trees, there's no place for a helicopter to land. And the trails are too narrow for an ATV."

Hope took a sip of soda. "Maybe the rangers use horses. Plus, the kids might be up to hiking by morning."

"True." Morning would be here before we knew it, but I dreaded spending another night on that lumpy cot. Especially with whatever might lurk in the woods.

Rico sat slumped against a log a few feet away, his head hanging between his knees. He'd declined my offer of ibuprofen, even though I promised it would help him feel better. Felony had plastered himself against Rico's side, hell-bent on winning the sullen boy over. Not immune to Felony's charm, Rico absently petted his head. The kid was still pale. Altitude sickness was no joke.

Not to be outdone, Hana looked on the verge of crying. She lay on a blanket I'd spread on the ground, her foot elevated on a log. Izzy was still MIA.

"I have a bad feeling about this," Hope said, her voice hushed so the kids couldn't hear. "They left us with the troublemaker."

I glanced Rico's way. "Doesn't look too menacing right now."

"His sickness will pass."

That's what Grizzly had said, but it could take a few days for Rico's body to adjust. I had a touch of it myself, but the Diet Coke settled my stomach. I grabbed another can from my backpack and walked it over to the boy. "Here, this might help."

His gaze narrowed with suspicion that I was being nice to him, but he held out his hand, accepting my offer. A mop of brown hair swooped across his sweaty brow as he popped the can open and took a long drink.

"You're welcome," I said.

"Can I have one?" Hana asked.

At least it would lighten my load on the way down. "Sure."

I helped her stand and let her lean against me, favoring her foot as we made our way to the picnic table. She sat on the bench and elevated her leg onto Hope's knapsack. "Feeling any better?" I asked.

She winced. "Like angry ants are eating my flesh. I think my foot might fall off."

I missed Google. If I had cell service, I would have looked up her prognosis and found tips to ease her pain. I knew scorpion bites made their victims wish they would die, but rarely killed anyone. I'd never been stung, but I knew people who had. It was a hazard of living in the desert.

"You should feel better by tomorrow," Hope offered.

Hana rolled her baby blues and nursed her Diet Coke. "If I live that long."

"You will."

"I just have the worst luck," Hana said. "My life's a train wreck."

I sat opposite her. "What's been going on?"

She tightened the rubber band around her pigtail. "You mean besides my parents being murdered? No one in the family wanted me to live with them, and now I'm in foster care with a bunch of entitled bitches."

My thoughts flashed to Phillips' arrest for that very thing. An uneasy feeling roiled in my stomach. I almost asked her if he was her parents' killer, but I didn't want it to become a thing where we compared horror stories. She seemed pretty fragile. "Wow," I said. "I'm sorry. That is rough."

"And when I get back, I'm meeting with the prosecutor. I'll have to testify against the guy who did it."

"You witnessed it?" Hope asked.

"Not really. But I overheard things. I was inside our house when someone killed them." Hana looked like she was about to break.

I bit my lip. Betz had yet to give me the police report on Phillips. I knew he had committed a double murder, but that was all I knew. "That must have been terrifying."

"Psychiatrist says I have PTSD. I can't sleep."

Another reason not to traumatize her by telling her I might have a connection to their killer.

Hope settled on the other side of the girl. "I'm sure. That's a lot to recover from."

Hana shrugged. "I thought you already knew about it. Izzy did. Thought it was in my file."

Hope and I exchanged a look over Hana's head. I would have remembered reading something like that, and I'm sure Hope would have, too. Maybe Izzy saw it on the news.

"Anyway," Hana said. "I'll feel better when they convict the guy. But what if they don't? What if I mess up on the stand?"

"Hope and I have testified a lot," I said. "Maybe we can give you some pointers. Let you practice."

Hope patted Hana's hand. "Best thing to remember is that as long as you're telling the truth, you'll be okay. They can't poke holes in the truth."

"I guess." Hana took another drink, then ran her finger around the rim of the can.

"Want to practice?" I asked.

Hana shrugged her slight shoulders. She looked so young, so vulnerable. I wanted to comfort her, but I didn't know how. "Maybe later. I don't like to think about it."

I couldn't fault her for that. "Whenever you're ready. But can I ask one more question?"

Hana sighed, but she didn't say no.

"Was there only one suspect in your parents' murders?"

"No. There were two. What's worse is they don't even know who the second one is."

So, it had to be Phillips. He'd committed the crime before he was on my caseload. Supervising him, I had no idea he had crimes he hadn't been charged with yet. There'd been no red flags. He was on supervision for a drug crime. Nothing violent.

Luckily, Hana moved on. "We could paint our nails," she said, brightening. "I brought polish."

Who doesn't bring nail paint on a camping trip? I got to my feet. "Sure. Where is it?"

She cocked her head toward the woman's cabin. "In my bag. Bring the Shamrock green."

I was probably Hana's age the last time I painted my nails. I remembered ruining them before they could dry, which was why I never wasted money on a manicure again. But it could help pass the time, and it would distract Hana from her pain. I headed to the cabin.

The bag lay against the wall. Placing it on the bed, I peered inside, worried a scorpion or two lay in wait.

Digging carefully through the contents, I quickly realized I'd grabbed Izzy's bag by mistake—the clothes were double the size Hana would wear. About to zip it up, a black hunk of metal caught my eye. Moving a hairbrush aside, I exposed a revolver. What the hell was Izzy doing with a gun? This wasn't standard counselor gear. In my contract, the agency had made it clear that no weapons were allowed. I understood wanting protection from forest animals, but with a bunch of kids with questionable backgrounds around, it could just as easily land in the wrong hands. I covered the gun with some clothes, zipped the pack, and returned it to its place on the floor.

I found Hana's backpack nearby. Grabbing it, I brought it back outside with me.

I put it on the bench next to the girl. "I'll let you find it."

I tilted my head toward the kitchen. "Hope, can you give me a hand?"

A look of confusion crossed my cousin's face, but she followed me into the building. I closed the door behind us. "I'm worried about Izzy."

Hope crossed her arms. "Me too. She's been gone for a while."

"Not just that," I said. "Something's not right about her. First her weird comments last night, and just now... I accidentally went into her bag, thinking it was Hana's. She's got a gun in there."

Hope's mouth dropped open. "Are you sure?"

I nodded.

"For protection?"

"From whom?"

Hope shrugged. "More like what. But how do we know if she's competent with the thing?"

"We don't."

"Is it loaded?"

I hadn't checked. Although Betz had taught me how to shoot and had even given me a gun to defend myself from Diablo, I still didn't feel comfortable handling firearms. "I assume it's loaded. We can ask her about it when she gets back. At least you're trained in firearms." Hope used to carry when she was a PO. I wished I'd scheduled the training so I could carry sooner. I kept my gun locked in a safe at my dad's house. I'd followed the program rules.

Hope crossed her arms. "I can't touch it. It's a condition of my probation."

Sometimes I forgot Hope was under court-ordered supervision. She wasn't allowed to possess weapons.

"I'll ask her about it when she returns. I'm sure they gave her the same rules as they gave us. I wonder what else she has that she shouldn't have."

"You didn't look?"

"No. But I'll ask her to empty her bag, so we know what we're dealing with. Just wanted to make sure you and I were on the same page."

Hope gave a lop-sided grin. "I'll always have your back, cousin."

"And I have yours."

"You've proven that," she said. "Let's hope the opportunity for me to return the favor doesn't present itself anytime soon."

Chapter Twelve

Betz

The house on Baseline was one of the last holdouts that hadn't sold when developers knocked down existing residences to make room for the ever-expanding suburbia. Betz pulled into the driveway and angled the car for a quick getaway if needed.

At the base of South Mountain, the ranch probably dated back to the fifties and had survived a changing landscape in an area that used to be mostly farmland. Betz remembered his sister Jasmine taking him to buy fresh flowers at a roadside shack for their mother, one of the many times she'd successfully completed rehab.

A camper was off to the side. Inside the house, the curtain on the front window parted, and a set of eyes peered at them.

"Must be the woman who called," Moody said.

Betz gave the dispatcher their location as they approached the house. They'd stopped at a Circle K on the way and had donned their bulletproof vests in the parking lot.

By the time they made it to the door, it had swung open, and an older woman greeted them dressed in a muumuu that brushed her bare feet. Betz's smile seemed to put her at ease.

"Ms. Cruz?" Moody asked.

The woman nodded.

"I'm Anita. We spoke on the phone," Moody added. "Can we come in?"

The woman stepped back, flashing nervous glances over their shoulders toward the house next door as they entered. Closing the door behind them, they stood in the entryway.

Saltillo tile floors were highly polished, and the scent of cleaner filled the air. A rustic bench sat against a wall filled with colorful folk art. Betz held out his phone and showed her Phillip's mugshot.

"Yes," she said with a slight accent. "That's him. I saw him leave the house next door yesterday."

"Alone?" Betz asked.

"No. There was another man and a young woman with him."

"Can you describe them?"

Moody got what she could, using her phone to record the descriptions. "You see anything else?"

"They got into a gray sedan. There was a lot of traffic on Baseline, and it took them a few minutes to pull away. That's when I got a good look at the driver. The man in the photo you showed me. He saw me, and that makes me nervous."

"Do you live alone?" Betz asked.

"No. My son lives here. He's a chef. He's at work."

"Who lives next door?"

"My neighbors?" The woman hugged herself. "The Hutchinsons? A middle-aged couple and their two adult daughters. One daughter has two little kids. They live there too if they're not with their dad."

"Any concerns about them?" Moody said.

"What? Oh, no, they're very nice people."

Betz tucked his phone into his pocket. "We'll pay them a visit."

"Lock up after we leave," Moody offered. "Have you seen your neighbors since Phillips visited them?"

"No. And it's odd that they didn't put their trash out last night. They missed pick-up this morning."

"Anything else?"

She shook her head.

"Well, Ms. Cruz," Betz said, handing her his card. "Please call if you think of anything. If any of them come back, call 911."

* * *

At the house next door, Betz pounded on the door and waited. Moody had already found out what she could about the occupants on the internet. The Hutchinson family had purchased the home seven years ago. A social media search suggested a tight-knit family. A mom, dad, two adult daughters, and two kids.

When knocking met with zero results, Betz looked at his partner. "Going around back."

Moody keyed the radio and alerted the patrol officers who were covering them, then followed Betz through the side gate and into the backyard, guns drawn.

The space was well-maintained. A swing set and pool toys suggested kids frequented the area. At the patio door, Betz flattened himself against the stucco wall. Once Moody was in place on the other side, he chanced a look.

Someone had drawn the vertical blinds, but one slat was damaged, leaving a gap. Before Betz could get a good look, a shadow passed by. Betz nodded to his partner, then knocked on the glass. "Police. Open up."

There was no response. Firearm at the ready, he chanced another look. Inside, the family from the internet sat at the kitchen table. Minus one. The looks of fear on their faces told the story. A man with a handgun paced back and forth in front of the door. Spotting Betz, he raised his weapon.

"Shit!"

Before Betz could duck, a gunshot exploded in his ears; the bullet barely missed him as he slammed himself back against the wall.

The door shattered, and shards of glass cascaded onto the concrete patio floor. Screams came from inside the house. Betz and Moody parted ways, running and diving for cover behind the tool shed on the other side of the pool.

"You okay?" Moody asked.

Betz shook pieces of glass out of his hair. "Yeah. You?"

"I'm good."

He got on the radio. "Shots fired. Caucasian male. Has hostages. I counted five. Three adults and two kids."

Patrol officers rushed to tactical positions around the property. Hunkered down, they waited for the hostage negotiation team to arrive.

Chapter Thirteen

I'd never been into girly things like painting my nails, but it seemed to calm Hana and distract her from her pain, so I held her hand and applied the polish with quick strokes. After getting more on her hands than her nails, Hope took over the job. I declined Hana's offer to paint mine. I'd chewed my nails down to stubs, and a manicure wouldn't be enough to make them look good.

Turning my face to the sky, I noticed that the sun was directly overhead. I was no naturalist, but I was pretty sure that meant it was close to noon. My growling stomach brought me to the same conclusion.

Hope was two steps ahead of me and had gone to the kitchen, where she found cans of soup that she heated in a pot over the fireplace. The fire added to the heat of the warm day. I pulled my hair into a high ponytail and knotted it on top of my head. A slight breeze coming through the open window chilled the sweat-soaked back of my neck.

After thoroughly heating the soup, I spooned it into two bowls and took them to the kids seated at the picnic table.

"Thanks," Hana said, digging in. Rico looked less enthused about my offering, but he took careful spoonfuls to his mouth.

"Feeling any better?" I asked.

He gave me a hard stare. "No."

Okay, then.

Once we'd eaten and the dishes were done, Hope curled up with a book in the hammock, and the kids played a game of checkers on the board I'd found in the kitchen.

I was restless and getting more and more worried about Izzy, who'd now been gone for hours.

"I'm going for a walk," I said to no one in particular.

A click of my tongue and Felony fell into step beside me. I started down the trail that had brought us to camp, thinking I'd walk to the cliff and try to commune with nature, whatever that meant. With no internet or other distractions, it seemed like a good place to do some soul-searching.

Lord knew I had some thinking to do.

For the past few weeks, I'd felt an overwhelming need to be alone, to disconnect. Staying with my dad and his girlfriend, Millie, gave me little chance to be alone. Before that, my handful of a cousin, Joy, had lived with me. I couldn't remember the last time I'd had a moment to myself.

Then there were the two men pushing me to make a commitment. Thing was, both were good choices. Each had a place in my heart. Betz was safety, and I knew his love for me was deep. We had a history and could finish each other's sentences. There was a lot of comfort in that.

Marcus represented the unknown. He was a wild ride, and I never knew what to expect from him. His touch, hell, just a look from his hypnotic eyes, electrified me. Around him, I could let my hair down.

A girl would be crazy to turn either away. But one failed marriage was enough for me. If I got into another serious relationship, I had to be sure it would last.

And if I were pregnant, stability was even more important.

I found a flat rock, far enough back from the ledge that it didn't stir up my fear of heights and make me more anxious, but still gave me a glorious view of the mountains that rolled in the distance. Sitting cross-legged, I played with the stick in my pocket, flipping it over and over as I tried to enjoy my surroundings.

I'd tried yoga once, but it was too calm for me. Meditation? Forget about it. I didn't normally like being alone with my thoughts and preferred running for exercise. It was hard to analyze your psyche with music pounding in your ears.

But today I tried to center myself. I even laid my hands palms up, on my thighs as I gazed at the treetops, stretching out for miles until they climbed the next mountain range. But Zen, whatever that was, was elusive.

Minutes ticked by as I took cleansing breaths. Felony had an itch, and the clanking of the tags on his collar as he scratched his ear jangled my nerves. Reaching back into my pocket, I fingered the pregnancy test.

Maybe it didn't matter how I felt about Betz. If I were pregnant, Marcus was the father. He was the only man I'd been with for a very long time. What a slap in the face it would be for Betz when he learned I was having another man's child. My reluctance to start a family was one reason we'd parted. He'd never understand.

And I hardly knew Marcus. How would he take such momentous news? It was too soon to get so serious, and nothing was more serious than bringing a new life into the world.

A rustle in the leaves of a nearby tree startled me. My gaze shot skyward just in time to see an eagle take flight. Its wingspan was at least six feet. I sucked in a breath as the bird soared overhead, swooping over trees with grace. My breath caught in my throat.

Once the moment passed, and I was alone again with my thoughts, my mind raced.

Relaxing wasn't easy.

In fact, it made me nervous.

I got to my feet and paced.

I should look at the damn stick. Stop my wild thoughts and just pull it out of my pocket and face the truth. A rip the Band-Aid off approach was the best option.

But before I could do the deed, footsteps sounded from the woods. Then voices.

Izzy emerged from the brush. She stopped short when she entered the clearing and saw me, obviously as startled as I was. Behind her was a man.

"Casey," she said. "What are you doing here?"

Like she owned the mountain.

The man wore a tan shirt with a Forest Service badge sewn on.

"You came to rescue us," I blurted.

The man looked a little rough around the edges—I imagined the nature of the job would do that. He cleared his throat. "Didn't know anyone needed rescuing until I ran into this young lady. She told me about your predicament. How are the kids holding up?"

"Hana still can't put pressure on her foot," I said. "I think Rico, the one with altitude sickness, is coming around."

The man adjusted his belt. His name tag said Stewart. "Well, that's good."

"The camp's not far," I said, starting toward the trail.

But the man didn't follow.

I turned back to face him. "You coming?"

"Sorry, Ma'am. As I was explaining to this young lady, I need to respond to another call. Their situation is more dire than yours. But now that I know about you all, I'll get help on the way. Seems like you'll need more than me to carry that girl out of here. Might take a few hours for them to get to you, though. For now, you're safest staying at camp."

Izzy must have filled him in. She fidgeted, rubbing her arms. Had she gone into the woods to use drugs?

"As I told Ms. Izzy here," the ranger went on. "You should all stay together. There's an escaped convict on the loose."

Maybe my feeling of being watched wasn't so far-fetched, after all. I'd thought it was an animal, or more likely, my imagination. But now there was something else to worry about. "In the area?"

Stewart shrugged. "Probably not. But stranger things have happened. Should have jail scrubs on. Easily distinguishable from a hiker. Just wanted you to be aware."

"What kind of crime are we talking about here?" I asked.

"Robbery, I think. Anyway, I need to go." He tipped his ball cap. "You ladies stay safe. Help will be here soon." He moved down the trail and out of sight.

I turned to Izzy. "Where have you been?"

She crossed her arms. "I went for a walk. Got lost but then ran into the ranger. He steered me back to the trail."

"We were worried. Please don't take off by yourself again."

She snorted. "Looks like you did the same."

But I hadn't ventured off the trail. Before I could point that out to her, she turned back toward camp. I followed, relieved that the ranger knew our situation. Help should be on the way before the others even made it back to the parking lot. I wished he'd stuck around long enough for me to ask more questions, like how long it would take for the cavalry to arrive, but he hadn't given me the chance. With any luck, I'd be able to sleep in my own bed tonight.

Chapter Fourteen

Betz

Hours passed, and the standoff dragged on. Chance McKinley was the lead hostage negotiator. He could talk a Red Sox fan into cheering for the Yankees. With a bullhorn, he'd established contact with the man barricaded inside the house.

Not escaped convict Phillips. A man who went by the name Pug.

Betz worried most about the two kids inside. So far, they'd uncovered no ties between the family and Phillips. But there had to be one. He'd been there.

After hours of negotiation, Pug released the two toddlers and the grandmother.

Betz made a beeline toward the woman as paramedics tried to calm her. "My daughter," she cried to anyone who would listen. "Izzy. They're going after Izzy."

Betz knew better than to tell her to calm down. He'd been married to Casey after all. He knew that phrase added fuel to the fire. "Start from the beginning," he said instead.

She took a long, shuddering breath. "My other daughter. She lives with her boyfriend. The people who left. They were asking all kinds of questions about her."

"Izzy?" Betz asked.

"Yes."

"Where is she?"

"She's supposed to be working. I don't know."

"Back to the beginning. Who else is inside the house?"

The woman worked arthritic hands. "My other daughter and my husband."

"Do you know the man holding them? The man with the gun?"

She shook her head. "I've never seen him before. He came to the house yesterday with three other people. They forced themselves inside. They had guns."

Betz pulled his phone from his pocket and brought up Phillips' mugshot. "This man?"

She nodded vigorously. "That's him. He seemed to be in charge. He and that woman had a lot of questions about Izzy. It doesn't make sense; she's just a social worker."

Betz folded his arms across his chest and gave the woman his full attention. "What questions?"

"How to find her. We didn't tell them that she had recently moved in with her boyfriend. We said we didn't know where she was. The man who stayed with us…Pug…he was supposed to hold us hostage until the others got what they wanted."

Betz held out his phone. "Call her. See if she's okay."

She took the phone with shaking hands and tapped out the number. The call went straight to voicemail.

"Was Izzy involved in anything illegal? Drugs?"

The woman looked taken aback. "Izzy? No. She's a good girl."

"What about her boyfriend?"

"I don't know him well, but Izzy wouldn't associate with him if he was up to no good."

But parents didn't always know what their kids were up to. Betz got the boyfriend's information and was about to head out to find him when a commotion came from the front of the house.

Betz turned and ran toward the line of officers, drawing his gun on the way. Pug had emerged through the front door, hands held high in the air. McKinley must have talked him into surrendering. But he wasn't in custody yet.

Betz didn't forget that not long ago, Pug had shot at him. He could still feel the sensation of the bullet exploding the glass sliding door, missing him by an inch.

"Turn around," McKinley ordered.

Pug slowly turned his back to them. "Keeping your hands up, walk back toward the sound of my voice," McKinley commanded.

Pug took careful steps. So far, it was a textbook arrest, but Betz didn't miss the tension that permeated the air. This was far from over.

When Pug was within reach, Betz and McKinley both rushed forward. Betz holstered his weapon, then withdrew his handcuffs from the pouch on his belt. But before he could secure the second cuff, Pug twisted away and reached for the waistband of his shorts. "Gun!" Betz yelled.

McKinley pulled his pepper spray and aimed it at the suspect. And Betz inadvertently took a face full of the stuff. Chance might have been a master negotiator, but he had terrible aim.

Gagging and coughing. Betz couldn't see a damn thing. He staggered back, vaguely aware of his peers subduing Pug, so he was no longer a threat.

Moody appeared, holstering her weapon and taking Betz by the arm. She pulled him away from the melee.

"Crap," he said. "My eyes are burning."

She steered him to the road where the paramedics waited. They poured bottled water over his face, flushing out his eyes. Slowly, the burning subsided. His vision cleared. Well, clear was a lofty goal. His contacts had washed away, and he was half-blind without them.

He kept an old pair of glasses in his duty bag for such an emergency, and he dug them out. Cops he'd known for years looked at him like he'd grown an additional head. "They're just glasses," he said. "If McKinley weren't such a lousy shot, I wouldn't need them."

Still, the jokes flew. "Take it easy, Buddy Holly. Relax, specs. Chill, Clark Kent." Maturity wasn't a hiring requirement.

Betz stalked off and motioned for Moody to follow him. "Let's find the missing sister and see what Phillips would want from her."

Chapter Fifteen

Back at camp, I asked Hope and Izzy to meet me in the kitchen while the kids played Monopoly.

Once we filled Hope in on Ranger Stewart's promise to send help, I turned to Izzy. "What's with the gun?"

A shadow passed over her face. "You looked in my bag?"

"Answer the question," I said.

Her shrug was nonchalant. "We're deep in the woods. Never know what we might need protection from. And with what that ranger said, we have even more reason to defend ourselves."

Hope and I exchanged a worried look. "Yet you've been in the woods for hours. Wandering around with God knows what animals, and with an escaped convict on the loose, and you left the gun in your bag," I said.

"I didn't know about the escapee when I left," she snapped. "And I didn't expect to get lost and be gone so long."

"But why bring a gun if you're not going to carry it?" Hope asked.

Izzy threw up her hands. "I knew you two uptight bitches would react this way if you knew I had it. Anyway, you should be grateful I found that ranger. He's our ticket out of here."

I didn't miss her change in subject, and my bullshit meter was going nuts. But if she didn't want to be truthful, pushing her wouldn't help.

Izzy shoved her hands in the pockets of her pants and rocked back on her heels. I noticed bruises the size of fingerprints on both biceps. Did Izzy have an abusive boyfriend back home? I knew if I asked her about the marks, if I pressed her, she'd get even more defensive, so I held my tongue.

"Would you mind opening your pack?" I asked. "Just want to make sure you don't have more prohibited items."

Izzy glanced about nervously. "I'm not gonna do that. You have no right to ask. You're a PO and only have power over people on probation. That's not me."

With that, she turned and stormed out the door.

"I don't like this," Hope said. "If she has nothing to hide, why not show us?"

I rubbed my chin. "We need to keep an eye on her. Something about her isn't right."

"I agree," Hope said.

* * *

It was mid-afternoon, and clouds had moved in. Without the intense sun overhead, there was a sudden chill in the air. My hoodie wasn't enough. "We should start a fire," Hope said. "If a rescue team comes, we can bury it, but it'll be dark soon. I don't think anyone will come until morning."

I nodded. "I'll go find some kindling."

"Don't go far," Hope said. "Please don't get lost."

Leaving Felony with the kids, I headed into the woods. I'd have my arms full and didn't want to deal with holding his leash. He'd probably stay by my side. Unless he spotted a squirrel. Then he'd be on the chase. The last thing I needed was another problem.

I stayed on the path, gathering fallen branches, laying the longer ones on the ground, and jumping on them until they cracked under my weight and became more manageable to carry. Arms full, I started back to camp. Something moved in the brush.

I froze.

First, a stillness settled over the forest. The calm before a storm? Before I could make sense of it, a small cat sauntered out of the foliage and onto the trail. My first thought? What was a house cat doing this deep in the woods?

Then it dawned on me.

My heart climbed into my throat.

This wasn't someone's fluffy pet. It was a mountain lion cub.

It couldn't be more than a few weeks old.

The mother wouldn't let it out of her sight.

Fuck.

My head whipped around, my eyes darting from side-to-side as I quietly backstepped, hoping to create as much distance between us as possible. I didn't want to be perceived as a threat. With a little luck, maybe I could get away undetected.

My foot pushed down on a branch, and a crack sounded as loud as a thunder boom.

No such luck.

The mother bounded out of the bushes and positioned herself between me and her cub.

My insides did a backflip.

"Get back!" I yelled. "I won't harm your baby."

The enormous cat's shoulders shifted as she sauntered toward me. Tawny-beige fur was a blur as soulful brown eyes locked on mine. Was I supposed to make eye contact? Look away? Make myself big or get in the fetal position? I had no idea. I should have paid closer attention when my dad watched those nature shows when I was a kid. But the threat of a wild animal attack on the suburban streets of Tempe wasn't something I'd worried about.

I knew the worst thing I could do was turn my back on her and run.

"Back!" I shouted, making guttural noises in my throat. "Go back to your cub."

For every step I took backward, the lion took four forward, closing the distance between us.

She snarled, enormous teeth flashing at me. Her growl reverberated in my head and sent currents of fear down my shaking limbs.

If I ran, she'd be on me in seconds. I imagined her giant claws sinking into my back as her powerful jaw clamped down on my neck. She'd shake me like an angry bartender mixing a martini. Would anyone ever find me, or would she drag my limp body into the woods and have me for dinner?

I continued to back away. Fear choked me and threatened to overcome my ability to move, leaving me immobile. I dropped most of the kindling, holding onto the longest, fattest stick.

It amazed me how many thoughts raced through my mind in what must have been seconds. The stick in my pocket? I'd never know the results. If it were positive, it wasn't just my life on the line.

I continued screaming at the animal and waving the branch over my head, but she remained undeterred. Head-sized paws took one cautious step at a time.

I'd felt fear before. Mostly at the hands of Diablo gang members. But with them, I always thought I stood a chance, even if that chance was slim. I could outsmart them if nothing else. But I was on this lioness' turf, and she was much faster and stronger than me.

My ankle rolled as I tripped over a rock. My knees buckled, and I went down hard. I was even less threatening now, my eyes level with the big cat's.

When they say your life flashes before your eyes, they aren't kidding. But mostly for me, it wasn't my past that I saw; it was my future. What I'd miss. Would I never gaze into Betz's loving eyes again? Marvel at Marcus' mischievous grin? Kate…my niece and nephew…my dad, Hope? Even my crazy cousin Joy. And an unborn baby I'd never get to meet? I wanted time with all of them. So many things remained unsaid. Undone. My heart ached for what I'd never know.

The cat was only a few feet away now. I crab-walked backward, increasing the distance between us, but she was faster, more agile. She'd be on me before I could get to my feet.

Still, I scrambled backward as fast as I could. The skin of my palms ripped as I pushed down on jagged rocks and broken sticks. The pain barely registered in my brain. My surroundings became blurry. The only thing I saw clearly was the giant cat. She and I were the only beings that existed in my current world.

Pushing off my hands, I sprang to my feet. First in a crouch position, then as I straightened to my full height, I waved my arms over my head in one last attempt to scare her off. "Please, please stop."

She prepared to pounce. Was mid-air when a gunshot shattered the silence. Instinctively, my hands clamped over my ears.

The lion startled. Giant paws flew into the surrender position before she turned and fled.

Adrenaline rushed from my heart and flooded my body, leaving me breathless and dizzy.

I chanced a look behind me. Izzy stood there, the firearm still leveled toward the place where the mountain lion used to be. "That's why I have a gun," she said. "You're welcome."

Lowering the weapon, she turned and headed back toward camp.

My legs were jelly, but I followed.

Chapter Sixteen

I owed Izzy one. No matter her motivation, she saved my life. No doubt that mountain lion would have torn me to pieces. But that didn't mean Izzy had gained my trust.

Back at camp, I gave her a wide berth. And a little respect.

Felony ran to greet me. His butt wiggled with such gusto I feared his tail would fly off. I patted his head with the back of my bloody hand.

"What happened?" Hope asked, rushing toward me. "We heard a gunshot. I've been going crazy with worry."

"Had a little run-in with a mountain lion," I said. "I dropped the wood, sorry."

Hope looked me over. "Are you okay?"

I held out my shaking hands. My palms looked like hamburger. "Just a little banged up from trying to get away." Then, in a whisper, I said, "Izzy saved me."

"Guess it's good she had the gun. Come on, let me clean those wounds."

I followed her into the kitchen, where she ran the water cold. My skin stung when I placed my hands under the flow, and Hope picked debris out of my cuts. She dried them with paper towels and grabbed the First Aid Kit from the shelf.

"That must have been so frightening," Hope said.

Reliving the event in my head made my heart race again. Relief that it was over, that I'd survived, rushed down my body and pooled at my feet. Suddenly, I had to know. Lay all my cards on the table. I'd almost died without knowing. I needed to have all the facts, and if I was… I couldn't even bring myself to think the word. I needed to take greater care of myself. Of us.

"My pocket," I said, motioning with a tilt of my head toward the side pocket of my pants. "There's a test. Can you get it?"

Confusion passed like a shadow over her face. "A test?"

"Please."

She finished tending to my hand and then reached over and unzipped my pocket. Pulling out the stick, she held it over the sink so she could read it in what little light came through the window.

"Pregnant," she announced.

Blood rushed to my head. Dizzy, I grabbed the counter for support.

"Pregnant," Hope repeated. "My God, Casey. How long have you known?"

I swallowed hard. "Seven seconds."

"My God…is this…good? Are we celebrating?"

I let out a barking laugh. "I don't know."

She looked so deeply into my eyes; I thought she'd snatch my soul. Then she pulled me into a tight hug. "I think it's wonderful."

I hugged her back. Was it? I guess you never know what you really want until you almost lose it. If that mountain lion had her way, I'd have never known. My story would be incomplete. But here I was, turning the page. No matter what the men in my life thought of this news, I knew one thing for sure. I wanted this. Even if I had to do it alone.

"Who's the father?" Hope asked. "Is it Betz? Please tell me it's Betz."

I bit my lip. I'd never told her about Marcus. I'd kept him a secret from my family. Not because I was ashamed of him, but because if we had a shot at something big, I wanted us to be the first to know. But I'd held him at arm's length. "It's not Betz. And I feel like I should tell the father before I tell anyone else. I hope you understand."

"Of course." Hope reached out and rubbed my arm. "Just know that no matter what the situation with the father is, I'll be here for you. I'll be the best second cousin your baby has ever seen."

"Better than Joy?" I asked, referring to her flaky sister.

We both laughed.

"Joy will be the most eccentric cousin. I'll be the best."

We hugged again. Nothing like a near-death experience to remind you of what's important. My family was small, but we were fiercely protective of each other. I often held people at arm's length, and maybe it was the hormones talking, but right now I felt like the luckiest person on the planet.

* * *

We heated another can of stew and then brought bowls out to the others. Settled around the dormant firepit, Hope wrinkled her nose. "Do you smell that?"

I sniffed the air. "It's a campfire. There must be another camp."

"I suppose that's possible." Hope looked at Izzy. "Did you encounter any other campers when you were wandering the woods today?"

Izzy shook her head. "No, but I doubt we're the only ones out here."

It could also be the escaped convict. I still couldn't shake the feeling of having been watched earlier. Sure, it could have been the mountain lion or another scary animal, but they didn't start fires. If we weren't the only humans around, you'd think anyone on the up and up would make contact and introduce themselves, not just watch us like some pervert. Unless they had nefarious intent.

Normally, I would have gone off to investigate, but I had a new respect for the forest. And more to live for. I exchanged a knowing glance with Hope. She understood the stakes were higher, too.

The woods were even more intimidating at dusk. We now knew we wouldn't be rescued until morning. With a prisoner on the loose, spending another night out here was even more troubling.

Without a fire of our own, it was cold, and there wasn't much we could do in the dark. So, we turned in early, knowing that this would at least be our last day, and we could soon put this adventure behind us.

Chapter Seventeen

Betz

On the drive to North Phoenix, Moody ran both Izzy Hutchinson and the boyfriend, Marty Goodwin. Both had clean records, although Marty's driver's license had expired.

The couple lived in a sprawling apartment complex that almost took up a city block. Betz's shoulders tightened at the thought of finding Goodwin's unit in the poorly designed monstrosity. The numbering system made no sense. Whoever designed it must have been drunk, high, or they wanted to mess with first responders.

After driving up and down rows of covered parking, the roofs blocking the signs with the address, they found the block that housed the apartment they were looking for.

Calling in their location, Betz led Moody up the stairs to a unit on the third and top floor. Hand on the butt of his gun, Betz thumped on the door. It hadn't been closed tightly, and it inched open with the weight of his knock.

"Police," he announced.

Moody met his glance with a knowing nod. Both drew their weapons, then Betz pushed the door further open with the toe of his boot.

A galley kitchen came into view. "Police," he repeated. "Anyone home?"

Dread dropped like a weight in his stomach. He eased through the door, his partner right behind him.

A pile of dishes sat high in the sink. The smell of peanut butter wafted from the half-made sandwich on the counter. The knife lay across the top of the jar. Something interrupted someone.

The kitchen opened onto a small dining area that housed a Peloton bike instead of a table. Betz ducked under the low-hanging chandelier and turned into the living room. The TV was on, a *Friends* rerun playing on the muted television.

This wasn't looking good.

Beyond the living room, a bedroom door was ajar. Betz took the corner slowly. With his gun at the ready, he swept the room. On the floor, he spotted a foot sticking out from the other side of the bed. Betz prepared himself for the sight of the motionless body. The man lay face down, his head twisted to the side. A gaping hole split the side of his head. Bile rose in Betz's throat. He'd never get used to this. The man was obviously dead, but Betz felt for a pulse anyway, while Moody cleared the only other room, the bathroom.

Izzy Hutchinson was nowhere to be found.

* * *

Turning over the crime scene to other detectives, Betz and Moody rushed to the precinct where Pug Sampson waited in an interview room.

"What does Phillips want with a social worker?" Moody said when Betz put the Interceptor into park.

"And who's he with?" Betz asked.

Inside the building, Betz got a Coke from the machine and brought it to the interview room, placing it on the table in front of Pug Sampson. Sampson sat sideways in the plastic chair, his legs stretched in front of him and crossed at the ankle. Like he owned the place.

Betz needed to gain control. He settled in the closest chair and scooted it forward, so Pug had to sit back and spread his knees to make room for him. Once he'd invaded Pug's personal space, the thug's smug expression faded.

"What did you want with Izzy Hutchinson?"

Pug blinked, squirming under Betz's intense stare. "Me? I don't want nothing with her."

"Okay, Phillips, then. What does he want?"

Pug tried to back up, but his chair was already against the wall. With the table on one side, two walls, and Betz surrounding him, he had nowhere to go.

"I don't know."

Betz leaned forward. He was so close; Pug's sour breath washed over his face. It repulsed him, but he powered on. "Know what I think? You're a flunky. Phillips is calling the shots. But you're the one in custody. You're the one who's gonna pay the price."

"I hate that," Moody said. "Hate when the boss gets away with murder and the peons take the fall."

"I ain't no peon."

"Yeah?" Betz laughed. "Cause I don't see Phillips sitting here, do you?"

Moody made a show of looking around the room. "I don't see him."

"And it's not just that you shot at me. Not just that you resisted arrest. Not just that you held hostages. Phillips is a murderer. Know what that makes you?"

Pug's jaw twitched.

"An accomplice," Moody said. "And the punishment for being an accomplice…well…have you heard of Tison versus Arizona?"

Betz stared hard into Pug's beady eyes that blinked furiously. "You don't have a law degree, do you, Pug?"

He wiped his palms on his thighs and cleared his throat.

Betz leaned in. They were now nose to nose. "Tison versus Arizona, Pug. Well, that basically says an accomplice can get the death penalty."

Pug's eyes grew larger. "I didn't kill no one."

Betz didn't flinch. "Unfortunately, that doesn't matter."

"Know what I hate?" Moody said. "Did you see that recent story on the news? The lethal injection didn't work. They kept trying to find a vein…and well."

"To suffer like that," Betz said.

"Okay, okay." Pug held up his hands. "They were going after Izzy

Hutchinson because she was a counselor. They thought she could lead them to Hana Stevens."

Betz and Moody exchanged a glance. "Hana Stevens?" Moody said. "The girl whose parents Phillips killed?"

Pug nodded. "I want an attorney. And a deal."

Betz leaned back in his seat and pushed his chair away. "We'll see about that."

Chapter Eighteen

Betz

As the sun broke the horizon, Betz and Moody climbed back into the Interceptor, weak station coffees in their hands. Sleep-deprived, they'd need gallons of the stuff. Or a power nap. But Pug had given them something to work with before he'd lawyered up.

"While you were in the bathroom, I contacted Izzy Hutchinson's employer, Harvey Boone. He'll meet us at the treatment center. We have enough time to get some decent coffee," Moody said, grimacing as she took a drink.

There was a Starbucks on the way, and they stopped for Venti Robusta coffees. If that didn't wake them, nothing would.

Boone met them in the parking lot of the behavioral health facility. Gray hair was slicked back. A bulbous nose and ruddy complexion hinted at a drinking problem. The odor of alcohol that he tried to cover up with cologne confirmed it.

Hypocrite or a recent relapse? Either way, Boone needed to heed his own message.

"Izzy should be working," he said. "A group of them left yesterday for a wilderness adventure camp."

The color drained from Betz's face. When he learned that Izzy Hutchinson was a social worker, he never thought there would be a connection to Casey. "Wait a minute. Is this a program for troubled teens?"

"You've heard of it?" Boone asked as he punched in the code to open the side door.

Betz cleared his throat. "Does Casey Carson work for you?"

Boone nodded. "We hired two POs to help keep a little law and order, given our clients' criminal tendencies. Ms. Carson was one of them. You know her?"

Betz nodded. His mouth went so dry he couldn't talk.

Moody stepped in. "You've met Casey? Casey Carson?"

"Haven't met her," Boone said. "My HR person hired her. But she came highly recommended, and I'll sign her paycheck."

As they followed the director down a hall, Betz tried to focus his thoughts. But they ran wild. "Do you have a way to reach them? The campers?"

"Of course." He led them down a long hallway to a closed yellow door. "I'm sure everyone's fine. Laurie's manning the radio and would have let me know if there were any problems. Other than me and the campers, no one else knows who's on the adventure. Privacy law protects that information."

He pushed the door open, and they stepped into the room. A woman sat in front of a computer at a messy desk. Her head rested on folded arms. She didn't move.

Boone reached down and shook her shoulder. Slowly, she stirred awake. Combing her fingers through her hair, she stretched and looked around the room.

"Have you heard from the campers?" he asked.

Laurie struggled to pull herself together. She worked her mouth, then took a sip of water from the bottle on the table. "Ah, not yet."

Boone crossed his arms over his puffed-out chest. "You know the protocol. You should have been reaching out."

Laurie bit her lip. "I'm sorry. I mean, I'm sure they're okay."

This wouldn't look good on her next performance evaluation. But Betz didn't feel sorry for her. He wanted to shake her himself. "Can you call them now?"

Boone grabbed the radio off the charger on Laurie's desk. "I'm sure they're fine. Probably having too much fun to remember to check in." He keyed the device. "Santos, you there? Santos?"

But only the buzz of dead air filled the room.

Chapter Nineteen

I woke with an odd taste in my mouth.

I'd hardly slept. Tossing and turning was impossible on the narrow cot. Especially with Felony glued to my side. Thoughts ricocheted around my mind like ping-pong balls. Lying there, I rehearsed sharing my news with Betz and Marcus. Even with me controlling the scenario, it didn't go well.

Betz would be mad. Maybe not mad, hurt. Crushed that I'd even slept with Marcus. Not that he hadn't had a fling himself. We weren't an item at the time. Still weren't. We could date other people. But I hadn't taken the news that he'd been banging my arch-nemesis well. I had no right to be jealous. That didn't mean I wasn't. And it didn't mean he wouldn't be as well.

I could picture Marcus stepping back as if I had a contagious disease. "Woah, pump the brakes, Sunshine. We're just getting to know each other." He'd be on his bike back to Jersey before I could finish my first trimester.

The charred flavor of burned wood choked me and dragged me back to the present and away from my worries. Coughing, I swung my feet to the floor. Had I forgotten to put the campfire out before we went to bed last night? But then I remembered. We hadn't started a fire because I'd dropped the wood while escaping a mountain lion who wanted to eat me.

With yesterday's scorpion incident still fresh in my mind, I felt for my hiking boots, turned them upside down, and shook the hell out of them before sliding them on. My gauze-wrapped hands made it difficult to tie the laces.

The other beds remained occupied. Rico hadn't been keen on sleeping alone in the men's cabin, so he'd taken Mika's spot. The only empty cot belonged to Izzy. Had she smelled the smoke too and gotten up to investigate?

The battery-operated clock on the wall told me it was just after seven a.m. I opened the cabin door and stepped out into the cool morning air. Felony darted past me and marked the nearest tree. As suspected, the firepit was dormant. Not the source of the smoke. The sky above me was thick, hazy, and unnaturally dark for the time of day.

I climbed onto the picnic table so I could see above the tree line. A strange orange glow rolled across the sky.

Crap.

With Felony behind me, I hurried down the path that we'd hiked in on. I was running now, gagging on the thick particles of soot that floated in the air. The back of my throat burned.

At the bend—the spot where I'd watched the eagle take flight—I came up short. Standing at the precipice, I watched a red glow dance across the towering trees below. Fast-moving flames gulped vegetation like a tsunami. It was alive and headed our way.

The way out was no more. No one would come to rescue us. Not in time.

Even worse, I had no idea what lay in the other direction. We had little choice but to find out.

* * *

I headed back to camp in an all-out sprint. *Oh crap...oh crap...oh crap...*

Flinging the cabin door open, I rushed from cot to cot, shaking everyone awake. "Get up! Get up!"

Hope sat up first, rubbing her eyes and blinking at me. "What's going on?"

"The forest is on fire," I said, panic altering my voice. "Everyone get up. Get your shoes on. We need to get out of here. Now!"

Bodies flexed and stumbled from their coverings. Hands reached for shoes, grabbed backpacks, and one by one, people trickled into the yard.

Hana was the last one to spill out of the cabin. "I smell smoke. What are we going to do?"

I pointed to the woods behind the huts. An area I'd yet to discover. "We'll have to go that way. The fire is closing in on us from the main path."

Rico scratched his head. "What about Izzy?"

"Izzy!" I yelled, pacing between buildings. "Where are you?"

Hope ran to the kitchen, slamming the door open. "Izzy?"

I checked the outhouses. Empty.

Embers drifted from the sky like a light snowfall. "Everyone get ready," I said. "We leave in five minutes." I ducked into the kitchen and grabbed packages of crackers, a few apples, and as many bottles of water as I could fit in my bag. Leaving my precious Diet Coke behind, I zipped up my pack, hoping the limited rations would get us by until we made it to safety.

"Izzy's backpack is gone," Rico reported, exiting the cabin. "She must have left already."

And not alerted us to the fire? No time to dwell on that. Not now. "Let's go," I said. "She must have headed out."

And maybe started the fire, leaving us to die. But then why not let the mountain lion finish me yesterday? She was up to something, but what? Maybe I wasn't her target. I didn't have time to make sense of it.

Overgrowth covered the path behind the camp, but I could detect a trail, probably not used in years.

I was hyperalert as I ushered the others ahead. First Hope, then Rico. Hana moved slowly in front of me, obviously still in pain.

Rustling noises came from the woods around us as tall grass swished against my hiking boots. Animals seeking higher ground? The fugitive? Izzy or other hikers in the woods?

I wasn't stopping to find out. We had no choice but to move forward.

Aspens shed golden leaves that floated to the ground. I almost cried, thinking the fire would swallow the surrounding beauty, devastating it, leaving the white bark dark with ash.

Felony pulled, wanting to be first. I tried to rein him in while fishing my phone out of my pocket. Awkwardly jostling it in my gauze-encased hands,

I turned it on with my thumb while keeping pace with the others. When the screen lit, the battery was in the red, but I had one bar. One chance to call for help. Making frequent glances at the trail so I wouldn't trip, I opened the last text message I'd read earlier.

From Marcus. I didn't have time to search my contacts for the best option of who to call. I clicked on the reply box and spoke into my phone. "Fire. Leaving camp. Send help." Knowing my window was short, I pushed send, not elaborating.

The line above the message moved, then stopped before the phone went dark. Did the message even go through?

Sliding my useless phone back into my pocket, I followed the group deeper into the woods.

Chapter Twenty

Marcus

Marcus pounded a nail into the last shingle on the flip he worked on in South Tempe. The sun blazed in a cloudless, deep blue sky, and he wiped his brow with his forearm before easing the vibrating phone out of the back pocket of his Levi's.

There was only one person he wanted to hear from, but he doubted it was her. Casey had made it clear she wouldn't be in touch for the next ten days. Not only wouldn't she have cell reception, but she'd stressed her need for some time to herself. With each day that passed after she'd declared her self-imposed break from him, from them, he felt her slowly slipping away. Not that he'd ever had her. Sure, they kissed a few times, and he vividly remembered the night they shared, which blew his mind. But none of that made her fall for him. If anything, she was more out of reach.

She was going through some things, sure. She recently lost her mother, and members of Phoenix's most dangerous gang nearly murdered her twice. He understood she had a lot going on. But that didn't make her distancing herself from him any easier to take. He'd driven across the flipping country for her, for fuck's sake. Left all he knew behind.

If he were being honest, she was out of his league. He lived paycheck to paycheck, job to job. He didn't have a college degree like she did. Like Betz—who made no secret of the fact that he still loved her. And he hadn't had the best track record in the romance department. Add a head injury to the mix, and even he had to admit, she could do better.

Still, he wanted a chance.

Even if that meant giving her space.

Covering the screen to block out the sun, he squinted to read the text on his phone. It **was** Casey.

Fire. Leaving camp. Send help.

Fuck.

Bubbles appeared, showing she was typing more. If that was even what it meant.

The bubbles disappeared.

Casey? He wrote back. *Fire? What do you mean, fire?*

Don't leave me hanging.

Casey???

No more messages came.

Marcus shot down the ladder and jumped to the ground. Ignoring the questioning look on his foreman's face, he ran to his motorcycle. They would probably fire him for deserting the job, but that didn't matter to him now.

Marcus knew Casey had headed toward the mountains outside of Flagstaff, but he didn't know her exact location. He'd never been to northern Arizona. And she hadn't even told him the name of the company she'd be working for.

Hopefully, her father knew more.

He'd only met Albert Carson once, and the man had barely acknowledged him. Casey probably hadn't told her family about their friendship, or whatever she'd call what they were doing. She wasn't one to gush about a crush. Her feelings for him were a mystery. One that drove him crazy. He had no idea where he stood. But something about her made him feel like it was worth his while to wait around to find out.

Not like he had any other prospects on the horizon. There was no shortage of women who would slip him their numbers. But that never worked out for him. His previous relationships had been based on lust. He had that for Casey, sure, but there were levels that ran much deeper than a physical attraction. They'd bonded over near-death experiences, but it was more than that. He wanted to know what she thought—about everything. Wanted to know what she felt. She made him want to be a better person.

Within ten minutes, he'd arrived at Casey's father's house.

Leaving his helmet on the seat of his motorcycle, he walked up to the front door and rang the bell. An older woman who dressed a lot like Casey's cousin Joy—Spandex shorts and a barely legal top—answered the door. For a moment, he thought he had the wrong house. Casey's dad was bald and boring, as he recalled. Flashy women didn't seem to be his style. But what did Marcus know?

"Ah…. Is Mr. Carson home?"

The woman dried her hands on a kitchen towel. Brightly polished nails suggested she could gouge his eyes out if she wanted to. "No, he's not. What are you selling, sweetie?"

Marcus tucked his hair behind his ear. "Not selling anything. I'm a friend of Casey's."

"Well, why didn't you say so?" She stepped back and ushered him inside. "Come in."

He hesitated. There wasn't time for this. He wasn't even sure what he hoped to accomplish by coming here. But then another swatch of spandex walked by. This one was lime green. "Joy?"

Casey's cousin stopped mid-stride. "Marcus! What are you doing here?"

It wasn't his usual reaction, but he was happy to see her. Joy was a huge flirt, and while she provided some comic relief, she came on too strong. If he let her get too close, he was pretty sure she'd eat him alive and then pout that he didn't enjoy it.

He looked at her feet. Instead of her usual hooker heels, she had on those weird shoes that were like gloves for your feet.

But she looked happy to see him. Too happy. Rushing over, she pulled him into a bone-crushing hug. His suspicions were confirmed. Her breasts weren't real. When she pulled away, he forced his eyes up and away from her ample cleavage. Her chest was so in-your-face, a monk would look. "Do you know where Casey is?"

Joy shrugged. "The woods. Somewhere around Flagstaff."

Marcus sighed. He knew that much. "Never mind." He turned to leave.

She put her hand on his arm. "Wait a minute. What's going on?"

"Casey messaged me. There's a fire. She's in trouble."

"Fire?" the older woman said. "I saw on the news just a few minutes ago that there's a fire in Coconino County."

"That's where Flagstaff is," Joy said. "You don't think—"

"Anyway," Marcus said, realizing the conversation would get him nowhere. Was a waste of time. Time Casey might not have. "She said to send help. I'm going to the police."

"Wait!" Joy grabbed a bag off the table by the door. "I'm coming with you."

Marcus took a step back. "Not necessary. I don't even know what I'm going to do."

She looped her arm through his. "I was just about to work out, but I can skip it. Let's go see Barry. He has connections."

"Barry?"

"Betz. His first name is Barry."

Casey had never called him that. If he could have shaken Joy off, he would have, but she had a way about her, and he'd never seen her take no for an answer.

Chapter Twenty-One

Marcus

Betz was the last person Marcus wanted to turn to, but he had no choice.

Not that Marcus was on the wrong side of the law, but he teetered close enough to the edge that cops made him nervous. Plus, Betz had been married to Casey. They had a history, and any idiot could see that they still had a thing for each other. Even if Marcus had distracted her from it sometimes.

Marcus pulled his motorcycle up to a meter outside the main precinct in downtown Phoenix. Glancing around to make sure no one was watching, he withdrew a handgun from his ankle holster that was tucked into his boot, then locked it in the locker mounted to his Harley.

He didn't need some derelict stealing his gun, or his bike. Satisfied that no one but Joy saw him secure his weapon, he pushed his hair back with his sunglasses and shrugged. "Diablo still has it out for me." He wasn't sure why he felt the need to explain why he was packing.

Joy flashed a sly smile. "I know, sugar. Your secret's safe with me."

* * *

The doughy cop at the reception desk must have drawn the short straw, and he didn't look happy with his assignment. He greeted Joy and Marcus with a grunt.

"Looking for Detective Betz," Marcus said.

The officer lowered his glasses and gave them the once-over. Marcus knew he had a bad-boy look. He could have cut his hair, shaved a little closer, concealed the tat on his bicep. He could have stepped up his wardrobe from Levi's and T-shirts, but he worked in construction, and he was comfortable in his skin. The risk was that people judged him, and this cop was no different. As the officer's gaze moved to Joy, his eyes just about bugged out of his head. He probably thought Marcus was a pimp and Joy was one of his workers.

Marcus had thought that very thing about Joy the first time they'd met. But Casey had been there, and once he saw her, Joy all but disappeared, and nothing else mattered. Marcus cleared his throat, reminding the officer he'd asked a question.

The cop tore his eyes off Joy. "Yeah, what do you want with him?"

"Can you tell him Marcus Sheldon is here to see him? It's important."

The cop sighed as if he'd asked for a meeting with the Pope.

After checking some things on his computer with all the urgency of a DMV employee, he said, "I can give you his number." He scribbled something on a piece of paper and slid it across the desk. "You can leave a voicemail."

"There's no time for that."

The cop was unfazed. Out of options, Marcus took the number and paced around the lobby while he made the call. Getting Betz's voicemail, he left a message. "This is Marcus Sheldon. Casey's friend. I heard from her, and it's not good. Call me." He rattled off his number.

Stepping back outside, he lowered his sunglasses against the mid-afternoon glare. Joy followed him. He cursed under his breath when one of those fancy cop SUVs almost hit his motorcycle as it pulled in front of the precinct. A woman climbed out of the driver's seat, a cell to her ear as she walked past him and went inside the building.

A convertible pulled up and double-parked next to the Interceptor. A woman with spiky blonde hair sat in the driver's seat. Betz exited the SUV and stood at the passenger's door of the sports car, talking to the woman.

From where he stood, Marcus could tell the conversation was heated.

An ache assaulted the back of Marcus' throat. He recognized Jasmine, Betz's sister, right away. She'd invited him to stay at their house once, when he and Casey were hiding from Diablo. She was a lieutenant, and she didn't take any crap. Even Casey found Jasmine intimidating.

"Barry!" Joy waved her arms in the air and hurried over to him.

Marcus took a deep breath and followed.

Betz accepted Joy's long hug. "What are you doing here?" he asked, arching his eyebrows at Marcus.

"It's Casey," Joy said, patting her chest. "There's a fire."

"What?" Betz glanced at his sister.

"Slow down," Jasmine said. "What do you mean, fire?"

"You know Casey's on an adventure in the woods with some juvenile delinquents, right?" Joy explained.

"Right," Betz said.

Marcus cleared his throat and took out his phone. Bringing up Casey's text message, he held it out for Betz to see. "She must have lost her signal because she hasn't answered me since then."

Betz squinted at the message, then rubbed the back of his neck. "I'm heading up there," he said. "Too many things aren't right."

Jasmine flexed her hands against the steering wheel and stared hard at her brother. "Let the Coconino Sheriff's Office handle it. It's their jurisdiction. And you're needed here."

"I believe there could be a connection between my case and Flagstaff." Phillips is looking for the girl. I'm going."

"Phillips?" Joy said.

Everyone ignored her.

"You're always rushing to rescue Casey." Jasmine spat her name out like it was rancid meat. "I hate to pull rank on you, little brother, but I'm ordering you not to go."

Betz pulled the badge off his belt and tossed it on the seat next to his sister. "Fine. I'll go as a civilian. But I'm going."

"You're a hopeless case. You think chasing her will make her love you again?" She cast a stoney-eyed glare at him, put her car in gear, and drove off, tires screeching.

Marcus' stomach clenched. As much as he wanted Betz to heed Jasmine's words and stay away from Casey, he needed him to help find her. Betz had connections that no one else he knew had.

Watching his sister drive away, Betz clenched his fists and shook his head. Then he leaned into the SUV and retrieved a duffel bag. Approaching Marcus, he said, "Let me give you my number. I want you to call me if Casey gets back in touch with you. Send me a screenshot of any messages right away."

"I'm going with you," Marcus said.

Betz snorted. "No. You're not." He recited his number, and Joy entered it into her phone. Then he stormed off.

Marcus kept pace. "I'll just follow you. It would be easier if we went together."

"I'm going too," Joy called from behind.

Marcus trailed Betz to the employee parking lot. Betz stopped at a gray Toyota 4Runner and unlocked the door. Tossing his bag inside, he said. "You're not coming. I don't have time to babysit the two of you. I need to get to Casey."

They were at an impasse. Before Betz could climb into the car, Jasmine pulled up, boxing him in. Climbing out of the convertible, she took purposeful steps toward them. Marcus and Joy moved out of her way. "Let's at least talk this through," she said. "Come inside. We'll call the Sheriff's office. Get someone on the line who knows the area."

"I can do that while I drive," Betz said. "Move your car."

Jasmine crossed her arms. In her heels, she was eye-to-eye with her brother. "I may be your sister, but I'm also your superior, and you're being insubordinate."

Betz took off his glasses and laid them on the hood of the car. He rubbed his eyes with his thumb and forefinger. "Look, I gave you my badge. I don't work for you anymore. I'm sick of this shit. Sick of you trying to control my life."

Marcus felt like a third wheel, surprised he found himself rooting for Betz. How could he fault him for loving Casey? Joy wisely held her tongue, but she watched the exchange with her mouth wide open.

Jasmine sighed. "I understand your feelings. But this has become a conflict of interest. You're too close to this."

"What would you do if it were Karen?" he said. "I know you still love her, even if she's moved on."

Jasmine's lips tightened. Marcus didn't know who Karen was, but Betz had obviously hit a nerve. "I get it," she said. "I still think it's best we manage it from here. Let Coconino County do their job."

Betz reached behind him for his glasses. Instead of picking them up, he knocked them sideways, and they tumbled across the hood of the Interceptor. Dropping over the side, they fell, bouncing across the pavement. Joy startled and jumped back, her heel landing on the lens.

When she pulled her foot away, shattered glass littered the blacktop.

Even Jasmine looked worried as Betz scooped the worthless specs off the ground.

"Divine intervention," Jasmine said, turning and getting into her car. The three of them watched her speed away, leaving them staring after her in awe.

Chapter Twenty-Two

"I need…I need to rest." Hana steadied herself against a tree. Her breath came in labored gasps.

I helped her ease her pack off her shoulders and lowered it to the ground. "Where's your inhaler?"

Hana pointed to her bag. "Front pocket."

I dug through the pouch but found only some tissues and nail clippers. "Not here. Okay if I look elsewhere?"

Hana nodded, taking ragged breaths. I dug deep into the pack, finding the small device at the bottom of the bag. I held it up like a prize, then handed it to her.

She shook it, pressed the button, and inhaled. A whistling sound punctured the silence. Hand on her chest, she took shallow breaths, and the color slowly returned to her face. She studied the device. "There should be another one in my bag. This one only has a few doses left."

I rummaged through the pack, feeling my way through neatly folded clothes. "Can't find it."

What little color had flushed her cheeks, drained. She bent down and took over the search, removing items one-by-one and placing them on a rock. I got to my feet and approached Hope. "Just what we need, another problem."

Hope shook her head. "I'm starting to wonder about our employer. The camp wasn't what they had promised. They trusted one person with the supplies. And it doesn't seem like they vetted anyone. First Izzy…" She glanced at Rico, but his hard stare silenced her. "And then letting an asthmatic engage in intensive physical activity, not smart."

"She was okay on the way in," I said.

"It's the smoke," Hana said. "It's aggravating my asthma." She sat back on her heels and, with hands on hips, she looked at her belongings spread out around her. Tears glistened in her eyes. "I must have forgotten to pack it. I have only three puffs left. What am I going to do?"

"How long does a dose last?" Hope asked.

"Around four hours."

I bent down and started repacking her bag. "Then we move. Let's put some distance between us and the smoke."

Hana rose to her feet, and I helped her put her pack back on. Once again, we were on the move.

Chapter Twenty-Three

Maybe Joy had stepped on his glasses, ruining them. But if Jasmine hadn't caused him to become so tightly wound, it never would have happened. Why couldn't she understand his feelings for Casey? He knew mentioning Karen was a low blow. Jasmine had moved in with him after they'd broken up. And she was anything but over her.

His sister was happy with this setback. He needed his glasses after his contacts were destroyed. He couldn't drive without them.

She got what she wanted. He couldn't go.

He didn't have the time needed to go home and get a replacement, not that he could drive himself there. His house was in the opposite direction from Flagstaff. Damn her. Well, she was wrong if she thought he'd let that get in the way of his getting to Casey. He had only to figure out how to get back in the game.

Joy and Marcus stood speechless. Even blurred, he could make out the bewildered expressions on their faces. He could feel their discomfort. Airing his dirty laundry was the last thing he wanted to do. Especially in front of these two.

"Okay," he said, thinking out loud. "We can solve this problem. I hate to take the time, but I need you to drive me home so I can get new contacts. Then, I'll drop you off back here on my way north."

Marcus took the keys. "Sounds like a plan." He hopped into the driver's seat while Betz got in on the passenger side.

"Oh, no, you don't," Joy said, opening the back door. "You're not leaving me behind."

After everyone was seated, Marcus adjusted the mirrors while Betz fastened his seatbelt. He was fuming mad, but could feel a bit of control returning his way. He'd deal with Jasmine later. As siblings, they'd had their fair share of squabbles, had played pranks on each other. But pulling the insubordinate card was a bridge too far. She wouldn't take him seriously. He didn't mean to resign, and she'd know that. But she knew he was on the edge and worried about Casey. And what did she do? She pushed him over.

"You remember where I live, right?" Betz said as Marcus pulled onto the street. "Take I-10 east."

Marcus glanced his way, hand casually on the steering wheel. "Sure thing."

Betz looked down at his phone. Shocker. The screen was blurry. He could recognize the text icon, but when he opened the app, he couldn't read the letters on the keyboard. Couldn't even find the microphone button. He was pretty sure he'd received no new messages. His phone would have vibrated if Casey had reached out to him. He would have felt it.

It bugged him that she'd contacted Marcus and not him. He couldn't dwell on that. To help her, he'd have to put his feelings aside. He could lick his wounds later.

But he was as blind with rage as he was with his vision impairment.

He turned in his seat and looked back at Joy. "You got your phone?"

She fished in her bag. "Yup."

"Find the number for the Coconino Sheriff's office."

"I can do that."

Betz faced forward, glancing up to see the sign for Interstate 17. They were traveling north. Not what he'd asked Marcus to do. "What the hell? I told you to go east."

"Sorry," Marcus said, although he sounded anything but sorry. "Like I told you, I'm going with you."

Betz gave up trying to control his emotions. He was about to break.

"Without my contacts, I can't fucking see."

"Well," Marcus said calmly. "I guess you'll just have to rely on me and Joy. We'll be your eyes."

"That's absurd."

Marcus gave a little laugh, smug at being in control of the situation. "Then you should have played nice when I asked to come. Now, it is what it is."

Betz would have strangled him. But then he'd have to rely on Joy, which would surely slow them down.

Chapter Twenty-Four

The air ahead was clear, but when I turned to look behind us, a yellow haze hung heavy, like slow-moving fog. I was lucky to have healthy lungs, but the taste of fire tickled the back of my throat, and I knew the air quality was poor.

What would that do to my unborn baby? I would have Googled the stages of pregnancy if I had been home with internet capabilities. I was only six weeks pregnant at most, and the fetus couldn't be bigger than a peanut. Did it even have lungs yet? Most likely, it was safe deep inside me. I took some comfort in that.

Felony was another story. He was doing the reverse sneeze thing that told me the smoke was getting to him. I wished I had left him at home with my dad. But I thought he'd enjoy a few days in the woods. And frankly, he'd wormed his way so deeply into my heart, I'd be the one having separation anxiety if we were apart.

I wanted to move faster, but Hana's sore foot limited us. Hope and Rico seemed to have forgotten about us, keeping a good pace and disappearing ahead. "You doing okay?" I asked.

She shrugged. "My foot hurts, but I'm breathing better. Not like I can do much about it."

"Sorry."

"Not your fault. Just glad you're here. You're easy to talk to. Can't say that about many people in my life."

I took a leap of faith. "I'm sorry about your parents. Were you close?"

Another shrug. "My mom had issues. But my dad and I got along. We played video games when he wasn't working."

"What did he do?"

"He managed a restaurant and a gym."

"Do you mind my asking how they died?"

The path became a little wider, and we could walk side-by-side. She glanced at me, a look of pain crossing her face, aging her. I was sorry I had asked. "You don't have to tell me."

"No, it's okay. Someone shot them. Executed them. They begged for their lives while I hid. The cops think it happened over drugs. But my parents didn't do drugs."

So, definitely Phillips. The story was too familiar to be a coincidence. "Did you tell the police that?"

She pulled on her pigtails. "I did. But they didn't listen to me. The cop was a jerk. I just gave up."

"Gave up? So, you didn't tell them everything?"

"Mostly."

"Mostly?"

She stopped and grabbed my arm. "Did you hear that?"

Felony obviously had. He pulled towards the woods, straining against my hold on his leash. Ears pinned back, he gave a low growl like nothing I'd heard from him before.

I put my hand on Hana's backpack and encouraged her to move faster. "Keep going." I didn't know what was out there, but with the mountain lion scare fresh in my mind, I wasn't about to wait around to find out.

Chapter Twenty-Five

Marcus

Marcus glanced at Betz, reading his mood. He'd just ended a call with the Coconino Sheriff's Office, and it didn't seem to help him overcome his sour state. So, Marcus expected more bad news.

"What'd they say?" he asked.

Betz gave him the side-eye. His displeasure that Marcus had commandeered his mission to find Casey was obvious. When he spoke, his tone was so sharp, Marcus half-expected to bleed. "The fires are in the camp's area where Casey and Hope should be. The sheriff's office has set up a command station and is preparing to send in a rescue team. Meanwhile, they're fighting the fire from the air and ground."

Marcus's heart dropped into his work boots as he looked back to the road. He tried to picture the area in his head, but he had no idea what to expect. He'd never been to the high desert and didn't know what northern Arizona looked like. Since arriving in Phoenix a few months prior, he hadn't had the chance to explore other parts of the state.

As they moved north, the scenery morphed into something greener and less populated the higher they climbed. The highway snaked past saguaro cacti that stood like cowboys on hillsides defending their land. Sporadic farmland and the occasional ranch dotted the landscape. "So, we're headed to the command station?" Marcus guessed.

"We are." Betz glanced over his shoulder. "Joy, can you pull up your GPS? And keep trying to reach Casey."

"Sure thing," she said, eager to please.

Betz gave her the coordinates, and in moments, a computer-generated voice guided them north. They still had about an hour to go.

"No answer from Casey. I tried Hope, too, but the calls just go to voicemail. But I want you to know I'm psychic," Joy announced loudly from the backseat. "So, I know they're okay. In danger, sure, but Casey is tough. She can handle this. And Hope? Well, she always lands on her feet. Quite frankly, I'm getting tired of coming to their aid. Who would have thought Kate and I would be the stable ones in the family?"

Betz let out a snort.

"Don't make this about you, Joy," Marcus said. "Or you'll be using your psychic abilities to determine whether you should trust the trucker who picks you up when I leave your ass on the side of the road."

Joy smacked his shoulder. "I can understand why Barry's cranky, but you need to relax."

Marcus tightened his grip on the steering wheel. From his peripheral vision, he thought he saw a smile break Betz's bad mood.

Maybe they had more than loving Casey in common, after all.

Chapter Twenty-Six

Deep in the foliage, I could no longer see the orange sky behind us, but I could still taste the smoke. Not that I knew how to use a compass, but some guidance would have been nice. I had no sense of our direction, or if we were moving in circles. For all I knew, we were doing a loop that would lead us right back to the fire. I never understood the east, west thing. When I ask people for directions, I only need to know if I should head toward Target or McDonald's.

I knew the Grand Canyon was a good drive north of the camp, and then Utah was further north. What good did that knowledge do? Even if I had a satellite radio and could call for help, I wouldn't know how I'd convey our location. What would I say? We're by some trees? But the police could probably ping the phone.

Every so often, fallen trees blocked the path, slowing down Hope and Rico and allowing Hana and I to catch up to them. We rounded a bend to find Hope sitting on a log, elbows on knees, head hanging down. She looked defeated. Rico, obviously feeling better, balanced eight feet off the ground on a giant fallen log, treating it like a balance beam. "Be careful," I called out, realizing how old I sounded as soon as the words left my mouth. When did I turn into my dad? But the last thing we needed was another injury.

Rico glanced down at me and rolled his eyes. "Just trying to see if I can get a better view of what's ahead. I can't see anything but more trees."

"What are we even doing?" Hope said. "This is all so hopeless."

Rico laughed. "Hope is hopeless."

Hana plopped down next to my cousin, pulled out her inhaler, and took another hit. If I remembered correctly, that left two more doses. I hoped we'd find civilization before she ran out of the stuff, but I, too, was losing hope. The forest couldn't go on forever, but it felt like it would.

Since my phone was already dead, I asked the others to check theirs for a signal. But time had rendered all devices useless. No one would be able to track us down. Not that way.

Rico walked heel to toe—as if he was taking a field sobriety test—down the log, then jumped to the ground. "I'm hungry. Did you bring food?"

Definitely feeling better. "I have a few granola bars, some crackers, and apples." I opened my pack and sorted through my supplies.

"What do you think happened to Izzy?" Hope asked.

I bit my lip. "Don't know." But something was off about her. I couldn't shake the thought that she was somehow responsible for our current plight.

Taking two granola bars out of my pack, I broke them in half and passed the pieces out. Grubby hands accepted my miserable offering. "That's all?" Rico said, swallowing his ration in two bites.

"For now. I have a few more, but we should save them. We don't know how long we'll be out here."

Hope got to her feet. "It's going to be dark soon. We should find a place to camp for the night."

We couldn't go much further in the fading light, I knew that. But the fire wouldn't take a break. It didn't need to rest. It was gaining energy, getting bigger, more out of hand, with every acre it devoured. We had to get further ahead of it. "Let's keep going for a bit," I said. "Maybe we can find some shelter."

I slipped Felony a few pieces of kibble and squirted a stream of water into his mouth before taking a quick drink myself.

Hana was so petite; she needed a boost to get over the log.

The deeper into the woods we went, the harder it was to tell if we were still on the trail. I tried not to think about what lay in the underbrush we waded through, but I pictured all kinds of slithering things. Did I mention I hated snakes? And spiders? Basically, anything creepy and crawly. But this was where those things lived. *Puppies and rainbows,* I told myself. *Puppies and rainbows.* But all I could think of was a poisonous snake side-winding its way across my boot and up my pant leg.

* * *

The tree line finally broke, and we came upon a clearing against a wall of boulders. We stumbled into it, one by one. Stopping, we caught our breath. A valley lay before us. Nothing but sprawling mountains on the horizon. Miles and miles of rugged landscape. No sign of civilization.

I squinted, holding my hand across my eyebrows like a visor, my vision less clear in the fading light. Hopeful at first that I'd find a road, a building, some movement. But there was nothing but rocks, trees, and mountain peaks for as far as the eye could see.

"Well," Hope said, shrugging off her pack and dropping it to the ground. "We must have walked ten miles. I can't take another step."

I turned to Hana. "How's your foot?"

She dropped her pack next to Hope's and flexed her foot. "Numb. I can't feel my feet." Tears pooled in her eyes. "We're going to die out here, aren't we?"

Everyone looked at me as if I had the answer to that. "We're not going to die," I said with false bravado. "People have survived worse."

"Yeah," Rico said, sitting on a rock. "But some of them died, and a few even ate their friends."

"That's not helpful," Hope said. "No one is eating anyone."

Still, we sized each other up. None of us had much meat on our bones. Why did my brain even go there? Fatigue, mixed with hunger, made it difficult to filter my thoughts.

The temperature had dropped, so we started adding layers of clothing. "Anyone have a lighter?" I asked. "I hate to start a fire, given that we're outrunning one, but it's getting cold."

"That asshole PO took it with my weed," Rico said.

I wondered if that "asshole PO" and the others had made it back to the parking lot and called for help. Between them and the ranger, people had to be looking for us. It was only a matter of time.

"Isn't there a way to start a fire by rubbing two sticks together?" Hope asked.

"Or is it rocks?" Rico said.

No one had done their homework. I should have at least looked up some camping advice before we left. This scenario should have occurred to me, as not much in my life went as planned. But the only preparation I'd done was to research hiking boots. Even though the saleswoman had boasted that this brand lasted her hike of the Oregon Trail, mine were no longer comfortable. I longed to kick them off and wear flip-flops for the rest of my life. But I was afraid that if I took them off, I'd never get them back on.

Rico and I gathered kindling, while Hope tried the stick-rubbing thing. After what seemed like thirty minutes, we'd built a decent stack of logs for a fire, but the only thing Hope had accomplished was breaking a nail. "This isn't working," she said.

I stood over her, hands on hips. "There must be a trick to it."

She tossed her sticks onto the heap of wood. "Yeah, well, I'm all out of ideas."

Time to problem-solve. "So, we don't have a fire. We can create body heat by sitting close together." The sun was nearing the horizon, and it would be dark soon. Pitch black dark since cloud cover blocked the moon.

I sat against a bolder and Hope wedged herself against me, while Felony crawled onto my lap. I patted the ground. "Come on, guys."

Hana hurried over and sat next to me, positioning herself so close that we were connected at the hip.

Rico gave a heavy sigh, then sandwiched himself between Hope and a giant rock. At least we were out of the wind.

From our spot, we faced the valley. The colors drained as the sun clipped the trees and disappeared. The sudden darkness felt like someone had flipped off a light switch.

In the morning, we'd have to hike down this peak into the valley with nothing but the next hill to climb. How many of those would we encounter on our way out of the woods? And with our supplies dwindling, how far would we make it before we were too weak to go on? The miles of wilderness laid out before us told me one thing. This might not be our only night spent on the ground.

Chapter Twenty-Seven

Betz

As the hours ticked by, Betz felt the last inch of hope he'd been clinging to slip through his fingers. Maybe he couldn't see well enough to drive, but the countryside would be a blur to anyone, as Marcus drove like a madman. Betz cherished his 4Runner and would be furious if Marcus wrecked it. On the other hand, he didn't want to waste time. The sooner they got there, the sooner he could start looking for Casey.

"GPS says to take the next exit," Joy said from the backseat.

Marcus overtook a semi-truck, cutting in front of it just in time to make the turn. "Shit," Betz said, flattening his hands against the dashboard. "We won't be much help if we're roadkill."

Marcus glanced his way. "You want to drive? Oh, wait, you can't see."

"Fuck you," Betz said under his breath. But he was pretty sure Marcus heard him.

An uncomfortable silence ensued until Marcus cleared his throat. "Your sister, she's a lot."

"Yeah." Betz braced for a sharp right turn. "She can be."

"That was gangster the way she acted."

Betz hung his head. Was this guy going to keep poking the bear? It had been two hours, and Betz was still trying to calm down after his words with Jasmine. But he didn't want to talk about his relationship with his sister. Not with these two clowns. "We need to concentrate on what comes next," he said, trying to refocus the conversation. "When we get to the command station, I want you two to hang back. They may be weird about us joining the search. Especially since I don't have my badge."

"Your vibe says cop. No badge needed," Marcus said. "Especially with your sidearm."

"And you speak the lingo," Joy said. "Just say ten-four a lot."

Betz couldn't help but laugh. "Thanks, Joy. I'll keep that in mind."

* * *

Passing an abandoned car on the side of the road, they pulled into a spot marked Scenic Overlook.

As promised, a command center had been set up. There was a van, a few marked patrol SUVs, and a horse trailer. A forest ranger tied a horse to a post. In the distance, the sky glowed orange, and it wasn't from the setting sun.

As Betz climbed out of the vehicle, he got his first taste of smoke. He quickly deduced that a middle-aged guy in sheriff's gear was in charge, and he walked over to him. Reaching out, he shook the man's hand. "Detective Betz," he said. "I think we spoke on the phone."

A calloused hand pumped his. But the man cleared his throat and pointed to a woman, not quite five feet tall and one hundred pounds. "Think you were talking to my boss, Sargent Savage."

Without his glasses, he couldn't make out the stripes on their sleeves.

"Good of you to come." She stepped forward and pumped his hand with gusto. Probably trying to compensate for her size. Her gruff voice was the last thing he expected. All this time, he'd pictured a portly, gray-haired chain smoker. When he caught a whiff of her breath, he knew he had the smoker part right.

"So, it's your wife out there?" she said.

Was that what he'd called her? Why correct it? "That's right."

"We got a drone up. Afraid the news isn't good."

His heart seemed to shrink, and it took every ounce of strength he had not to let his knees buckle. "Tell me."

"The camp they were staying at has burned to the ground. The scene's hot. Too dangerous to go in and check for bodies. But if it had caught them unaware, nobody could have survived that."

Betz tapped his chest as if to restart his heart. "As I said on the phone, she got a message out. They were on the move."

"Yeah, but the fire's traveling fast. Drones haven't picked up any activity. No signs of life. Sorry, but on the phone, you asked me to be straight with you."

He tried not to follow the trail she laid out for him. That it could be hopeless. "Wouldn't tree cover conceal them from drones? Do you have a map? We need a good spot to go in and get ahead of the fire. Hopefully, we can meet them on their way out."

Savage looked doubtful, but Joy and Marcus diverted her attention when they appeared at his side.

"They with you?" she asked.

Reluctantly, Betz nodded.

Savage's gaze stuck on Joy for a moment, but with a shake of her head, she recovered. "We got SAR all over the place."

"SAR?" Joy asked.

"Search and Rescue. Your people aren't the only ones trapped by the fire. To make matters worse, we have an escaped convict on the loose."

"Martin Phillips," Betz said. "I'm working that case."

"There haven't been sightings of him, but that vehicle over there," she motioned to the Buick parked at the side of the road. "It was jacked out of Phoenix yesterday. Waiting for a description of the suspect who stole it, but thinking there's a connection."

Why was he hearing this just now? Bad news on top of bad. The good news? Savage and her crew were so scattered, so overwhelmed with two major problems to manage, they wouldn't mind the help.

Marcus wasn't the seeing-eye dog Betz would have hoped for, but he'd have to do.

Chapter Twenty-Eight

Marcus

Marcus was amped up when, with a headlamp on and a flashlight in hand, he led the way into the woods. SAR had provided them with a tarp and fully stocked backpacks, including food and water.

They'd tried to talk Joy into staying behind. Someone had given her a coat, but she had those ridiculous shoes on, which would no doubt slow them down. But short of tying her to a tree, which he half expected Betz to do, they were stuck with her. "I have more right to go than you two," she'd said in a high-pitched voice on the verge of hysteria. "Barry's just an ex-husband, and you have no relation to them at all, Marcus. That's my sister and cousin out there."

"Fine," Betz said. "But if you slow us down, we'll leave you behind."

Of course, she slowed them down. And no matter what Betz threatened, he wouldn't leave Joy to fend for herself.

Daylight had all but evaporated, and the forest was eerie in the dark. Marcus wouldn't admit to being spooked, but he disliked horror movies and being scared. *Suck it up, buttercup.* If Betz could do it with his vision impaired and Joy could keep moving even though she had to feel every stick and stone through the gloves on her feet, he could, too.

Realizing he'd outpaced the others, Marcus stopped and waited, aiming his flashlight at Joy, who was carefully picking her way over the terrain.

"You really should turn back," he said. "We know you care. You don't have to prove yourself. It's just those shoes—"

She shone her flashlight in his face, blinding him. "Listen here, Mister. These shoes allow me to grip the ground like a monkey. And I saved your life once, remember?"

Marcus squinted and blocked the beam with his hand. "You hit me with a car."

"Yeah, but you don't remember anything after that," she said, hips swishing with gusto. She walked faster when she was mad. Maybe he was onto something. "Both Casey and I scooped your unconscious butt off the ground. I forget. How many head injuries have you had?"

A head injury she caused. The second one had nothing to do with her. Still, he made more sense concussed than she did clear-headed. But she was generally a positive person. Her dark mood meant she was worried, and he felt for her.

Betz pushed past her. "Marcus is right," he said.

His words only seemed to strengthen her resolve. She followed Betz, hurrying past Marcus. With a sigh, he turned and followed.

Chapter Twenty-Nine

My head bobbed, and my chin hit my chest, jolting me awake. Attempting to orient myself, I squinted in the darkness. Last thing I remembered was watching the tree line gobble the last light of day. Now it was pitch dark. Clouds obstructed the moon and stars, cooling the air. A chill permeated my bones. The only warm spot came from Felony, who covered my lap like a heating pad. His little heart beat against my leg, comforting me. I wasn't alone. Pressure from the weight of Hope on one side, and Hana on the other, reminded me that Hope, Hana, and Rico were also there. Everyone else seemed to be asleep.

I rubbed my stiff neck, and Felony stirred.

Reaching down, I pet him, freezing when I spotted two beams of light in the woods.

I nearly jumped up. Someone was here to rescue us. Unless they weren't.

Felony sensed someone was coming toward us, and he let out a single bark, then a low growl.

"Is someone there?" I called.

The lights disappeared.

Hope stirred.

Everything was still. Quiet.

"What's going on?" Hope asked, yawning.

"There were two beams of light. Flashlights, I think. Someone's out there."

I got to my feet and helped Hope to hers. Without me to prop her up, Hana curled into a ball, unfazed. Rico slept on.

Holding Felony's leash, I let him drag me toward the woods. "Anybody there?" I called.

Light spotted the ground in front of me. There was a rustling in the bushes, and then Izzy stepped out of the foliage. "Oh, thank God," she said. "I thought I'd hopelessly lost my way."

I looked past her. "But you're not alone."

"Yes, I am."

"I saw two flashlights."

She shone her light past me, coming to a stop on the kids. "I don't know what to tell you," she said. "It's just me."

"Where have you been?" Hope asked.

"I got up early and went for a walk. I got lost. By the time I found my way back to camp, no one was there, and the fire was getting close."

"You didn't learn from the last time you got turned around?" Hope said.

"And you took your backpack," I added.

"Of course I did," she scoffed. "Couldn't trust you two not to invade my privacy again."

I looked behind her, expecting another person to emerge from the woods, but the forest was still.

Izzy walked past me and over to where the kids slept. "It's freezing. Why haven't you started a fire?"

Hope followed her. "We don't have matches or a lighter."

I turned to join them. A distant sound of a branch snapping in the forest made me freeze in my tracks. "There," I said. "Someone else **is** in the woods."

"That could have been anything," Izzy said, dismissing me. "Anyway, I have a lighter. Let's get a fire going."

While Hope and Izzy started a fire, I kept watch on the woods. Izzy might want to make me sound crazy, but I knew what I saw. What I heard. There was someone out there watching us. And Izzy was covering for them.

But I wasn't about to go traipsing off in the dark to confront them.

With plans to further interrogate her, I pulled Felony back and helped get the fire going.

Chapter Thirty

Betz

They headed toward the fire, hoping they'd cross paths with Casey and the others on their way out. Betz couldn't see flames, but the air was thick, and smoke irritated the back of his throat.

If it were up to him, they'd be running, or at least keeping a good pace, but Joy was struggling, slowing them down. She was too damn proud to admit it, but she wasn't appropriately dressed for the occasion. Her outfit was more suitable for working Van Buren Street than hiking in the woods. At least Marcus was a trooper. He never complained and, leading the way, he did his best to keep Joy moving. Still, Betz didn't like the guy.

Then again, who liked their competition?

Letting Joy tag along was a mistake, but he couldn't undo it now. They'd been walking for hours. He couldn't spare the time to escort her back to the command station, and he wouldn't let her go alone. Casey would kill him if he let anything happen to her cousin. Even though Joy was responsible for a great percentage of Casey's eye rolling, she was fiercely protective of her family.

And Joy had dug her gloved heels in. She wouldn't go back.

A sudden scream interrupted his thoughts. Joy threw her arms up as she stumbled, landing with a thud on all fours. Betz aimed his flashlight her way and hurried forward as Marcus stopped and ran back.

Joy let out a second scream, this one louder than the first, as she scooted back, kicking at whatever had tripped her.

Because of his damn useless eyes, Betz couldn't make out what all the fuss was about. What had she tripped over?

Marcus got to her first. "Holy shit," he said. "Is that a leg?"

He offered Joy his hand and helped her to her feet. Betz arrived in time to follow Marcus' flashlight beam to the bare calf lying on the ground, partially covered by leaves. Marcus moved the light up the leg, over a torso, stopping on a contorted face. Lifeless eyes stared up at the sky. The last moments of his life etched a look of surprise on his face. The man was in boxer shorts. No shoes on his feet.

Betz aimed his flashlight at the man's face and squatted down for a better look. A slash wound extended across the man's throat. Rigor mortis had set in. He'd been dead for a while.

"Oh, gross," Joy shrieked.

"Phillips," Betz said.

"The convict they're looking for?" Joy asked.

"No, it's not him. I'm guessing he killed this poor guy and took his clothes." Taking out the satellite radio SAR loaned him, he did his best to convey their location to the command center, telling them what they'd found.

In normal circumstances, he would have stayed with the body. Worked the case. The victim deserved to be treated with care. But there wasn't much he could do for him now except find his killer. Hot on Phillips's trail, they needed to catch up to him. It was even more important that they find Casey before Phillips did. If he hadn't already. But Betz couldn't let his mind wander there.

He returned the radio to his pack. "Let's go."

"We're just going to leave him here?" Joy asked.

Betz adjusted the straps on his shoulders and gave the body one last look. "If we don't find Casey and the others soon, they may meet the same fate as this poor guy."

Chapter Thirty-One

With a fire blazing, moods lifted. Izzy had turkey jerky and crackers that she doled out like prizes. Providing fire and food, she quickly became everyone's hero. Everyone's but mine.

"Maybe you were dreaming," she said when I further insisted that I'd seen the beams of two flashlights in the woods. "Or since you just woke up, you were seeing double."

Next thing she was going to call me was irrational. "I didn't just see two flashlights," I said, digging in. "I heard someone else in the woods."

She shrugged. "Don't know what to tell you."

"How about the truth? You conveniently disappear and then reappear. Why?"

She laughed. "You're like a dog with a bone. I'm not hiding anything."

At the word "bone," Felony's ears perked up, and he looked at me, expecting one. Fresh out, I slipped him a cracker.

With a little food in our bellies, everyone took a place around the fire, close enough to feel the warmth, but far enough away not to roll into it while sleeping. Exhausted from hiking all day, no one had a problem drifting off. No one but me. I couldn't stop my mind from flipping through scenarios as to why Izzy would lie about being with someone in the woods.

Had she found some introvert camper who shared drugs with her, but was too shy to meet us? Or was it the escaped convict the ranger had warned us about? That made no sense. Why would she help a stranger over us? We weren't exactly friends, but we were on the same team.

If there was a chain of command, Grizzly had been in charge. He was trusted with the satellite phones, and he was the only one who knew the woods. But with him removed, the rest of us were on an equal footing. If that weren't the case, no one had explained it to us.

My thoughts drifted to the life I carried. Lying one hand on my stomach, I pulled Felony a little closer with the other, his soft fur tickling my chin. Would this be my little family? Just the three of us? The reality of becoming a single mom, hell, any kind of mom, terrified me. Kate had a husband. She wasn't raising my niece and nephew on her own. But she did the bulk of the parenting and made mothering look like a skill that required a four-year degree. It was so foreign to me. No matter the situation, she always knew the right thing to do. A fit in the middle of a store? No problem. A small game piece up the nose? That's what the emergency department was for.

I'd watched her juggle keeping the house in order, providing meals for her family, and reigning in two kids under six. I couldn't do even one of those things. And I had a full-time job. I wouldn't have the luxury of being a stay-at-home mom. Not that the lifestyle appealed to me.

I'd managed to keep Felony alive, but I didn't always do so well with beings in my care. I had killed every plant I'd ever owned, and when Betz and I had frogs, I had forgotten to feed them, and one ate the other.

Mostly, I operated in my own little world. If I were being honest, I could be a little selfish and generally preferred my own company to spending time with other people. I rubbed Felony's head. Didn't apply to him.

Go for a run in one-hundred-degree weather?

It was my funeral.

Binge-watch Dateline until two a.m.?

Diet Coke would revive me in the morning.

Leave my clothes in the dryer for a week?

Throw in a towel and restart the machine to get the wrinkles out.

I was the only one suffering the consequences of my poor decisions. And I liked it that way. I wasn't one to hold myself accountable.

My circle was small. My sister and my mom had been the people I'd depended on most. Now that my mom was gone, I felt lost sometimes. I couldn't imagine taking on motherhood without her to lean on.

Kate would be there, but she had her own family to tend to.

I didn't want to discount Marcus. Maybe he'd want to be involved, but I couldn't count on that. And even if Betz and I wouldn't be together, I would bet my last nickel he'd be there if I needed him.

I'd recently declared my latest project: myself. It was time to get my act together. Expand my horizons. It would all be so much harder with a kid in tow.

But that was my reality now. Unless I miscarried from all this damn stress.

The fire warmed my back, Felony my chest. But my feet were blocks of ice. And I had to pee—one of the many fun things I had to look forward to for the next several months. And once the baby came, would my body return to normal, or would I wet myself every time I sneezed?

Feeling we were a safe distance from the forest fire, I started losing the thread of my thoughts, and my eyelids became heavy. I looked forward to welcoming a few minutes, maybe a few hours of sleep before we conquered the next mountain.

But then Felony became alert in my arms. I forced my eyes open and followed his gaze to someone leaning over a backpack.

Sleep called me back, urging me to give in to it. But I fought it, narrowing my gaze and holding my breath so the person wouldn't know I'd seen them.

Izzy.

She had unzipped Hana's backpack and was digging through it.

I silently watched her, not wanting to spook her so she could lie again about what she was up to. I wouldn't put it past her to claim she was sleepwalking. Her arm was elbow-deep in the bag. The firelight illuminated the determination on her face.

It wasn't me who stopped her. Rico stretched, then slowly sat up.

Izzy startled, pulled her arm out of the bag, and quickly folded the top back over.

"What are you doing?" Rico asked.

"Nothing," she said, returning to her place around the fire. "Go back to sleep."

What did she want that Hana had? I knew one thing for sure: I was right not to trust her. I'd never sleep now. I had to keep watch.

Chapter Thirty-Two

Marcus

A dead, almost naked body in the woods was a plot twist he hadn't seen coming. That day, nothing happened as expected. Never in his wildest dreams did he think he'd be hiking toward a forest fire in the middle of the night with Casey's ex-husband and her spandex-clad cousin for company.

With others on their way to recover the body and work the crime scene, the trio had continued on their way.

Marcus knew Joy was freaked out after stumbling upon a corpse because she was unusually quiet.

Betz was also silent. He seemed to grasp how difficult finding the missing group would be. There were acres and acres to cover, and Casey and her group could have gone in a different direction. But Betz hadn't voiced that concern. He acted as if he had a plan. Marcus wouldn't be the one to poke holes in his optimism.

But the deeper into the forest they went, the more he realized even Betz was out of his depth. They had the radio to communicate with the command station, but it would take a while for any help to arrive if they needed it. He knew one thing: Betz would find Casey or die trying, and he respected him for that. Neither of them could live with letting her down.

Darkness was fading. It was almost morning. They'd been walking all night. He wasn't sure they were going toward the fire, although smoke hung heavy in the air. He'd made a makeshift mask out of a bandana SAR had given him, but it wasn't really helping.

A low-flying small plane passed overhead. "Look," Joy said. "They're searching for them."

"Looks like a tanker plane," Betz said.

"What's that?"

"They drop water on the fire."

"That's good," Joy said. "If they can put the fire out, that takes a worry off our list."

"Except it can take weeks, months even, to get a fire this size under control," Betz said.

They didn't have that kind of time.

* * *

They walked on as daylight broke. No longer needing his headlamp, Marcus slipped it off and stored it in his pack with his flashlight. It felt good to free up his hand. They paused while Joy and Betz did the same thing. Then Joy collapsed against a tree stump. Gulping water, she gave a heavy sigh. "How do we even know where to go? If we're on the right track?"

"Thought you were psychic," Marcus said.

She shot him a death glare. "It doesn't work that way."

Betz cleared his throat. "While you two were gathering gear, Savage showed me a map. This trail, although not recently maintained, should lead us to the camp. We're coming from the east. This is the way they'd go to flee the fire. Hopefully, we'll walk right into them."

"That makes sense," Marcus said.

"There's a survivalist in the group. He knows this mountain. What bothers me," Betz said, "is they have a satellite radio, yet no one has heard from them. Why are they so out of touch?"

"Something happened to it," Joy said.

Or to them, Marcus thought, but he kept that to himself. No one wanted to speculate about the convict and what he would do to Casey and her group if he found them.

* * *

After hydrating, they lurched on. Marcus, then Joy, with Betz bringing up the rear.

The path was rocky at first and then smoothed out with rich brown earth that was soft under his boots. Marcus stopped short, and Joy knocked into him. "Look." He pointed to a shoe print in the dirt. "Someone was here recently."

"Nobody move," Betz ordered. "Look for more prints."

Marcus held his foot inches over the imprint, noting it was slightly bigger than his work boot. At least a men's size eleven. There was only one set heading up the trail. They vanished again when the path became covered in fallen, rotting leaves.

"So, just one person," Marcus said.

Betz studied the prints, then stood and adjusted his pack. "Not the group we're looking for. Could be Phillips. Keep in mind that if we find him, he's armed and dangerous."

Marcus cursed himself for not taking the time to get his gun from his bike before they started this mission. "Can you see well enough to shoot?" Marcus asked. "I'm not questioning your abilities, but you don't have your glasses."

"Whose fault is that?" Betz snapped.

Marcus and Joy looked at each other. "It was an accident," Joy said.

"Never mind," Betz said. "I can see well enough to protect us. Let's go."

They turned and moved further down the path, the smell of smoke growing stronger.

Chapter Thirty-Three

I kept Izzy in my sight for the rest of the night. Not that she moved. By the light of the fire, I watched her fall into a deep sleep. Not fair at all. Eventually, I gave up on getting any rest. Using Izzy's flashlight, I got up to pee in the woods, wondering if Izzy's sidekick, whoever that was, was nearby, watching me. But when nature calls, you answer. I gathered a few more sticks on my way back and added them to the dying fire.

Although the morning sky had brightened, dense clouds blocked the sun, and a chill remained in the air. Rain would be good for the forest fire, but nobody had the proper gear, and life would be even more miserable once we were cold and wet.

Hana was the first to wake. Stretching, she slowly got up and walked over to me, hugging herself against the brisk morning air. At least she was no longer limping. "I have to pee," she said.

I pointed to the woods. "Bathroom is that way."

She cringed. "You mind going with me? I'm afraid to be in the woods by myself."

"Sure thing."

She followed me a few feet into the forest. I turned my back while she did her thing, keeping watch. Trees loomed, looking foreboding, and I had to wonder if Izzy's pal was still out there, stalking us. It miffed me that no one else seemed to be worried about her. Not even Hope.

Back at the fire, I took two granola bars from my pack and handed one to Hana. We settled on a log and spoke in hushed voices so we wouldn't wake the others. I wanted to get moving soon, but didn't have the heart to wake them yet from much-deserved sleep.

I sat sideways, tucking my legs and looking directly at Hana. "I need to ask you something, and I want you to be honest. Do you have something in your pack that someone else would want?"

Hana glanced at the ground and bit her lip. "What makes you ask that?"

So, yes. "Hana, it's important."

She shrugged and took a bite of her breakfast. "Just clothes and toiletries. Remember, you searched my bag before we even got on the bus. Nothing illegal in there."

"I didn't say it was illegal." I had looked for contraband, but I hadn't paid attention to items that looked benign.

She was starting to trust me. At least it seemed that way. But she'd been through a lot lately, and I only knew the Cliff Notes version of what happened to her. Her parents were dead, and she was in foster care. I didn't have time to keep building rapport. Izzy could wake at any moment. "You mentioned something earlier that's been bothering me. Did you hold something back from the police related to your parents' murders?" Although, what that had to do with Izzy looking through her things, I didn't know.

Hana kept her gaze on the ground. "Like I said, police think my parents are....I mean, were....drug users. They weren't."

"Yet someone came after them. Why?"

When she answered, her voice was small. "They may have been involved in… something sketchy, but it wasn't drugs."

"What was it?"

Before she could answer, Izzy sat up and stretched. Hope rolled over and got to her feet. Only Rico continued to sleep.

Hana stood. "I'll tell you later," she said over her shoulder. And she walked back to the firepit.

* * *

With Hana's promise to give me an answer in the back of my mind, I shook Rico awake so we could start moving again. The sky threatened a major

119

storm, but so far, no rain fell. I passed out the last of the granola bars and apples. We ate in silence. Izzy assured us she had some jerky and crackers left that would hopefully get us through another day. Our water supply was getting low, too. I didn't have the numbers, but I knew we could last longer without food than without water. Hopefully, the incoming rain would take care of that.

And slow the fire.

As we started down the steep trail, loose rocks moved under our feet, causing us to lose our balance. Hope reached out to me more than once to keep from falling. Rico, more careless with his steps, kicked up cones of dust, doing a comical dance as he fought to stay upright. In the end, he lost the battle. His legs kicked out from under him, and he landed flat on his back.

That had to hurt, but would hopefully knock some sense into him. I rushed to his side. "Are you okay?"

He blinked, looking skyward, struggling to sit up. "I guess."

I helped him to his feet, and he brushed the dust off his pants. "I fucking hate this," he ranted, kicking at rocks, sending them flying over the cliff. "I want to go home."

Here we go. "We all do," I said. "That's the goal."

He pushed past me and lumbered down the path.

Hope and I exchanged worried glances before we urged the others along.

The trail narrowed, hugging the side of the mountain and forcing us to slow our pace. A solid rock wall was on one side, with a sheer drop-off on the other. One wrong step, and we'd plummet to our deaths. I kept one hand on the wall and tried to stay as far away from the edge as I could, while giving Felony a short leash. I imagined him tumbling over the edge and pulling me with him. Fear left me dizzy, and I struggled to keep my breathing even. Hana wasn't so successful. She was wheezing.

We came around a bend and halted, staring at what lay before us. The ground several feet below crackled orange as fire ripped through the foliage. Had it caught up with us, or were we backtracking?

Even from this height, we could feel the heat of the flames. It felt like we stood on the precipice of hell.

Hope, in the lead, stopped short, and I nudged her with my elbow. "Keep going. Once we get around the next bend, the fire will be behind us."

Steading herself against the cliff face, Hope continued with cautious steps. I let the others pass me and Felony before we brought up the rear.

Rain fell. First, just a few drops, but then sheets pummeled the top of our heads, making the ground slick and more treacherous. One of us owed some money to the karma bank. I pulled up my hood. Not that it did any good. Water quickly soaked the fabric, and it clung to my head like a sopping wet towel.

There was no place to seek refuge. The only way was forward.

Chapter Thirty-Four

Betz

When the others turned and looked back at him, Betz held a finger to his lips. "Stop. I hear something."

"Rain," Marcus said, shivering.

"Shush," Joy said. "I hear it, too. Someone's crying."

Betz cocked his head toward the woods to his right and squinted as if that would help. The undergrowth was a blur of deep green. He waded into it, following the sound. "Is someone out there?"

The sobbing stopped.

Betz pushed forward through prickly bushes, wet leaves soaking his jeans. "Where are you?" he said.

He heard the others behind him. Joy yelped as a branch snapped back toward her after he'd pushed it aside. He ignored her and focused on the spot where the sound had come from.

The trees thinned into a small clearing before an eight-foot wall of rock. Boulders lay against each other, creating a small cave. Two teenagers, a boy and a girl, were crouched inside, clinging to one another.

Betz ducked inside. "What are you doing out here?" he asked.

"Who are you?" the boy said, his voice shaking with fear.

"I'm Detective Betz. This is Joy and Marcus," he added as they entered the space. "What are your names?"

"I'm Tristen. This is my sister, Mika. We're trying to outrun the fire."

"Well," Joy said. "At least you found a good place to wait out the storm." She dropped her knapsack and settled herself on it like a fussy peacock, fluffing her drenched hair. Betz could just make out the mascara running down her face, staining it like she was the lead singer in an Alice Cooper tribute band.

"You're out here alone?" Marcus asked.

"No," Tristen said. "We were part of a group. It's a long story, but half of us were hiking out to get help after some things happened. We had to turn back because of the fire. But then, things went from bad to worse."

Betz exchanged a look with Marcus. "Were you part of a wilderness program?"

The boy nodded. "You're looking for us?"

"What do you mean, half of you?" Betz said.

"One girl got stung by a scorpion, and one boy, well, he had altitude sickness. They stayed behind with the three women."

"Casey and Hope?" Joy asked.

"Yeah," Tristen said. "And the woman with the rainbow hair."

"Her name's Izzy," the girl said in a timid voice.

"Anyway," Tristen continued. "We'd lost our satellite radio, so we couldn't call for help. Half of us started hiking out. We got turned around by the fire. And then, we ran into a man on the trail. He got into an argument with our survivalist, and the man… He stabbed our survivalist."

"Right in front of us," Mika added. "I've never been so scared in my life."

"I grabbed my sister's hand, and we ran for our lives," Tristen said. "We got separated from the group, and we've been wandering around ever since. We even left our packs behind. We've only got the clothes on our backs. No food. No water."

"When did this happen?" Betz said.

"At least a day ago," Tristen said. "We've been lost ever since."

Betz ran a hand across the stubble on his chin. Did Izzy Hutchinson leave for the trip before someone murdered her boyfriend? "You must be starving."

Marcus laid his pack at his feet, withdrew some snacks, and tossed them to the kids. Joy offered them water.

"Did you hear what the argument was about?" Betz asked. "Between the survivalist and the man who stabbed him?"

"Something about the rest of the group," the boy said. "The man demanded to know where the other kids were. He kept asking about the girl."

"The only other girl on the trip was Hana," Mika said. "He had to be talking about her."

Phillips. He'd already killed Hana's parents, had killed the social worker's boyfriend, and now he'd stabbed the survivalist. Probably that poor schmuck they found dead in the woods. There was no reason to think he'd show any kindness if he encountered Casey and her group. He was desperate.

"We'll lead you back to the trail," Betz said. "If you stay on it, you'll come across some deputies. They'll help you. It will take a few hours, but if you stay on the path, you won't get lost."

"We want to stay with you," Tristen said.

Betz shook his head. "Where we're going is too dangerous. It's safer if you head out."

Joy cleared her throat. "I'll go with them," she said. "You kids shouldn't be alone. And I can see I'm slowing you two down."

Betz laid a hand on Joy's arm. "I think that's a good idea. And I know how hard it was for you to come to that decision."

Joy choked back tears. "Those are my girls out there. Promise me you'll find them in time."

Betz looked toward Marcus. He wanted to promise that. He wanted nothing more. But he knew it would take a giant stroke of luck. Reaching into his pack, he pulled out the satellite radio and handed it to Joy. "Take this. Call for help if you need to. But if you keep to the trail, you should walk right into the area where they are processing the crime scene we found."

Joy nodded and gave Betz a hug, then walked over to Marcus. "Listen to Barry. He knows what he's doing."

Marcus nodded. "You're tougher than you look, Joy. You've impressed the hell out of me."

"Thanks, sweetie." She hugged him, too, then shooed the kids down the path, following.

Down to the two of them, Betz followed Marcus deeper into the woods.

Chapter Thirty-Five

We found a recessed area on the mountainside with an overhang of stone to take refuge from the storm. Not deep enough to be considered a cave, but the two-foot-wide path was enough to protect us from the storm if we hugged the rock and stood shoulder to shoulder. I felt fairly confident that the flames couldn't climb the rock, so for now, we felt safe from anything Mother Nature could throw at us.

Izzy was tight-lipped, and it wasn't the place to question her, but I was still miffed that she was hiding something. She seemed to be focused on charming Rico, increasing the rift between him and me. I wished I could get Hope aside to discuss my distrust of Izzy. Or separate Hana from the group so we could continue our earlier conversation. But there was no room for either talk to occur. Everyone was within earshot.

I found comfort in knowing that anyone following us, and I was convinced someone was, wouldn't be able to reach us unseen. There were no trees to hide behind, no bushes that could conceal someone.

Wind howled as it rushed through the canyon. Sudden distant thunder booms jolted my heart. I was wrong. Mother Nature had more up her sleeve. Apparently, she hadn't gotten the memo that monsoon season had ended. Lightning cracked the sky, but it seemed far off. Regardless, I knew we were in a bad spot. Exposed.

"We should move along," I said. "We're vulnerable here."

Everyone groaned. No one wanted to step back into the wind and rain.

"Lightning doesn't care if you're tired or wet," I said. "Come on."

I shooed the others ahead of me, keeping a tight hold on Felony's leash. I would not look down. If I did, my fear of heights would paralyze me.

Those in the lead disappeared as they rounded a bend. When I caught up, everyone had stopped. "What's the problem?" I asked.

Hana, who was in front of me, reversed, so her back was to the wall, and I could see around her. Peering over the shoulders of the others, I got a good look at a wobbly footbridge linking our side of the canyon to the one across the way. Fuck no.

"The path goes on," Hope yelled against the wind. "But it's so narrow, with lots of loose rocks. It doesn't seem safe."

"And that rickety bridge does?" I asked.

"Well," Izzy said. "Unless a spaceship beams us up, these are the only two options. We can't go back toward the fire."

Hana shook her head. "No way am I crossing that. Half the boards are missing."

Not only was the roped handrail frayed, but the wind batted the bridge from side to side like a ship tossed on rough seas.

Another round of thunder shook the ground. Or maybe it was me shaking, but I had an urge to get on all fours and crawl.

Rico pushed Hope aside and put his hands on the rope, testing it. When it held, he placed one foot on the first board of the bridge. "Rico, don't," I said. He either didn't hear me or he ignored me.

The contraption held him. He slowly started across, giving each slat a try before putting his full weight on it and moving on to the next one. He was halfway to the other side when a board cracked under him, and a piece of wood separated and fell into the abyss. His leg followed, dangling over jagged rocks below. He caught his armpit on the ropes and kept his other foot on the board behind him.

Hana screamed, and I held my breath.

"I'm okay," Rico yelled over his shoulder. But his face was red from the effort it took not to fall. Pulling himself up, he took a moment to compose himself. Then, stepping over the open space, he moved on to the next board.

It was slow going, and I'd bitten the shit out of my thumbnail watching, but he made it to the other side.

I didn't think my heart could take anyone else crossing over, but what choice did we have? We needed to stay together.

Hope stepped up. "I'll go next."

"Leave your pack," Izzy said. "The lighter you are, the better chance you have of making it across."

Hope dropped her backpack to the ground and dug through it, taking out a sweatshirt that she tied around her waist. Shoving a granola bar in her jacket pocket and sliding her water bottle in the side pocket of her pants, she stood at the first step of the bridge and glanced back at me.

I wanted to offer encouragement, but my heart was in my throat. All I could manage was a nod.

She was mid-step when another blast of thunder echoed throughout the canyon, the sound bouncing off the walls. Hope froze as lightning sizzled like a giant white zipper across the gunmetal gray sky.

We were in the storm's eye now. We needed to get to a place where we weren't the tallest things around.

Hope darted across the slats, her feet barely making contact; she went so fast. Making it to the other side, she let out a "whoop" of excitement.

Everyone clapped.

"You're next," I said to Hana.

Hana's eyes were giant saucers. She trembled as she looked up at me. "I…I can't."

"I don't like heights either," I said. "But we have to do this."

"What about Felony?" she asked. "A dog won't cross that thing."

I'd thought of that. I'd been calculating the possibilities ever since I'd spotted the damn thing. I knew only one thing for sure. I wasn't leaving him behind. "I'll have to empty my pack. He should fit inside."

"But that will make you too heavy."

My thoughts exactly, but there was no other way. "I'll go last."

"I'll wait for you." Her voice was soft, and her eyes locked on mine.

Izzy grew tired of our conversation. "I'll go." She leaned over her pack. Digging inside, she pulled her revolver out and slid it into the waistband of her jeans.

I wasn't sure how I felt about that.

Instead of starting over the bridge, she stepped toward Hana and placed a hand on each of her shoulders. "I'm done playing games. I know your father gave it to you. I need you to hand it over."

Hana stiffened. She glanced at me with fear-filled eyes.

"What are you talking about?" I asked.

Izzy shot me a look of hatred. "This doesn't concern you."

I pushed between her and the girl, forcing them to break their physical connection. I met Izzy's hard stare. "I think it does."

"I…I don't have anything," Hana said, her voice weak. "I told you this morning."

"Then I'm done protecting you," Izzy spat.

"Protecting her?" I said. "From what?"

Another bang in the sky. This one was so loud, all three of us startled. The lightning that followed shattered the wall behind us. Loose rocks tumbled down, and I pushed Hana out of the way before softball-sized chunks bounced onto the path.

"We've got to move," I said. "We can do this later."

Izzy stepped onto the bridge. "Okay, I'm going, but you've got to give it up, Hana. Believe me, you'd rather deal with me than him."

What the hell was she talking about? A cloud passed over Hana's face. She wasn't in the dark. She knew exactly what Izzy was after.

Izzy started across the bridge. She was more than halfway when another clap of thunder put her off balance. Her foot searched for a board that wasn't there. She slipped through the space, both legs dangling. She caught the rope with one hand, swinging like a pendulum over the canyon.

Chapter Thirty-Six

Marcus

The rain was relentless, soaking Marcus through to his skin. If he'd known he'd be hiking for days, with no end in sight, he'd have gotten the proper gear. But his Levi's and hoodie acted like a sponge, clinging to his tired body. He'd have to peel them off. Thankfully, the borrowed waterproof backpack protected the supplies given to him at the command station. He'd checked the contents and knew there was no rain gear inside.

Betz was struggling, too. Too miserable for conversation. Not that they had anything to say to each other. Voicing their concerns would only make things worse.

Having made it to the top of a switchback, the woods emptied into a meadow, which meant even less protection from the rain. Or the lightning that was getting closer and more dangerous. Betz plowed ahead, trying his best to keep them on the trail that was getting harder and harder to find.

If they found Casey. Not if, when? They would find her. And he would stop treating her with kid gloves. Maybe she'd been so hesitant to move forward because he hadn't made himself clear. He'd go after what he wanted. And he wanted her. If she needed him to change, he could do that. He'd do anything for her.

He watched Betz moving ahead of him through the field. He wanted to hate the guy, but it became harder and harder with each hour that passed.

Betz's drive to find Casey was remarkable. How could he fault him for that?

If the weather and fire weren't enough, they had an escaped convict to worry about. He could hide in the woods, waiting to take shots at them. More likely, though, he was a day ahead of them and close to finding Casey and her group. The rain had washed away any footprints he would have left.

A lone tree stood like a monument in the middle of the field. Beyond it, more woods.

"I think the trail picks up there," Marcus said, pointing across the pasture. He could barely see it in the sideways rain. No way Betz could.

"Thanks," Betz said. "We should hurry. We're nothing but lightning rods out here."

They broke into a jog.

The next strike sizzled as it struck the top of the solitary tree. Its trunk illuminated as if the hand of God had struck it, and the bark split. "To the right," Marcus yelled, ducking flying splinters of wood.

A chunk of the tree crashed to the ground. Marcus came up short. "Betz?" Where did he go?

Marcus backtracked, pushing drenched hair out of his face. He scanned the area, spotting a lump on the ground next to the fallen tree limb.

He darted toward him. Splashing through mud and puddles. Betz lay on his back, arms and legs out. Not moving.

Falling to his knees, Marcus bent over his motionless companion and felt for a pulse.

Chapter Thirty-Seven

I zzy hung from the rope by both hands. Her boots clicked at the ankle as momentum caused her to swing back and forth. I handed Felony's leash to Hana and dropped to my stomach so I could look over the cliff and assess the situation. "Hold on," I yelled, as if she had another plan.

Jagged rocks jutted from the canyon fifty feet below her like greedy hands waiting to receive her. No way she'd survive a fall.

A pop sounded, and something whizzed past my ear. The bridge dropped a few feet. Izzy screamed but held on. I turned toward the source of the projectile. Bolts securing the ropes to the mountainside were bulging, pushing free from the plate attached to the rock. There were only three when there should have been four.

Izzy's terrified gaze latched onto mine.

Another rivet from the opposite side of the bridge broke free, and the walkway dropped a little lower.

"Hold the rope," I yelled. Pushing to my feet, I rushed to the beginning of the bridge. On the other side, Hope matched my move.

I grabbed the rope but couldn't get a good grip. It was wet and slippery in my bandaged hands. I pulled at the gauze with my teeth until my hands were free, then got a better hold of the rope. Looping it around my wrist, I dug my heels into the rock, hoping I could relieve some of Izzy's weight and stop more bolts from breaking free.

"Can you pull yourself up?"

Izzy adjusted her grip. "Maybe…if I can….hook my feet around the rope." She tried to swing her leg toward her hands.

Another screw broke away from the rock.

A look of acceptance relaxed Izzy's face as she locked her eyes on mine. "Take care of the girl. He will come for her."

She closed her eyes as the remaining bolts popped in quick succession, and the bridge fell away. I twisted my wrist free of the rope just before it was yanked from my hands. To the sound of Izzy's scream, I lay my forehead on the wet, cold ground and pounded the stone with my fist.

* * *

I don't know how long I laid in the puddle, but I slowly realized Felony was licking my face. Getting onto my hands and knees, I struggled to my feet. Wiping my face with my forearm smeared mud across my cheek.

I placed my hands on Hana's trembling shoulders. "Are you okay?"

Stupid question. How could she be? She just watched someone die.

Although she nodded, her stream of tears told the truth. No matter what Izzy was, what she was after, she didn't deserve that fate.

I remembered Hope and Rico across the way. I turned, relieved to see them still standing there. They were only about fifty feet away, but with no way to reach them, it may as well have been miles.

"Keep going," I yelled.

"But…" Hope said, looking down at the rocks.

"We can't help her," I said. "She's gone."

Hope nodded. From this distance, I couldn't read the fear in her eyes, but I knew it was there. Not only were we separated, but Hope and Rico had left all of their gear behind. They would run out of food and water, and had no change of clothes.

Hope cupped her hands around her mouth and called out, "What are you going to do?"

I pointed to the narrowing trail. "Move on." The only other choice was going back the way we'd come. Toward the fire. The rain may have slowed the flames, but it wouldn't stop them.

"Stay safe," Hope called.

"You, too."

Rico turned and disappeared into the foliage. A moment later, Hope was gone, too.

I picked up Izzy's backpack and laid it on a rock.

"What are you doing?" Hana asked.

"Trying to figure out what Izzy was talking about." I dug through her things. Clothes, mostly. There was a zipper compartment that held a work ID for the Maricopa County jail. I recognized Izzy in the photo, although she had black hair at the time and no nose ring. But the name was different. Crystal Monroe.

Izzy wasn't Izzy, and she wasn't a counselor. She was a corrections officer at the local jail.

What happened to the real Izzy?

I rocked back on my heels and looked up at Hana. "Did you know Izzy wasn't who she pretended to be?"

Hana bit her lip and wiped the rain off her face.

"If you want me to protect you, like she said, I need to know what I'm dealing with."

The girl trembled. She looked so young, so small, I couldn't believe she held a secret worthy of taking lives. And now, someone else lost their life. When Hana spoke, her voice was soft, almost lost in the wind. "My mom…she had gambling debt. My dad embezzled money to cover it. But instead of handing the money over, they decided to keep it. We were going to start a new life. Before he died…"

She took a minute to compose herself.

"Go on."

She sucked in a shuddering breath. "My dad told me that if anything happened to them, the money would be mine. But I shouldn't claim it until I'm eighteen. It's safe where it is. They'll never find it."

"Unless they get to you. God, damn it, Hana. You put us all in danger."

Hana nodded, hung her head. "She told me, Izzy, or whoever she was, that her boyfriend would kill me if I didn't tell them what they wanted to know. She thought that if she could get me to tell her, she could stop him from killing anyone else. But my dad wanted me to have the money. I didn't want his murderers to get what they wanted. What they killed my parents for."

"Jesus, Hana." Her boyfriend? Was that why she was gone all those times? She'd met him in the woods. It would make sense that Phillips was after Hana, since he'd killed her parents. He must have escaped from jail. He was the convict the ranger had been talking about. The pieces were coming together.

"Hana, do you know the name of your parents' killer?"

"Martin Phillips," she said. "Remember, I'm supposed to testify against him."

I remembered Betz taking him into custody. How he had reached for a gun. He would have done anything to avoid capture. And now that he'd tasted freedom, he wouldn't want to give it up. He probably wanted the money Hana's father had hidden to start over somewhere else.

But where did Crystal Monroe fit in? I thought out loud. "She used her role as a corrections officer to help him escape. And she posed as a camp counselor. What happened to the real one who was supposed to be on this trip?"

"I don't know."

"But you never told her what she wanted to know, did you?" I asked.

Hana shook her head. "I didn't know what to do. I didn't want to give up the money. My dad wanted me to have it. If I told them, they'd have no reason to keep me alive. I wouldn't be useful anymore." She looked down at the ground and toyed with a pebble under her shoe. "Now that she's gone...she can't reason with him. He'll come for me. Torture me until I give up the information."

So, Izzy...I looked at the ID. That wasn't her name. Crystal Monroe had questionable motives, sure. But she was the lesser of two evils. At least she'd tried to keep her boyfriend from killing a teenage girl.

I stuck her ID in my pocket. Shoving the rest of her belongings into the bag, I threw it off the cliff. If Phillips was following us, I didn't want to leave any signs of our direction of travel. I heaved Rico's and Hope's belongings over the edge as well.

"Grab your pack. We need to move."

The location of the money was none of my business. Martin Phillips was behind us, and he'd have no choice but to follow. Our only hope was to outrun him. Unless he somehow had gotten ahead of us.

I slid my bag over my shoulders and called Felony to my side. Ushering Hana in front of me, we started down the narrow path. What I didn't know was whether we were walking to safety or into a trap.

Chapter Thirty-Eight

Betz

Betz blinked rain from his eyes. Someone had to have a voodoo doll with his likeness, and they were stabbing the hell out of it. His luck couldn't get any worse. Well, that wasn't true. He didn't actually get struck by lightning. He'd only rolled his ankle while dodging the falling tree. Some would call him lucky. He wouldn't go that far.

He lay flat on his back, trying to catch his breath. Marcus leaned over him, reaching down to check for a pulse.

"I'm not dead," he said, smacking Marcus' hand away. He struggled to sit up. His back spasmed, as if he were a hundred years old, but not because he was injured. His clothes were so waterlogged, he weighed twice what he normally did.

Marcus offered his hand, and out of desperation, Betz took it, getting to his feet.

"Damn," Marcus said. "Thought the lightning got you."

He almost commented that Marcus would like that, move him out of the way in his pursuit of Casey. But that wasn't fair. Marcus had been nothing but helpful. "Let's get out of this damn field before one of us gets struck."

By the time they reached the trees, the rain had slowed to a sprinkle. Thunder sounded less often and from further away. A welcome break.

Finding the spot where the trail picked up, they headed down it. Adrenaline gave them what little energy they had, but it wouldn't last long. Eventually, they'd have to stop and get some sleep. But there was always the hope that around the next bend or over the next hill, they'd run into Casey and her group.

Betz couldn't stop thinking about Casey and what he'd say when he finally laid eyes on her. He'd been more than patient while she worked things out. Although she usually laughed it off when he questioned her relationship with Marcus, he saw how she acted around him. And Marcus wasn't out here risking his life for community service. He had no reason to be in Arizona other than for Casey. In fact, Diablo would kill him if given the chance. It was stupid of him to set foot in the state. But he wasn't thinking with his head; his heart was guiding him.

None of that would matter if Phillips got to her first. Desperation choked him. He couldn't imagine a world without her in it.

Betz's personal phone buzzed in his pocket. Surprised he had service; he pulled it out, afraid to take another step because he knew he'd hit a lucky spot. "Hold up," he called to Marcus before taking the call.

"Savage here. Been trying to reach you." Her voice became garbled. Betz took a step back, hoping to improve the connection. Every other word was lost. "Lieutenant Faulk…Phoenix…patch her through."

Betz groaned. As much as he didn't want to talk to his sister, she might have news. "Okay."

"Where are you?"

"Gee," he said, not bothering to block the sarcasm in his voice. "On the beach in Costa Rica with a margarita. Where the hell do you think I am?"

The connection had improved because he could hear her clear her throat.

"You'll be glad to know Joy made it back to the command station. She and the two kids are okay. How are you and Marcus?"

"Fine."

"Well, there's something you should know."

"Go on."

"We found the body of a woman named Izzy Hutchinson. She was a counselor for the treatment center. She never made the trip."

"Phillips got to her," Betz said.

"Looks that way. But the director says the survivalist told him he'd accounted for everyone in their last conversation. That was after they boarded the bus for Flagstaff. Someone must have taken her place, pretended to be her. The staff hadn't met before, so the others wouldn't have known."

"Had to be Phillips' girlfriend who helped him escape from jail."

"That's what I'm afraid of."

No matter how tired they were, there'd be no resting. The rising body count showed just how desperate Phillips was.

Chapter Thirty-Nine

The trail became more and more treacherous. Each step had to be carefully placed. The path became so narrow, I could only fit one foot in front of the other. I kept my eyes on the back of Hana's shoes and held Felony's leash, so he had to walk behind me. Looking over the edge would have brought on a panic attack.

We had no choice but to go on. The rain had stopped, but the smell of smoke lay stagnant in the air. Phillips couldn't be far behind us. Even if I'd tried to throw him off the trail by tossing Crystal's backpack off the cliff, he would follow the same route as us. With the bridge gone, he'd have no choice.

My arsenal consisted of a dog who had no discernible animal qualities and a scared young girl. My instincts, which had seemed to fail me as of late, were my only weapons. Add to that, the new life I carried, whom only Hope knew about. Our only chance was to make it out of the woods before the next bad thing happened.

At least we'd been able to fill our bottles with rainwater. We'd have water for a while.

As we wrapped our way around the mountain, the trail widened as we descended. I took that as a good sign, but Felony wasn't having it anymore. He found a dry spot and laid down, refusing to take another step.

Hana and I looked down at the exhausted animal and then at each other. She shed her pack and sat on the ground beside him, lovingly petting his head.

I opened my water bottle and forced some liquid down the dog's throat.

"You should drink, too," I told Hana. "We don't want to become dehydrated."

"I'm so sorry," she said. "It's all my fault. He's after me."

I settled on the other side of Felony, who laid his head on my lap. "You couldn't have known they'd come after you. You said you felt safe up here."

"That was before I knew my parents' killer escaped from jail."

"Did Izzy, I mean Crystal, tell you that?"

"Yeah. Right before she started pumping me for information."

If Hana would have warned me back then, clued me in to who the fake counselor was, maybe things could have gone differently. But there was no point in trying to rewrite history. "We can rest for a few minutes, but then we should keep going. I think we're almost off the mountain."

"And then there'll be another one," she said with a sigh.

"Come on. We've got this."

"Tell that to Felony."

I was going to have to carry the dog out of here. Checking his paws, I could tell they were sore. He wasn't used to all this walking, especially on the rough terrain. He was exhausted, and I wasn't about to leave him behind. I unloaded my pack, saving what little food we had, but hiding my clothes behind a bush. I'd scoffed at the backpack's large size when Betz had loaned it to me; now I was grateful.

Felony didn't argue when I slid him into the bag, his head sticking out the top so he could see what was going on. I was touched by his trust. I knew from our last visit to the vet that he was about thirty-five pounds. A lot more than the belongings I'd tossed to make room for him.

Hana had to help me stand with the weight on my back. Once I was upright, it wasn't so bad. But it threw me off balance. I'd have to be extra careful. "Okay," I said. "Let's go."

My now too-tight boots cramped my feet. Heavy, wet clothes made each step laborious. Dampness from the rain mixed with my sweat left me shivering.

Coming around a bend, I spied the base of the narrow canyon. A trickle of water passed through the riverbed. Low-lying vegetation was lush in different shades of green. Steep walls blocked the sun, shading the area. The rim seemed a mile above us, and I marveled that we'd come so far.

Back on flat ground, we stopped at the creek's edge. It looked innocuous, just inches deep. Being from Arizona, I was used to dry riverbeds. We could easily walk through it and pick up the trail on the other side, where the path continued along the base of the stone wall.

My feet splashed in the runoff from the mountain as we walked alongside the riverbed. Getting wetter wasn't a concern. It was impossible to be more uncomfortable than we were. Felony's weight caused the straps of my pack to dig into my shoulders. I hiked it higher onto my back to relieve some of the pressure and spotted a path on the other side. "Let's cross," I said.

Hana nodded. She was zoning out, and she struggled for each breath. Down to one dose of her inhaler, she wanted to save that until she was desperate.

Knowing nothing about asthma, I wasn't sure if that was the best course of action or if she should use it now to get ahead of an attack.

Figuring she knew more about it than I did, I was about to ask her when a rumble sounded from further down the canyon. It sounded like a train was coming. I scanned the area for tracks, but high walls and the occasional tree were all that bordered the riverbed on either side.

The water beneath us churned and rushed about our ankles, turning from clear to silty.

"Move it," a male voice called from behind us. "Seek higher ground."

I whipped my head toward the voice. A man hurried toward us, agile as he navigated the uneven trail.

For a minute, I feared it was Phillips. As he got closer, I realized it was the ranger from the day before. "Ranger Stewart," I said with relief.

He came to a stop behind us. "Incoming flash flood. Hurry, water will quickly fill this canyon."

He pointed to a ledge several feet up. "Go."

Hana scrambled up the rock, scurrying on her hands and feet like an animal. I did my best to follow her, but Felony's weight slowed me down.

There was no path. We had to dodge trees and bushes. The rumble grew louder, and I summoned strength I thought was long gone, grabbing whatever I could—tree limbs, rocks—to pull myself up the last few feet and onto the ledge.

Ranger Stewart met us at the top. The roar of rushing water grew louder, and the canyon below us filled with muddy water. Giant tree trunks and other debris bobbed along as the current carried them downstream.

The beauty from seconds before was now just a memory.

The ranger stood with hands on hips, surveying the sides of the canyon wall below us as it caved into the raging water. "Where's the rest of your group?"

I took a minute to catch my breath before I could answer. "We got separated. One didn't make it."

He glanced at me. "Which one?"

"You knew her as Izzy. But that's not who she was."

An eyebrow shot up. "I'm sure there's a story there, but we need to keep moving. The water might continue to rise. There's a fire tower not far from here. We'll be safe up there, and as soon as a helicopter is available, they should be able to rescue us."

Another short hike and we'd be safe. But what about the others? "My cousin and one kid crossed the footbridge before it broke. They need rescuing, too. Can you alert the authorities of their direction of travel?"

"Sure thing." He keyed his radio and started talking. Hana and I began our climb and could no longer follow the conversation. But he'd made contact. This was almost over.

The only thing that kept me going was the hope that tonight I'd sleep in my own bed.

Chapter Forty

Marcus

Marcus looked up at the walls of the canyon that surrounded them. Rocks stood tall and proud, like monuments. Scattered pine trees had rooted on the bare, rugged ridge. The contrast of reddish stone among the bright green vegetation would be beautiful if he weren't soaked, exhausted, and worried about Casey. Each step sucked a bit more energy out of him, his boots heavy as cinderblocks.

The trail ran along the creek's edge. The water trickled crystal clear, tempting him to refill his water bottle. But he'd watched enough movies to know the water wasn't safe to drink. But after the miles they'd covered, he was almost out of the stuff. He should have collected rainwater when he had the chance, but he'd been preoccupied with finding Casey.

At least the sky was clearing.

What if Casey hadn't stuck to the trail? What if they were walking in the wrong direction and they'd never cross paths? He guessed they'd know once they reached the camp where this whole nightmare had started. The camp that had burned to the ground.

A rumble shook the earth. Not more thunder, he thought to himself. Not more rain.

But the sky above him only held intermittent clouds.

Betz cocked his head to the side. "Do you hear that?"

They stopped on a small footbridge that stretched a few feet above the creek.

"Don't think that's thunder," Betz said.

The bridge shook beneath their feet. Marcus looked over the rail. What had been a trickle of water moments ago was suddenly a raging, wild, mud-filled river. "Run," Marcus yelled.

They'd almost made it across the bridge when it lifted and put them off balance. They couldn't turn back. They had to carry on. A few steps and Betz slipped, landing prone on the slick boards.

Marcus leaned over him. "Shit! Get up."

Betz tried to get his feet under him, but he couldn't get traction. Marcus scooped his arms under Betz's armpits and hoisted him to his feet.

The roar of the water was deafening now.

Marcus shoved Betz forward as torrents of muddy, debris-filled water smashed into the bridge. The wood lifted and splintered, swaying like a carnival ride. The force thrust Marcus forward, and he fought to stay upright as he lost his footing. There was no more wood beneath his feet. He reached for Betz, but he wasn't there anymore. The current grabbed him like outstretched hands, twisting him around and around, leaving him dizzy. The angry river sucked him under, and the world around him disappeared.

Chapter Forty-One

Betz

Betz scrambled off the bridge just before it broke free. "Hurry," he said, glancing over his shoulder. But Marcus was no longer behind him.

"Shit. Shit. Shit." Betz scrambled up a rock and stopped once he reached the high ledge. Where the hell was Marcus?

The remnants of the bridge snaked down the river, banging against the rock walls.

Betz ran along the cliff, following the current. Massive tree trunks rammed into the rock below him. He couldn't imagine anyone surviving if the debris-filled soup swept them away and smashed them against the stone walls. Where the fuck was Marcus?

How would he explain this to Casey?

He tried to swallow, but the giant lump in his throat choked him. "Marcus!" he bellowed, side-stepping on the narrow ridge, slipping, almost falling in.

Out of rock to walk on, Betz came to a stop. "No!"

With the speed of the river, the wave of mud and tree parts, Marcus could be a mile away by now. There was no way for Betz to move further downstream unless he plunged into the water himself. But that would be suicide.

There had to be another way.

Chapter Forty-Two

At the top of the hill, the ground flattened, and the trees thinned. Ranger Stewart guided us, telling us when to go straight and where to turn. I was relieved to be with someone who knew the area and that I was no longer the one making decisions. As uninformed as they were.

Each breath Hana took was labored, producing a whistling sound. She wasn't getting much air. "I think you've pushed it as long as you can," I said. "Might be time to use your inhaler. Rescuers will arrive soon. You don't have to worry about running out."

She stopped, removed the device from her pocket, and took the last hit.

We paused, giving the medicine time to take effect. "I was surprised to see you," I said to the ranger. "I thought you'd get ahead of the fire when I saw you the other day."

He took a drink of water from his hydration pack. "I got turned around, was forced back your way. Wasn't even able to respond to my original call. The camp was destroyed by the time I got there."

So, maybe it was the ranger who'd been trailing us and not Phillips the maniac. But that didn't jibe with Crystal's story. I supposed there could have been more than one person in the vicinity. "You encounter anyone else?"

He shook his head. "You thinking of the escaped convict? No. Only thing I came across was some wildlife hightailing it to safety. They were headed this way. Since they have an innate sense about such things, I figure we're going in the right direction."

"Makes sense."

"I'm ready," Hana said. But her breathing was far from normal.

We continued along. Eventually, we came to a meadow. In the middle of it was a fire tower. Just like the ranger promised. I was so happy; I wanted to kiss the ground.

A steep ladder led to the structure. Hana went first. I focused on the rung in front of me. If I looked down, I'd have a panic attack. Ranger Stewart brought up the rear.

The lookout was one square room. A table, a chair, and a cot were the only furniture. A telescope pointed toward the canyon, where the newly formed river raged. Beyond it was a panoramic view of the forest we'd come from.

There was smoke in the distance, but the fire was nowhere near us. For now, we were safe.

"The helicopter will be here as soon as possible," Stewart said, lowering his pack to the table. "But we're not the only ones in need of help. We may not be the highest priority since we're safe here."

Hana sank onto the cot. "But my asthma."

I let Felony free, then sat next to Hana, rubbing her back. "That was her last dose," I said to Stewart.

He nodded. "I'll see if I can get an ETA on the chopper. Tell them we might have a medical emergency." He stepped outside onto the narrow deck, talking on his radio and closing the door behind him.

Hana grabbed my hand and squeezed it. "What if…what if I die?"

I encouraged her to lie down and covered her with a blanket. "Not gonna happen. We didn't come this far for nothing. Help will be here soon."

But as I looked down at her, I wasn't so sure. She was pale, wheezing.

She let go of my hand and fished in her pants' pocket. Pulling something out, she pressed it into my hand. "A key?"

She nodded. "Just in case—"

"What does it go to?"

Hana closed her eyes. The lids fluttered as she said. "The shed. Number 56."

As she fell asleep, her breathing evened out. Panic had made her asthma worse. Relaxed, she seemed better. Making sure her head was propped up on a pillow, I stood. The key she gave me lay in my palm. Small, silver. I slid it into my pocket and joined the ranger on the deck.

"What about the helicopter?"

"Soon," he said. "Get some rest."

Chapter Forty-Three

Betz

Betz sat back on his heels and rubbed the stubble on his chin. This couldn't be happening. Not on his watch.

He'd taken an oath to protect and to serve. That meant everyone. Betz couldn't bear the thought of Casey losing someone else. She was still recovering from her mother's death a little over a year ago. If Marcus was gone….if he died trying to save her….save him….well, Casey would never come back from that. And neither would he.

On his butt, he scooted down the embankment toward the now violent river. There was a chance, a slim one, that Marcus had gotten caught in the debris. Maybe he hadn't drifted out of sight.

But at the bank, he saw nothing but destruction. With his vision blurred, he thought he spotted the shape of a man, but as he got closer, he could see it was only a giant log bobbing against the rock.

Sending Joy and the twins off with his satellite radio seemed like the right decision at the time. Now he wished he'd kept it so he could start a helicopter search for Marcus. But the best he could do was to keep looking for Casey. She's the reason they were out there. He climbed back up the ridge and looked for the trail.

Chapter Forty-Four

The sound of a helicopter pulled me from a deep sleep. The last thing I remember was thinking I'd just rest my eyes. But as I rolled over, I noticed the last traces of daylight had faded into night.

I stretched, reaching for Hana at my side. "Wake up. We're being rescued." Just like Ranger Stewart had promised. But the space next to me was empty.

Squinting in the near darkness, I spotted Felony across the room with his paws on the window frame. He whimpered, watching whatever was happening outside.

Hana and the ranger must have already gone down. Had she gotten worse? Was the helicopter going to airlift her first and then come back for us?

I hurried to the window, where I watched the chopper approach. Their spotlight lit up the room as it passed overhead.

"Wait!" I ran to the window on the other side of the room. But instead of stopping, or hovering over the tower, the helicopter continued past us, eventually disappearing from view.

Why didn't they stop?

I ran to the door and tried to push it open. But something blocked it. It wouldn't budge. What the hell?

I took a deep breath. Fire. I smelled fire. Not again. But looking out the windows, I could see in the moonlight that the forest was untouched. The flames hadn't moved this way.

I tried the door again, ramming my shoulder against it. But I only bounced back. I was trapped.

The windows.

I yanked on them, but they wouldn't budge. Someone had painted them shut. With my elbow, I tried to break the glass. But it was double-paned. My efforts were futile. I looked around for something I could use to smash the glass. Grabbing the table, I hefted it into my arms. It was awkward, and I couldn't muster the momentum needed to break the window.

I looked down at the ground. Now I could see flames dancing, casting shadows. The bottom of the tower was on fire.

It was suddenly clear. Ranger Stewart had taken Hana. I'd seen him place calls on the radio but heard no one on the other end. He hadn't called for help. He'd locked me in the tower, set the fire, and left me here to die.

Chapter Forty-Five

Betz

Betz spotted an orange glow through the trees. Had the fire jumped the river? It happened. Embers traveled. Except the conditions weren't right for that. The air was still. There was no wind. Something wasn't right.

He quickened his pace and entered a clearing.

A fire tower loomed large. Flames licked the wooden foundation.

Betz aimed his flashlight at the cab on top. Windows reflected the light back at him, blinding him. But then he heard a muffled bark.

Someone was up there.

Rushing forward, he dropped his pack. Untying the tarp he'd carried, he used it to beat the flames. They danced toward him; the heat searing the hair on his arms. Once he had smothered them, he found the ladder. The wood had charred, burning his hands. But he forced himself to withstand the pain, and he made the climb.

At the top, he rushed to the window. There was Casey, her hand pressed against the glass. He flattened his palm against the other side, the cool surface soothing his wounds. The sight of Casey kick-started his heart. He looked to the door, noting the chair wedged against it, trapping her inside.

Kicking it out of the way, he pulled the door open. And drew her into his arms.

* * *

He had her.

Nothing else mattered.

Betz pulled her even tighter and buried his face in the nape of her neck, breathing in the scent of her. He wanted to remember this moment, every detail, for the rest of his life.

Both of them were dirty and disheveled, but that didn't matter. He'd found her, and she melted against him. She belonged in his arms. Part of him thought he'd never see her again. Now that he had her, he never wanted to let her go.

She clung to him tighter than she ever had before. Resting her head on his shoulder, she let out deep, shuddering sobs.

He stroked her hair. "It's okay." But he had to fight his own tears. If he'd been a few minutes later…if he'd taken more time to look for Marcus…

But this was what Marcus had wanted, too. For Casey to be found.

He didn't know how long they stood there like that, but he never wanted it to end. Felony had his own agenda. He wedged his way between them. Not wanting to be on the outside. "Okay, boy." Betz dropped one hand and petted the dancing dog. "I'm glad to see you, too."

"How?" Casey said, finally releasing him and taking a step back. "How did you find us?"

Betz shook his head. "I don't even know. Instinct, I guess. I just kept thinking that if I stayed on the trail, I'd run into you. But then there was a flash flood, and the trail disappeared."

She nodded. "We got caught in that, too."

He had to touch her again. Make sure she was real. He reached out and ran his hands up and down her arms. "You're okay? You're not hurt?"

"I'm not hurt."

"We. You said, we. What happened to the others? Where's Hope?"

"We got separated. I ended up with Hana. She's one of the kids. And then the ranger. But…" She whirled about, motioning to the empty room. "I woke up, and they were gone. I couldn't get out. They left me to die."

He took her back into his arms. "It's okay. You're safe now." But he had so much to share with her. Except he wouldn't tell her about Marcus. Not yet. Not while they were miles from safety, miles away from climbing off this damn mountain. She had to stay strong. Finding her was a victory, sure. But this was far from over.

"The ranger?" he said.

'Couldn't have really been a ranger," she said. "He'd warned us about an escaped convict.... I thought it was Phillips, but.... The guy who said he was a ranger, it wasn't him."

"Phillips is out here. That part is true. But we found a man, dead, his clothes missing. Could have been the real ranger."

"But who—?" She shook her head. "Now I remember. The ranger. Whoever he was.... He said it was a robbery suspect. He'd been lying all along."

"No one has ever identified Phillips's accomplice. He's never been found."

Casey's hand flew up and covered her mouth. "My God. He has Hana." She reached into her pocket and produced Crystal Monroe's jail ID. Passing it to Betz, she told him how Crystal had pretended to be the counselor, Izzy. How she'd kept Hana alive. How she was gone.

"We'll find them," Betz assured her. But he knew it might be too late. They might lose Hana, just as they lost Marcus.

"I'm going to climb back down. Make sure the fire is really out. Then we'll talk," he assured her.

* * *

Once he determined they were safe for the night, he promised Casey they would hike out at the first light of day.

He found some cheese and crackers in his pack, and together they sat on the cot, sharing the food with Felony. While they ate, Betz told his story about working the Phillips case and then coming to the mountains when he realized Phillips might be after one of Casey's kids. He omitted the part about Joy and Marcus, letting her believe he'd acted alone. It felt wrong to discount them, erasing them. But he needed her to stay strong. He'd catch hell for it when the truth came out, but now wasn't the time.

"So, you found the twins?"

"They reported that someone had stabbed the naturalist, Rick Santos. Guessing it was Phillips or whoever is pretending to be the ranger who did it."

"And Gary and Yuki?"

"The twins got separated from them. No update on them as far as I know."

Casey took something out of her pocket and held it up. A key. "Hana slipped me this. She was having an asthma attack and thought she was going to die. She said 'shed,' but I don't know where the shed is. I'm thinking whatever is in there is what Phillips and his buddy are after."

"Did the pretend ranger know she gave it to you?"

She shook her head, closing her fingers around the key. "Hopefully, that will keep her alive. If he thinks she can give it to him or tell him where the shed is."

"Is she smart enough for that?"

"I think so."

Casey slipped the key back into her pocket. "I feel like we should be out there. Looking for her now."

"As soon as it's light, we'll get going. It will be easier to find her with the help of the officers back at the command center. We'll head there. In the meantime, we should get some sleep. We still have a long hike ahead of us."

They lay on the cot, Casey in his arms, her head resting on his chest. Being with her like this felt as familiar as an old pair of jeans. He stroked her hair, and she relaxed against him. When he was sure she was asleep, he whispered, "I love you," as if she didn't already know.

Chapter Forty-Six

Daylight did its best to nudge me awake, but it was Felony's intense stare that broke me. I pressed my ear against Betz's chest and took a moment to let the sound of his heartbeat soothe me. A sound I hadn't heard in over three years. And yet it was like a familiar song, forever in my head.

I felt guilty for enjoying this momentary cocoon of safety in his arms. Hana was out there. Her life was in danger. Felony knew I was faking sleep. And, shocker, I had to pee.

That gentle reminder of my pregnancy brought me back to reality. I'd almost shared my news with Betz last night. We were so happy to see each other; would the news that I was going to have a baby with another man still push him away? If I gave the green light, could we be a couple again? Last night, anything seemed possible.

But I couldn't let my emotions do the talking. I'd been near death, and he'd saved me. I wasn't thinking clearly. Didn't I warn my clients not to make important decisions when they were under stress?

And there was Marcus.

I opened my eyes and met Felony's. His tail thumped. "Shush." I held a finger to my lips. Easing off Betz, I tore my body from his like a Band-Aid off a slow-healing wound. Wasn't that what we'd inflicted on each other? Wounds that would never heal.

Lowering the blanket back over him, I quietly crept to the door. Felony knew the drill, and he climbed into my pack, and together we made the descent. At the bottom of the ladder, I let him loose, and we both did our thing. Then I sat on a bench, letting the sun beat down on me, warming my bones.

With so much at stake, so many unknowns, you'd think I wouldn't feel at peace, yet here I was basking in Betz's love. He'd wandered the forest during a fire looking for me. Not that he'd had anything to prove. He wore his feelings for me like a neon sign.

For the moment, anything seemed possible. But there was still something that niggled at the back of my mind. That something was Marcus and a different life. I wasn't ready to let that go.

* * *

We started down the trail that led away from the tower. Betz was sure he knew how to get back to the command center. He said he had memorized the map. We were moving toward safety, and for a moment, my heart filled with hope. But this nightmare was far from over. We still had to find Hana.

He'd convinced me that the professionals would have better luck finding her. And now that we were sure Phillips and his accomplice were actually in the woods, they'd pull out all the stops to find them. As soon as we got to the command center, they'd have drones, helicopters, horses, and personnel. Hana might have a chance.

I felt stupid because the fake ranger had tricked me. But I was worried about Phillips. Someone I'd recognize. It never occurred to me he and Crystal weren't acting alone.

He knew the mountain. But lots of people did. Hiking was a big thing in Arizona. People especially liked to escape the summer valley heat and get lost in the wilderness of Flagstaff, where it could be twenty degrees cooler.

Still, I turned my time with the fake ranger over and over in my mind, looking for that moment when I should have figured things out and whisked Hana off to safety. I'd known something was off, but I'd been too tired to think clearly. Plus, I'd been missing a critical piece of information. A third party was involved. So why did I still feel responsible?

Chapter Forty-Seven

Betz

Betz almost expected there to be fanfare, balloons, and cheering crowds when they found their way back to the command station. But this wasn't a marathon, although it felt like he'd just completed one. Instead, they walked into the lot undetected.

He and Casey exchanged a look of relief mixed with exhaustion. He led her to a tent where Sergeant Savage stood talking to two deputies. When she noticed him, her face lit up. "Detective Betz, I thought I'd never see you again." Then she looked past him. "You found your wife?"

He raised his eyebrows at Casey and sent her a look that said, "Just go with it." He was too tired to explain their complicated situation. Then it dawned on him. Savage would mention Marcus.

But Savage didn't have to break the news. Joy popped out of a chair and ran to them, crushing her cousin in an overdue hug. "Good Lord," she said. "I've been worried sick."

Casey pulled back, shot Betz a second look of confusion, and then focused on Joy. "What are you doing here?"

"Looking for you," she said. "Didn't Betz tell you that me and Marcus were part of the search party?" Then she swiveled her head around. "Speaking of Marcus, where is he?"

"Marcus is here?" Casey asked, searching the surrounding group.

"Casey," Betz said, putting his hands on her shoulders. "You should sit down."

She squirmed out of his hold. "I don't want to sit down. I want to know what's going on."

Putting off the news was a disastrous decision. He saw that now. "I'm sorry," he said. "I didn't want to give you anything else to worry about. But there's something you should know."

Casey crossed her arms. The wall was up. "Hope?"

Joy reached out and patted her arm. "Hope's fine, honey. She's in Flagstaff getting checked out at the hospital. Hope and that boy. But I wasn't leaving. Not until they found you."

"What then?" Casey asked. "Is Marcus still out there looking for me?"

Savage crossed her arms and looked at Betz. In fact, every eye was on him. Betz cleared his throat. "I'm sorry. But the flash flood. I'm afraid—"

In that moment, everyone else vanished. With tunnel vision, it was just him and Casey. He always loved that she could finish his sentences. But not this time.

The color drained from her face. "No. Don't say it."

"I'm sorry."

Betz stepped forward and caught Casey as she fell to her knees.

Chapter Forty-Eight

Time stopped, yet rushed forward, leaving me dizzy. I stopped my brain from finishing a thought. Once I did, I wouldn't be able to pretend this wasn't happening.

I didn't remember getting to the chair on the other side of the tent, but the next thing I knew, I was sitting in it. People stood around me with worried looks on their faces, offering me water. Glancing down, I saw a blood pressure cuff on my arm and a young paramedic pulling a stethoscope from his ears and hanging it around his neck.

"You passed out," he said. "Probably from sheer exhaustion. We should get you to the hospital. Get you checked out."

But it was more than that. I found Betz in the crowd and met his gaze. I couldn't stand the look of pity on his face. "Marcus? Is he... Please tell me what happened."

Betz kneeled before me and laid his hands over mine. "He's missing. It was the water. It came so fast."

"How long? How long has he been gone?"

"About a day."

"A day?" I grabbed the armrests on the chair and squeezed them. Trying to feel something. But I was numb.

"We'll get the search going," the deputy Betz called Savage said.

I felt woozy and held tighter onto the chair so I wouldn't topple over. Felony came over and sat at my feet, pressing his weight against my legs. Letting me know he was there for me. Some comfort, but it was going to take more than that.

I turned back to Betz. "Why didn't you tell me?"

He cleared his throat. "I couldn't. You had to concentrate on getting off the mountain."

"But…" But what? How long could he survive in that water? How long before they presumed…I couldn't finish the thought.

I struggled to my feet. "Take me there. Take me to the place where he fell in."

Betz blocked my path. "Casey—"

I shoved him away. I was shaking now. "Is someone going to take me, or do I have to go alone? Because I'm going."

Betz followed. "Savage has started a search. They have helicopters, drones."

"But with all this time," Savage said. "I'm sorry, but—"

I spun about, shaking my finger at her. "Don't you dare. Don't say it. We're going to find him."

But when I tried to walk to the trail, Betz ran up beside me, reached out, and caught my hand. He pulled me into his arms.

I couldn't separate my thoughts. Anger, hope, despair. My feelings swirled like they were in a blender. Collapsing into Betz, I buried my face against his chest and sobbed. It felt like a knife stabbed my heart repeatedly, twisting back and forth, leaving a hole that would never close. We still had chapters to write. Marcus didn't even know he had a child on the way.

There had to be something I could do. But it was out of my hands.

Chapter Forty-Nine

Betz

Casey and Joy sat in camp chairs. Joy talked incessantly while Casey held her head in her hands. Every few minutes, she jumped to her feet, found Savage, and asked for updates, but there were none.

She blamed him for Marcus's disappearance. She hadn't said so, but he couldn't see it going any other way. He'd let two civilians accompany him on a search they had no business undertaking. He would have done anything to find Casey, but he should have insisted on joining the law enforcement search already underway or even going alone. But then, would he have found Casey? Or was it only the path they'd taken, losing Marcus and all, that finally led him to her? Had he been a few minutes later, she and Felony would have burned to death.

He would have thought that with Marcus out of the picture, he'd have a greater chance at rekindling his relationship with Casey. But he hadn't wanted it to happen like this. Marcus losing interest and returning to New Jersey, sure. But missing…presumed dead. Casey would never recover from that.

And because Marcus had been trying to help Betz when it happened, he'd never recover either. He'd always owe him his life.

Casey was just getting her feet back under her after her mother's tragic death. How much could one person take?

She'd refused the paramedic's recommendation to go to the hospital and get checked out. If they got news about Marcus, she wanted to be the first to hear it.

From across the tent, Savage motioned him over. "What's up?" he said.

"We've got a lead on the missing girl."

Betz's spine tingled. If he could deliver Casey a bit of good news....but what if it were bad? He doubted she could handle anything else. He braced himself. "Go on."

"Deputies found a woman walking along the fire road. She'd driven down it, hoping to get some photos of the fire damage. A man wearing a ranger's uniform and another man were with a teenage girl. They surprised her and stole her car."

Had to be Phillips, his partner, and Hana. "Did they say where they were going?"

Savage adjusted her gun belt. "The woman said the girl mouthed 'help me' and then, 'Phoenix.'"

"So, they're headed back to the valley," Betz said.

"Looks that way."

He jotted down the vehicle information on a piece of paper he'd found on the table. But without his glasses, he wouldn't be able to read the words he'd written if unable to recall them.

Rubbing the back of his neck, he crossed over to Casey and Joy. Joy was yammering on about her psychic abilities, and that she could feel Marcus's aura, claiming because of that, he couldn't be dead.

Casey looked like she was either going to throw up or tackle her cousin.

She slowly looked his way when he came to stand in front of her. "What now?"

"Phillips and the ranger impersonator stole a car. Hana was with them. They're headed back to Phoenix. The carjacked woman said Hana told her that much."

"I can't leave," she said. "What if—"

"SAR is handling the search. They'll let us know. There's nothing you can do."

Casey jumped up, startling Felony, who'd been napping at her feet. She ran her hands over her thighs. "Okay, let's go."

"The car is this way," he said. But as he patted his pockets, he realized he didn't have the keys. Marcus did.

Casey seemed to steel herself for what she had to do. "If you've got a screwdriver, I can get it going." She started toward the 4Runner. "Marcus taught me a few things."

Chapter Fifty

Screwdriver in hand, I popped the cover off the ignition. Marcus had dazzled me with his knowledge of stealing cars when Diablo had been hot on our heels. I never asked him about it, but figured it was a skill he'd learned on the mean streets of New Jersey. Because I'd checked, I knew he didn't have a criminal record as an adult. But juvenile records are sealed. Or perhaps no one ever caught him. I thought it was a skill I'd never need, but apparently I was wrong. Marcus was still helping me.

I tried not to think that it was his spirit assisting me, that I'd never see him again, but my mind went there without permission. I needed to keep my attention on the task at hand if I was going to help Hana.

Pulling out the wires, I twisted them together like he'd shown me, and like magic, the engine roared to life.

"I'm not gonna ask how you know how to do that," Betz said, putting his seatbelt on.

Joy ushered Felony into the back seat and then climbed in beside him.

I glanced at Betz. "You don't want to drive?"

"Can't," he said, although he didn't elaborate why.

Putting the 4Runner into drive, I adjusted the rearview mirror and started out of the lot. It killed me to leave the search for Marcus. Recovery, they called it when they thought I wasn't listening. But the authorities were doing their best, and I wasn't doing any good sitting around and worrying.

Hana still had a chance.

Once Betz got enough signal on his phone, he called Jasmine and filled her in on Phillips' recent movement, asking her to call out the cavalry. He handed Joy a piece of paper. "Read me the license plate info."

Once she did, he parroted the information into the phone.

I could hear that Jasmine was still talking when he ended the call.

"No contacts," I surmised. "You lose them in the woods?"

Betz squirmed in his seat.

I glanced at him. "Trouble in paradise?"

He didn't answer. But the bitter look on his face told me he and Jasmine weren't in a good place. I hoped it wasn't because of me, but I had a hunch it was.

"So, Hana talked about a shed," I said. "Apparently, her father hid something Phillips wants."

"Drugs?" Betz asked.

"I'm thinking, no. Hana said police thought the home invasion was over drugs, but she swore her parents weren't involved in that shit. Something shady, maybe, but I don't think it was drugs."

Betz scratched his head. "We can check out the Stevens' house. See if they have a shed. It's a good place to start, anyway."

"You'd think the entire property would have been gone over with a fine-toothed comb after the murders," I said.

"It would have been. It wouldn't be the first time someone missed something, though."

"Does the address start with fifty-six?"

"No."

That blew that theory. But we had to rule it out. I took the exit for I-17 South, my thoughts bouncing from Hana to Marcus.

Betz cleared his throat. "You ready for some more news?"

I took a deep breath. "I guess."

"Jasmine told me they found the rest of your group. Yuki and Gary were together, and they're okay. Rick Santos, the naturalist, didn't make it. He succumbed to his injuries while he was being airlifted to the hospital. I'm sorry."

I swallowed hard, trying to digest the news of another death. "How could everything go so wrong? They've killed so many. They won't hesitate to add

Hana to the list. They're only keeping her alive so she can tell them what they want to know. Once she does…"

"I know," Betz said. "We need to find her before that happens."

I punched the gas.

Chapter Fifty-One

The desert was a blur as we traveled south. I kept my eyes on the road, weaving in and out of traffic like I was after a trophy. Either my driving or my dismal mood scared Betz and Joy into silence. Even Felony was quiet.

I didn't want to talk, but silence wasn't my friend. My thoughts were stuck on Marcus. Images of him struggling to survive in unforgiving, violent water stuck on playback in my head. How long would he be able to keep his head above the rushing debris? Had the river sucked him down to the underbelly? Was he knocked unconscious by a fast-moving log? Would hypothermia set in even if he could keep his head above water? Would anyone ever find him?

Tears splashed down my face, and I didn't hide them. Betz reached over and squeezed my knee. "I'm sorry," he said. "It all happened so fast."

I wiped my nose with the back of my hand. "Did he even know what was happening?"

"I don't know."

But there had to be a moment. A moment of intense fear.

Don't think about it…don't think about it…don't let your mind go there…

I tried to hold on to hope. Until they found him, there would always be hope.

I lay my hand on my belly, still flat. I didn't know how he would have reacted to the news. But he deserved the opportunity to be part of his child's life. I would do my best to make sure he was, no matter what form that took.

For now, I had to focus on Hana. That was the best use of my energy. What little I had.

I felt a surge of the stuff as Phoenix came into view.

Chapter Fifty-Two

Betz

"Stop by the precinct," Betz said as they came upon downtown central Phoenix.

Casey looked as if she were in a trance. She'd been quiet for most of the drive. She was fighting like hell to keep it together. Taking the off-ramp, she navigated the 4Runner onto Washington Street, pulling up to a metered spot. Marcus' motorcycle sat where he'd left it.

When Casey spied it, she gasped.

She pulled into the employee lot and parked. "Let's run inside," Betz said. "Get some gear and some help." He hoped to distract her, but his thoughts went to next of kin notification. Somebody should have contacted Marcus' family. He imagined Savage would take care of that, but she hadn't mentioned it. He wondered if Casey knew how to reach his parents. Betz knew he had a sister. She was the reason Marcus had come to the valley in the first place. The reason Marcus had entered Casey's life.

Betz might have thrown his badge at his sister, but he still had his work ID, and he used it to let them in through a side door. Once inside, he led them up the stairs and to his cubicle.

"Where's the restroom?" Joy said. "I need to clean up."

Betz pointed down the hall. "On your left."

Putting his phone on the rapid charger, he looked up to see Jasmine standing at the entrance to his cubicle. She held out her hand, a box resting on her open palm. "A peace offering," she said.

He took the container that held a new set of contact lenses. It was a start, but there was a conversation to be had. One he'd put off far too long. No matter their relationship status, Casey was in his life for good. She would always be special to him. Jasmine needed to accept that.

"Casey," Jasmine said, nodding in her direction. "It's good to see you're safe."

Casey smiled, so forced it seemed to give her pain. "Thanks."

"Anything I can do to help?" she asked. "We've already got an APB out on Phillips and the stolen car."

Betz slipped his contacts in and blinked, his vision instantly clearing. "We've got it, thanks."

"Well, if anything comes up, you know how to reach me." With a shrug, she left.

Betz got on his computer and brought up photos of the house where Hana's parents were murdered. "There's a shed on the property," he said.

Casey stood and looked at the screen. "Still doesn't explain the fifty-six reference."

Moody appeared and leaned against the wall of Betz's cubicle, her arms crossed. Betz gave her a summary of the events that had occurred since he last saw her. "Let's go have a second look," she said.

Chapter Fifty-Three

I didn't realize we'd given Joy the slip until we'd almost arrived at the Stevens' house. Marcus was never out of my mind, but I didn't have the luxury of focusing on my feelings or admitting to myself that with each moment that passed, the odds of finding him alive decreased. Betz had promised me that Savage would call him if there were any updates.

I knew what had happened was eating at him, and he felt responsible. I didn't want to do or say anything that would add to that. My heart broke for him as well.

I'd plugged my phone into the charger in the Interceptor. Once the battery climbed out of the red, I gave Hope a call, but it went straight to voicemail. She probably hadn't had the opportunity to charge her phone.

"What does Kate know?" I asked.

"Nothing," Betz said. "Unless Joy told her."

Of course she did. Joy wouldn't be able to help herself. That meant my dad probably knew, too. They must have been going out of their minds.

I called my sister.

"Oh. My. God," she said, before I could even speak. "We've been so worried. Are you okay?"

"I'm fine," I assured her. Physically, I was. At least I thought so. But emotionally, I'd returned to that place, that horrible place I'd been when I'd received the news of my mother's death. I had stopped to take the call from Kate as I was preparing to leave the office for the day. The news had shaken my world.

That gut punch held its own space in the emotions compartment of my psyche. Something I would never forget or recover from. All those feelings came back to me now. I never thought I'd rise from that despair, and every day I made a conscious effort to be happy. It's what my mom would have wanted. But now all those emotions were back again. Raw and ugly. It wasn't the same, yet that sick feeling in the pit of my stomach was familiar.

I was losing the battle to push that feeling down. Maybe I'd never really dealt with my mother's death. I knew how to stuff negative thoughts down deep. But they were always there. Simmering.

And now they were gaining strength like a fast-moving hurricane about to make landfall.

Kate's voice snapped me back to the present. "Dad's here. I'm putting him on."

"Pumpkin." My father's gruff voice stretched across the miles, connecting us. "I'm so glad you're safe."

That was all it took. The damn broke. His heart had been through the wringer, too. The thought that he had to worry about me was more than I could take. I sat there blubbering like a little kid whose balloon had just floated away.

From the front seat, Moody turned and looked at me. She offered one of those half-smiles, draped with empathy. And then, a handful of tissues.

I fought my breakdown, trying to gather my wits and regain control of myself. My emotions had never been so out of control. Pregnancy hormones? Good God, this was the last thing I needed. I had to pull it together for Hana. I could have my meltdown later. Hopefully, in private. Grabbing the tissues Moody offered me, I wiped my face. "I'm okay, Dad. I've got to handle something, and then I'll be home."

"Are you with Betz?"

He'd always liked Betz. He trusted him with my life. "I am. Don't worry. I'm safe."

"Okay, pumpkin. I love you."

Kate came back on the line. "What are you doing? More sleuthing? When is it going to be enough? Get your butt home." The verbal equivalent of shaking me by the shoulders. But I knew she cared about me, and worry must have overwhelmed her. She'd also had her heart ripped out when our mom died. I tried to keep that in mind.

"I will," I said. "Just need to do one thing first. Love you, bye."

I ended the call. Kate never understood my draw to the chaotic. And she never would. She hated my job and often reminded me of that. And what do I do? Use my vacation time to take on a "safer" job only to have it blow up in my face. I was too frazzled to explain myself. And she didn't know about Marcus or the baby. I wasn't ready to go there.

I'd somewhat pulled myself together by the time we'd parked in front of an unassuming stucco house. Small and box-shaped. A *for-sale* sign stood in the yard. I wondered if the real estate agent would disclose to potential buyers the horrors that had occurred inside.

After Moody called in our location, we got out of the car. Not knowing what we'd walk into, I left Felony in the Interceptor.

We walked around to the backyard. And there it was, a shed.

My heart beat wildly with thoughts of what we might find. Slipping the Key Hana had passed me out of my pocket, I tried it in the lock, but the key was much too small.

Betz reached around me and tried the handle. It was unlocked.

He pushed the door open, and we peered inside. Just a bunch of gardening tools hanging on the wall. A giant sack of dirt. Empty pots. A planting stand. What one would expect to find in a shed.

"We scoured the place after the murders," Moody said. "I'd be surprised if anything's here."

Just in case, we moved things, opened drawers, and Betz knocked on the floor, looking for a false bottom. Nothing.

"Hana used the word shed," I told them. "Right before she drifted off to sleep."

We reconvened outside, and Moody shut the door. "We're going to have to figure that out. Let me go over the case notes and see if anything pops out at me."

Back in the car, Betz adjusted the rearview mirror so he could make eye contact with me in the backseat. "I'm taking you home, Casey. We're doing everything we can, and you need to get some rest."

I didn't want to miss anything, but I desperately needed a shower and some sleep. I couldn't think straight, so I didn't argue. "But you'll call me the moment you hear anything?"

"Promise," he said.

Twenty minutes later, we pulled up outside my father's house, and I raised my eyes at Moody, who watched me from the front seat. "Thanks," I said. I knew she and Betz would do everything they could to find Hana.

"We'll keep on it," she said. "Get some rest."

Taking Felony by the leash, I got out of the car. Betz met me outside. He held me at arm's length and gave me a look so intense, I felt like he could read my thoughts. "I'm so sorry about Marcus. If only I could have…"

I nodded. "I'm sure you did everything you could."

"Remember that I love you. I'll be here for you no matter what happens. No matter what you decide."

I swallowed hard. "I know. And same." I wanted to invite him inside. Have him hold me like he did the night before. But he didn't have time for that. Not if he was going to find Hana.

I took comfort in knowing he'd always be there for me. At least until he knew about the baby. Could he get past that? I almost asked him. But it wouldn't be fair to pile that on top of everything else he had going on. He was sleep-deprived, hungry, and dirty, too. And he had a job to do.

I stepped toward him and sank into his arms. He welcomed me, and we stayed like that until the porch light came on and my dad's girlfriend, Millie, came outside, watching us. Betz gave me a final squeeze and a soft kiss on the cheek before breaking contact.

"You've got to be operating on fumes," I said. "Be careful."

"I will be."

He climbed into the SUV, and from the driveway, I watched him pull away.

Millie walked toward me with her phone to her ear. "Yes, she just got here. Come home."

She must have been talking to my dad. I was glad to see her and thankful I had a bit of time before my father and Kate would overwhelm me.

Millie wrapped me in a hug. "We've been so worried."

I patted her on the back. She hadn't been around that long, and I didn't like that she had so easily stepped into my mother's shoes, but she made my dad happy. I didn't want him to be alone, so I was trying to make space for her in my heart. "I need a shower," I said. "Can you get Felony some food and water while I clean up?"

"Sure thing." She took hold of the leash and followed me inside. "Anything else you need?"

"Nope. It's all good." But the words coming out of my mouth didn't come from my heart or my head. I was on autopilot, like telling the cashier at the grocery store that your day was going well even if it had been a total shitshow.

Inside my childhood bedroom, which had been my home for the last several weeks, I went to the dresser and took out some sweats, a long-sleeved T-shirt, some clean underwear, and socks. Peeling off my filthy clothes, I stuffed them in the trash. I never wanted to see them again. Stepping under the hot water streaming from the showerhead, I was too numb to cry.

* * *

I ate while my family watched me. Like I was fragile and would shatter into a million pieces at any moment, which probably wasn't far from the truth. They didn't even know about Marcus or what he meant to me. I was just coming to realize it myself.

I kept my phone next to me in case there was news, but with each tick of the clock on the wall, my hope dwindled.

My family made small talk around me. Who knew we were in for a cold front? Who cared? I was glad they respected my need to be quiet. To fade into the woodwork. I wasn't ready to share my tale.

Finally, my sister laid her hand over mine. "You should get some sleep. Hope and Joy are at my house. They've been through a lot, too. I should get home to them. Unless I can do anything for you."

"Is Hope okay?"

Kate nodded. "She's tired and sore, but basically unharmed."

I looked down at my sandwich. I'd taken only a few bites. I'd been ravenous earlier, but once offered, food sickened me.

After my father had walked Kate out, I pushed away from the table and called Felony with a click of my tongue. "Good night," I said on my way out the door.

In my room, I plugged my work cell into the charger. I'd have to call my boss and tell her what was going on. I didn't know if I'd go back to work anytime soon, but I wanted to give her a heads-up on my latest disaster.

Climbing into bed, I invited Felony to join me. With him cuddled at my side, I held my silent cell against my chest and tried to manage my thoughts. Memories danced across my eyelids like fireflies...Hana...the pretend ranger...Marcus. Those images faded as sleep pulled me under. My last thought was of Marcus fighting for his life, and I had the sensation of being dragged down with him.

Chapter Fifty-Four

I was awake and staring at the ceiling before daybreak, absently petting Felony, who was curled into a ball at my side. Despite my best efforts not to cry, tears ran down my face.

Cell phone clutched in my hand, I checked the Arizona Republic website, the local news pages, and looked for any incoming text messages every few minutes. If someone had found Marcus, it would surely have made the news. Or Betz would let me know. But the only articles I found generalized what had happened, speaking of the many hikers and campers surprised by the flash flood. The story was bigger than me and my group. The storm had endangered over a hundred people, and several were still missing.

I found stories about the ongoing manhunt for Phillips and the Amber Alert for Hana. Nothing new from the night before.

When the sun broke the darkness, I forced myself to my feet, grabbed my iPad, and let Felony out in the yard. Stumbling into the kitchen, I retrieved a Diet Coke and filled Felony's bowl with kibble. Settled at the table, I checked the news outlets once again.

A headline popped up: **Rescued Hiker.** With shaking hands, I clicked on the story. My heart thudded while I waited for the advertisement for diabetes medication to conclude. After a few seconds of torture, I pressed the Skip Ad button.

A woman wearing a vest coat and ball cap came on the screen. She stood in front of the command station. "Search and Rescue has worked tirelessly to find folks missing in this canyon just outside of Flagstaff after an unexpected storm caused flooding in the area. Although rescuers still don't know the location of several people, they recently recovered a woman from Peoria. She was found clinging to a tree and unable to get down after the water receded. Seven hikers remain missing. As time passes, most are presumed dead."

I swiped the app away, dropped my phone onto the table, and covered my face with my hands. This couldn't be happening. How could someone who was full of life one moment suddenly lose it? Even worse, he was out there because of me. Why had I texted him I was in danger? I had hoped he would alert the authorities, not put his life at risk. I should have known he'd come. He'd made no secret of how he felt about me.

My whole body shook as I sat there sobbing. Felony put his paws on my thighs and licked my face. Which only made it worse, but I didn't have the heart to push him away.

"Pumpkin?" My dad stood in the doorway. Barefoot and in his pajamas, I was reminded of Christmas mornings. The only occasion he didn't get dressed before leaving his room.

"Dad," I said with a shudder.

He came to the table, bent down, and pulled my head to his chest. Smoothing my hair, he said, "Tell me. Something happened out there that you haven't shared."

If only I could speak. But there was so much he didn't know. So much I'd kept from those who loved me. And why? What good was the wall I'd built when it didn't keep me safe?

So, I spilled it. Bits and pieces. Out of order. Marcus. Betz. Hana. The only thing I didn't drop at his feet was news of my pregnancy.

When I was done, my father still stood there stroking my hair. We'd never been close. But after my mother died, I knew I had to hold on to those who remained, and we'd been working on our relationship. Nothing like an untimely death to prove what's dear to you.

He tilted my chin, so I had no choice but to look at him. "You're in love."

I wiped my eyes with the back of my hand. "I suppose." It hit me then. I'd been holding Marcus back. Fighting my feelings. I'd thought it was because of how I felt about Betz. But it was more than that. It was my family who might not approve of Marcus. But his swagger was a front. Maybe a survival mechanism for how he grew up. He'd shown his true heart. He was a good man.

"I knew something was different about you."

"But…" I shook my head, got up, and paced. "I never told him how I felt. And now…he might be gone forever."

"Aren't they still searching?"

"It's been too long, don't you think? I can't do this." I circled the kitchen island, where a box of tissues sat. I grabbed a few and blew my nose. "I'm not comparing this to Mom. That would be crazy. He's only been in my life for a few months. But we had a chance at something."

"Allow yourself to feel what you feel," he said. "Sometimes the heart knows before our head does. Your mom's death was the worst thing that happened to any of us. But you're allowed to feel emotions…love…for others. All we ever wanted was for you and your sister to be happy."

I sucked back a fresh sob. Would I find happiness again? Running back into Betz's arms couldn't happen now. I knew that. This pregnancy would force me to turn the page. I'd been coming to that realization that although Betz would always be important to me, it wouldn't be like that. We'd had our shot. It was time to move on.

* * *

I knew the responsible thing to do was to get checked out. Get confirmation that I was, in fact, expecting. Maybe the last few days of roughing it in the wilderness had changed that. Initially, I wasn't thrilled about being pregnant. I didn't feel ready to take on motherhood, especially since Marcus and I were still figuring things out. But if that was all I had left of him, I'd move mountains to keep this baby. This piece of him.

I got dressed, combed my hair, and headed to the doctor's office, surprised they had a last-minute cancellation, and I could get an appointment.

Sitting on the examination table, I shivered in the paper gown that I awkwardly held closed while I waited for the doctor. I'd already submitted a blood sample, and my mind raced with each scenario. A positive test would be the best outcome. But that too would have its challenges. Either way, my life would be forever changed.

When Dr. Mitchell finally knocked on the door, I was a mess. Seemed to be the norm for me these days.

"Nice to see you, Casey. It's been a while."

I forced a smile.

"You're going to have to do better about coming to see me now."

I went rigid. "Is that your way of confirming a positive pregnancy test?"

She nodded. "Congratulations."

"Thanks." But I was too numb to unpack my feelings. Especially in front of her.

* * *

With some recommended reading, a list of what I should and shouldn't eat or drink, and a ranking of prenatal vitamins I could order off the Internet, I made a follow-up appointment four weeks out.

Back in my Jeep, I sent a text to Betz. *Any updates on the search for Hana?*

I waited a few minutes for a reply, but when he didn't respond, I started my Jeep and gave up the parking spot to someone waiting for it.

I didn't know what to do with myself. I was technically still on vacation. I could cancel that and go to the office. Throwing myself into work might be a good distraction. But I didn't feel like being around people or dealing with the problems of others. I had enough of my own.

I wanted to help in the search for Hana. Being out of the loop made me crazy. I remembered Hana and Rico passing the time at camp playing games. And then fake Izzy had tried to get close to both of them. Was she pressing Rico for information, too, thinking Hana might have shared something with him?

I didn't know how to find Rico, but maybe he told Hope where he lived when all they had was each other.

I took the next exit and got back on the freeway, heading in the other direction. Kate's house was only ten minutes away.

Chapter Fifty-Five

Kate's husband, Kevin, answered the door. I hadn't seen him in a while, and he greeted me with an awkward side hug. "Sorry for what you've been going through," he said.

Kevin was a good guy, but we never really connected. I appreciated his treating my sister and their kids well, but he had the personality of a napkin. I didn't understand Kate's attraction to him, but who knew what their life was like when I wasn't around. Maybe he came out of his shell. But in front of me, he kept his opinions to himself, and with the kids and the household, he let Kate run the show. Since she had an opinion about everything, I guessed they complemented each other. It seemed to work for them.

I needed a partner, not someone who would let me boss them around.

"Is Hope around?"

He made a grand gesture in pointing me down the hall. "The women are in the kitchen, which is why I'm watching TV in the den."

At the back of the house, I found Kate, Joy, and Hope standing around the center island. A bottle of wine was open, and Joy and Kate took sips as they food prepped. Chopping colorful vegetables, they tossed them into glass bins.

I reached around Joy for a carrot.

"Get yourself a glass," Kate said. "You know where they are."

I almost did before I remembered wine wasn't on my list of approved beverages. Neither was Diet Coke, but I'd yet to make peace with that.

"Um, I'm gonna stick to water."

They all stared at me as if I had just announced I was becoming a nun.

Maybe a break from alcohol would be a good thing. I didn't have a problem, but I rarely turned it down.

I got a glass, hit the filtered water from the fridge, and sat on a stool. "How are you two feeling?" I asked.

"I'm okay," Joy said. "Although my feet hurt. Those boys weren't messing around in their quest to find you. We must have walked a hundred miles." Then her face clouded over. "No word on Marcus?"

I looked down at my lap. "No."

Joy rushed around the counter and pulled me against her.

"Ah, Joy, please. I can't handle this right now."

She backed away and held up her hands in surrender. "Sorry, I forgot that you're not a hugger."

"Any word on Hana?" Hope asked.

I sighed. "No. If Betz knows anything, he hasn't shared it. I wanted to talk to you about Rico. I remember him and Hana playing games and talking. Did he tell you anything that might be useful in tracking her down?"

Hope held a red pepper against the cutting board, stopping mid-chop. "You know, he said something about Izzy pressing him for information."

Fake Izzy. But I didn't correct her. "Did he have anything to give up?"

"I don't know. We were talking about it just before we stumbled upon SAR. Then, all that was on our minds was going home."

"Do you know his number? Have a way to contact him?"

"He told me he lives in a trailer with a view of I-17 just off Indian School Road."

I knew the area. I had several clients who had lived there over the years. "Okay, thanks."

I finished my water and put my glass in the dishwasher.

"You're not going there, are you?" Kate asked. "That's not the best area."

"I am."

"Want me to come with you?" Hope asked.

"Not necessary. Enjoy your prep party." I grabbed a few carrots to go. On the list. Dr. Mitchell would be proud.

"Be careful," Kate called as I headed out the door.

* * *

After stopping home for the gun Betz had gifted me a few months ago so I could protect myself from Diablo, who frequented the area, I headed toward Phoenix. The trailer park was an epicenter of crime. People congregated in the parking lot among broken-down cars and stray shopping carts. Parking my Jeep as far away from a group of young men as I could, I avoided their hard stares. Little kids dressed in mismatched clothes ran around playing with a skinny dog that looked like a coyote, and had me wondering if it had been mistaken for a pet.

"The PO is here!" one kid shouted like Santa had arrived. "You have any stickers?"

When I did home visits, I typically had a stash of badge stickers I handed out. Kids in these communities could spot a PO from a mile away, even if we dressed like your average Joe. I probably had some stickers in the glove compartment, but I didn't want to take the time to return for them. "Sorry, not today," I said.

A syringe broke under my foot. The crunching sound sent a shiver up my spine. It was why I usually wore thick-soled work boots when visiting clients. But my guard was down. I made a conscious effort to watch my step. How these kids played in these conditions and didn't get hurt was beyond me.

I picked my way across the lot and walked up to a teenage girl sitting on the hood of a car. She focused her attention on the thick paperback in her hands.

"Hi," I said. "You know which trailer Rico lives in?"

The girl held up her finger like a stern librarian. I waited while she finished the passage she was reading, and then she slowly looked up at me. "It's about five units in. The one with the toilet in the yard."

Charming, but seeing how his family left Rico at the bus to Flagstaff, I wasn't surprised. "Thanks." The girl returned her attention to her book, and I left her to it, entering the trailer park.

Sure enough, there was a unit close to the entrance with a discarded toilet in the yard. Other appliances and junk I couldn't identify completed the landscaping. Unique, but nothing I hadn't seen before.

One sign on the door told me the trailer was protected by the Second Amendment, while another showed a scary pit bull snarling and wearing a studded collar. So welcoming. Thankful for the gun on my hip, I rapped on the door.

"It's open," a deep voice yelled.

Talk about conflicting messages. I tried the handle and pushed the door open a few inches. No way would I go inside. "I'm looking for Rico."

"Rico!" Another bellow, this one with a tinge of annoyance.

I heard things rustling and footsteps before Rico appeared at the door. His hair stood up in different directions, and he had sheet marks on his cheek. Basketball shorts and a threadbare, torn T-shirt sagged on his slight frame. He looked like dirty laundry just unpacked from a suitcase had come alive.

"What do you want?" He asked, scratching his head.

"Just wanted to talk to you for a few. Can you come outside?"

The kid shrugged and squeezed past me, settling on an overturned industrial paint container. The only other seat available was the toilet. I opted to stand.

"How are you doing?" I asked.

He gave a smirk. "I got blisters that aren't healing. Otherwise, I'm okay."

"Emotionally?"

Fingers drummed on his knees. He shrugged. "Fine."

He'd seen a woman die. But given where he lived, I wondered if it wasn't the first time. The needles in the parking lot suggested an overdose or two must have happened in the space.

"Hana is missing," I said. "Was wondering if she told you anything that might help us find her."

He squinted at me. I could almost see him flipping through the information in his brain. "What kind of things?"

"Did she tell you anything about a shed?"

"The one with the money?"

My heart raced. "That's the one."

He crossed his arms and rocked forward like he had a stomachache. "She said her dad hid something, and she'd be rich when she claimed it. He told her to wait until she was eighteen, so she didn't draw attention. Then she could go anywhere."

"Did she tell you where the shed is?"

He laughed. "Gotta be honest. If she had, the money wouldn't be there anymore. I'd be the one leaving this shithole. But she didn't share that detail. Not with me."

"Did you tell Izzy, or Crystal, which is her real name?"

He shrugged. "She asked a lot of questions, but I didn't tell her shit. Didn't trust her."

He stood and kicked a crushed soda can across the yard. "Hana talked about an aunt. Said she worked with her dad. Sounded like whatever her dad was up to, she might have been in on it."

* * *

Back in my Jeep, I watched the group of kids playing with a soccer ball that needed a shot of air. They didn't ask for much to brighten their dismal days. Reaching over to the glove compartment, I pulled out a stack of stickers. Unzipping the window, I called to the little girl who'd approached me earlier.

She happily skipped toward me. I handed her a few stickers. "Here, share these with your friends. And you shouldn't talk to strangers."

"But you're not a stranger, you're a PO," she said.

"How did you know that?"

She shrugged. "You look like one."

Good to know.

She looked down at the stickers in her hands and squealed in delight. "Thank you." And she ran back to her friends.

My good deed for the day. Hopefully, I could pull off one more and figure out where Hana was.

I drove a few blocks away and parked in a Circle K lot. Detective Moody must have spoken to Hana's extended family when she investigated the murders. There wouldn't have been a reason for her to share that information with me. But I had to know.

Betz still hadn't responded to my texts. Maybe he felt like he had to give me space to deal with the inevitable. But keeping me in the dark would land me in the fetal position with a bucket of Ben & Jerry's. I figured a phone call might seem more important, and he might answer.

I was right. After four rings, he came on the line. Groggily, he said, "What's up?"

"Didn't you see my texts?"

He cleared his throat. "Sorry. I crashed."

"About time you got some rest. Sorry I woke you. But I'm going crazy and feeling useless. Can I come over? Can we talk?"

He hesitated a few beats too long. I was going to tell him to forget it, but then he said, "Sure. But I'm not home. Airport Holiday Inn."

"Things that bad with Jasmine?"

"I'm not ready to forgive her."

"Isn't it your house?"

He laughed. "Squatter's rights. Anyway, I'm in room 202. Gonna grab a shower. How long will it take you to get here?"

"About twenty minutes."

"Perfect," he said.

Chapter Fifty-Six

Betz answered the door, drying his hair with a towel. Barefoot, he wore jeans and an open button-down shirt. His beard was past the stubble stage, and he looked exhausted. But he seemed happy to see me.

Especially when I held up a to-go cup of coffee.

"Bless you," he said. Taking a drink, he walked back toward the bathroom, rubbing the towel over his head.

I walked over to the window and opened the curtains, letting light flood the room.

I dropped into the desk chair and spun around so I faced him. "I'm sure I know the answer to this, but no word on Marcus?"

He shook his head and sat on the edge of the bed. "Wish there was."

"He could have gotten to shore," I tried. "He might be lost in the woods."

Betz looked at me like I'd just suggested Santa was real. "Anything's possible. Just don't want you to get your hopes up."

I nodded and looked to the floor. "Yeah, I know. Anyway, how much do you know about Hana's parents' murders?"

He took a sip of coffee and leaned forward, placing the cup on the dresser. Scooping his Mac off the surface, he laid it on his lap.

"It was Moody's case. Phillips has a record of dealing meth, so the logical thought was that he killed Marilynn and Jacob Stevens over a drug deal gone wrong. As the investigation's been unfolding, Moody's thinking that isn't true."

"What does she think the killing was about?"

Betz pecked at the keyboard with one finger. "Still coming up with a theory."

"Has she interviewed the family?" I told him what Rico said about an aunt.

"I'm sure she has, but let me look." Some more pounding on the keyboard and scratching his head. "She talked to a woman named Jill Stevens. Jacob's sister. But she didn't say anything of value."

"What did Hana's parents do for work?"

His attention returned to his computer. "Jacob was a manager at a restaurant. That Greek place on Thomas you used to like. Marilynn worked at a bank."

"A bank is a good place to embezzle money from."

"Yeah," he said. "I'm sure Moody looked into that. But given what you told me, she'll probably want to talk to Rico."

"Any info on the sister?"

"She works at the Greek restaurant, too." Betz laid his laptop aside and ran a hand across the back of his neck. His signal that I'd gone too far. "You should get some rest," he said. "You look tired."

"I don't think I could sleep." I'd spent the last night tossing and turning, which was worse than staying up.

"Well, you know better than to interfere with an investigation, so I don't have to tell you."

"Yet, you always do."

He laughed. "And you always ignore me and stick your nose where it doesn't belong." He got up and took a pair of socks from his gym bag. Sitting back on the bed, he pulled them on.

"What happened between you and Jasmine? I hope it had nothing to do with me."

"Of course not," he was quick to say. So quick, I knew he was lying.

Grabbing his shoes, he flashed me a smile, knowing I was calling bullshit, but not taking the bait. Even if he was mad at his sister, he wouldn't give me any more ammunition to further weaken my relationship with her.

Shoes on, Betz got to his feet. Taking his holstered weapon off the nightstand, he clipped it onto his belt. "I need to get to work. Figure out how to locate Phillips. They haven't recovered the stolen car yet, so he probably still has it. News outlets have heavily covered the story, so our best hope is that someone will spot the vehicle and report it."

I followed him to the door. "Will you keep me posted?"

"To a degree."

"Yeah, I know. But I feel responsible for letting him take her. It happened under my nose."

"You fell asleep. You expected someone to rescue you soon. Not your fault."

Yet I felt like it was. I'd been so relieved to have someone else take charge, I hadn't asked a lot of questions of the fake ranger. Looking back, I saw red flags. The first time I encountered him, he was headed in the other direction. It had made sense that the fire forced him to head back our way, but was the timing right? And I knew there was an escaped convict on the loose. But that was Phillips. I knew he had an accomplice, and it should have occurred to me that claiming to be a ranger would be a good cover for him. I'd never forgive myself if Hana didn't make it out alive. And I couldn't sit back and do nothing.

Chapter Fifty-Seven

While Betz headed out to look for Phillips, I concentrated on the only information I had. A shed was involved, but I had no idea where it was located. The Greek restaurant wasn't too far from Betz's hotel. I could nose around there.

Betz had warned me to stay out of things. But he and Moody were busy tracking down the car Phillips had stolen. They couldn't be everywhere. Plus, I'd never heeded his warning before. Why start now?

Within ten minutes, I was at the restaurant. Betz and I used to frequent it when we were married—it had the best moussaka in town—but I hadn't been there in a few years. From the outside, it looked the same. I parked in the lot with five other cars. There was no shed on the property that I could see.

It was just after eleven, and patrons were dribbling in for the lunch special. I still had my gun on my hip, but an oversized sweatshirt covered it. Arizona's gun laws were pretty much nonexistent, so I had no worries about breaking any.

Inside, white tablecloths covered tables for four, and I could see the kitchen through an open pass-through where servers picked up plates of food. The aroma of oregano made my stomach lurch. That was new. Usually, it just made me hungry.

A young girl stood at the hostess podium. "How many?" she asked, barely glancing at me.

"Not here for a table. Is Jill here?"

With her chin, she pointed to a woman jostling two tables together to accommodate a large group. I rushed over and helped her slip them into place. "Thanks," she said, eyeing me with suspicion.

"Are you Jill?"

She looked wary but nodded.

"I'm Casey. I wonder if I could have a word with you. It's about your niece."

"Hana?"

"Yeah."

Her hand covered her mouth. "Have they found her?"

"Not yet. But I'd like to talk to you about her."

Jill sighed. "Let's go out back. I need a smoke break, anyway."

I followed her out the door and around the corner, where a bench sat next to an overflowing ashtray. I wondered if that was a normal amount of smokes for her or if she'd been relying on nicotine to soothe her nerves since her niece went missing.

Sitting down, she lit a cigarette. I stood upwind.

"Another detective already came here. I told her everything I know."

Nice to know I didn't always look like a PO, but I must have given off a law enforcement vibe. I didn't correct her. "Just a few more questions."

"Go ahead. Anything to get Hana back safe and sound."

"Are you close?"

She took another puff. "Kind of."

Hana had complained about being in a group home. Jill hadn't stepped up to save her from foster care. "Yet, after her parents died, she didn't come to live with you."

My statement hung heavy in the air. Jill closed her eyes for a moment. I waited her out.

"I didn't think she'd be safe with me."

"Why not?"

She took another hit from her cigarette. "Because when my brother and sister-in-law were killed, I thought I'd be next."

"Why?"

She hung her head and shook it. "I was afraid their killers would think I knew more than I did."

"Yet, you're not in hiding. You're going about your normal routine."

"When it first happened, I stayed in motels, didn't come to work. But when Martin Phillips got arrested, I eased up on the paranoia."

"But you still didn't take Hana in."

She sighed. "I was going to. But then she got in trouble for stealing pills again. I didn't need that in my life. I work long hours and wouldn't be able to keep an eye on her like she needed. I figured foster care was the safest place for her."

"But then Phillips escaped."

"Yeah, but they sent her to a wilderness camp in the mountains. I figured she'd be safe there, and once Phillips was captured, I'd take her."

I crossed my arms. "Did your brother come into a lot of money recently?"

She smirked and shook her head. "That's when I knew he was up to no good. A few years ago, he borrowed money from me to start a business."

"How much?"

"Twenty grand. I never expected to see the money again; he always had some scheme to get rich that failed. I was shocked when he actually paid me back."

"All of it?"

She nodded. "He said his new business was doing well."

"What kind of business?"

"He owns a gym."

"So, he managed this restaurant and ran a gym?"

Her cigarette had fizzled down to her fingertips, and I feared she'd burn herself. The heat seemed to get her attention, and she dropped the butt into the tray at her side. "Since my brother's death, I've taken over the books for the restaurant. The place hadn't been doing so great. Which is odd, since we've been super busy. I looked closer. There are employees on the payroll who don't actually work here."

"So, Jacob was collecting their wages?"

"If I had to hazard a guess."

Hana had said that there was a lot of money they were going to use to start a new life. Phillips must have found out about it. "Anyone else your brother would have owed money to? Could he have owed some to his killer?"

She cleared her throat and stood. Checking her watch, she said. "Lunch crowd is starting. I need to get back inside. But yeah, it's possible. His wife had a gambling problem."

I followed her to the door. "One more question. Which gym did your brother own?"

"You know," she said. "He never gave me the details."

"Did you share the thing about the fake employees with Detective Moody?"

"Not yet. I can give you the books."

I might have pushed this too far. "It's Moody's case," I said. "You need to call her."

I left, ignoring the bewildered look on Jill's face.

Chapter Fifty-Eight

Betz

Moody turned to look at Betz from the passenger seat of the Interceptor as they rode toward South Phoenix, where a lead had been called into the tip line. "You still have it bad for Casey, don't you?"

Betz grumbled under his breath, thankful that his phone rang, and he had a reason not to validate the obvious. "Betz," he grunted into the phone.

"Savage," came the now familiar gravelly voice, followed by a phlegmy cough. "We recovered a body."

Shit. Not the call he wanted. A rush of emotion overwhelmed him. It was his fault. Marcus died, pushing him to safety. How would he break the news to Casey? He fought to catch his breath before he spoke. "Go on."

"SAR found it. Must have taken quite a fall. Impaled on some jagged rocks."

"Wait...what? He didn't drown?"

Savage cleared her throat. "He? No, it was a woman. The camp counselor, or the woman posing as one. At least as far as we can tell. We found her backpack nearby."

Betz let out a long breath of relief. Inevitably, he'd have to break the news to Casey that Marcus was gone at some point. Even if they never recovered his body, eventually they'd presume he was dead. But for now, at least, he had a reprieve.

"Did you gather any intel that might help us find Phillips?"

"We found a cell phone. Forensics is trying to access what's on it. Might take a while."

"Well," he said. "Let me know."

* * *

They pulled into the parking lot at the base of South Mountain. Several trails were accessible from there, and the locals used it as a playground for hiking, horseback riding, and mountain biking. Betz had fond memories of the place from his early morning hikes with Casey when they were married. But he'd been too busy, or perhaps evading places that reminded him of her, to make the trek in years.

"That's our caller," Moody said, motioning to a horse trailer.

Betz called in their location, and they exited the Interceptor and walked over to a woman with leathery-lined skin and flowing red hair. She wore Wrangler jeans and pointy-toed boots. All that was missing was a cowboy hat.

"You said you had information?" Moody said in greeting.

"Is there a reward?"

Moody and Betz exchanged a look. Everyone wanted something. If they were called out on a wild goose chase, he'd find something to charge this so-called good Samaritan with. His decent mood had evaporated before he'd gone to Flagstaff.

"If it leads to the apprehension of Martin Phillips," Moody said. "There is a reward. What have you got?"

She pointed toward the mountain. "On the other side of my trailer. Think it's the car you're looking for."

Betz and Moody headed around the trailer, noticing a horse's tail swishing through the back window.

On the other side a car was parked. Betz walked around it and peeked inside. Empty except for some photography equipment in the back seat.

"Matches the description," Moody said. "Same plate, too."

But its occupants were long gone.

Betz reached for the trunk release and pulled the lever.

"Oh, shit," Moody said as the hatch bounced open.

He hurried toward the back of the car. Inside, knees to chest, was a teenage boy. Betz reached down and held a finger to the boy's neck. "Got a pulse." But he was unconscious, and his skin was clammy.

Moody got on the radio and requested paramedics and an ambulance, while Betz lifted the kid out of the car and laid him on the ground.

"Who the fuck is this?" he asked, as Moody shook her head.

Chapter Fifty-Nine

A gambling problem, debt, a shed, the number fifty-six, and embezzling money from his employer. Those were the pieces I had to work with. Too bad they didn't seem to fit together and gave me no inkling of where Hana might be. Or if she was still alive and unharmed.

There were probably thousands of gyms in the valley, thousands of sheds. And I didn't have the brainpower for white-collar crimes, which is why I always avoided that caseload. Where would I even start?

I couldn't come up with my next move. But I felt restless, useless, and guilty. Betz would have a cow if he knew I'd poked around in his case. But it wouldn't surprise him. It wasn't the first time. I doubted it would be the last.

Not knowing where to turn, I went back to the only place I'd find some sense of normalcy. I headed to Kate's.

Joy's car was still in the driveway. I parked behind it. Kevin had left the den and was out front mowing the lawn. He paused long enough to give me a wave and then got back to business.

Finding the front door unlocked, I let myself inside.

The kitchen was empty. I followed the sound of voices to the patio out back. My niece and nephew played in a sandbox while Hope and Kate watched them from wicker chairs in the shade.

"You're back," Kate said. "Find anything useful?"

I settled into an empty chair and focused on the kids. "All signs point to money, not drugs. Seems like Jacob Stevens created fake employees at his job and embezzled the funds."

"They're called ghost employees," Hope said. "When I had the white-collar caseload, I supervised a few people who did that. They log shifts for workers who don't exist and pocket the money that person would have earned. Happens a lot in large companies and, surprisingly, in church offices."

"That's so wrong," Kate said.

"I've seen them rack up hundreds of thousands of dollars," Hope added. "One client stole millions before they caught her."

"Gambling problem?" I asked.

"A variety of issues. Gambling, addiction, living above their means. I had one woman who did it to support a shopping habit for expensive shoes and purses. Most of them meant to get out of some dire financial situation and planned to stop. But they get greedy. It's easy money. Things snowball."

"Did you share this hunch with Betz?" Kate asked.

"I'm pretty sure the police already know. The woman I spoke with said she had talked to them. I encouraged her to share the books with them. I just want to do my part."

Kate shook her head and sighed. "You don't have a part. Stay out of it."

"Why did I come here?"

"Because you actually like it when I shove your face in the truth," Kate said, giving me a bug-eyed stare.

Hope laughed. "Gotta admit, you're a glutton for punishment."

She had me there.

Joy strutted out of the house and took the last chair. She wore leggings and a tank top despite the cool temperatures. In her hand, she held running shoes. "I need you to move your Jeep, Casey. I'm trying to get back to real life, and that means a trip to the gym. My excursion in the woods resulted in two pounds of weight loss, and I want to keep the needle moving in the right direction."

"You have shown a lot of dedication since the new gym opened," Hope said. "Wish I had that kind of drive."

I sat up a little straighter. New gym? "What gym?"

"It's called the Shred Shed," Joy said. "It's intimate, and lots of cute guys go there. Today I'm going to lift some weights and get on the tread."

Shed? A shot of energy rushed through my veins. "Ah, hold on. I'm coming with you."

"Really?" Joy said. "You're gonna work out with me? You never do anything with me."

"It will be fun," I said, getting to my feet.

"Do you have gym clothes to change into?"

I looked down at my jeans and sweatshirt. "No."

"Don't worry," she said. "You can borrow some of mine."

* * *

The Shred Shed was within walking distance, but Joy insisted on driving. She didn't want to mess up her hair on the way over. Fine by me. This way, less people would see me in the tight yoga pants and bright pink crop top she'd loaned me. Thank God I could cover up with my sweatshirt.

"A workout will take your mind off things," she said. "I'm so excited to share my passion with you."

I was hardly listening. Instead, I fingered the key Hana had given me. I didn't have the heart to tell Joy I had no intention of working out.

She pulled into a strip mall parking lot, angling her car into a spot near the door. The gym only took up a quarter of the building and was next to a dry cleaner and a convenience store.

Inside, Joy sashayed her spandex-clad butt up to the front desk. "Hi, Lexie. This is my cousin, Casey. I'm allowed a guest pass, right?"

Lexie nodded, reaching for a clipboard. "Fill this out and sign the waiver. Then I'll give you a tour of the facility."

I pocketed the key Hana had given me and took the pen Lexie held out for me. Scribbling down my information, I filled out the top form and then, without reading it, signed the waiver of liability, flashing back to the one the wilderness adventure folks had me sign. Would I ever learn? But the only cougars I'd find here were women like Joy.

"Go ahead and get started," I said to Joy. "I'll catch up to you when the tour is over."

"Okey dokey." And she strutted into the weight room.

"Follow me," Lexie said, putting a sign on the desk that said she'd be back in ten minutes.

"I don't remember seeing this place," I said.

"Only been open for about a year."

"Who owns it?" I matched her quick steps past treadmills, stationary bikes, and elliptical machines.

"We have two owners," she said. Then she added in a whisper, "But someone murdered one recently. The other operates things from a distance. He's never here."

She pushed the door to the woman's room open, and I followed her inside. Lockers lined the wall. In another room, there were showers and a row of stalls for toilets. Nothing fancy. I scanned the lockers, which all had numbers on them. They ended at the number fifty.

"Ah, my boyfriend might be interested in joining," I said. "Is the men's locker room the same?"

"Except for the urinals," she said with a chuckle.

"Are the lockers numbered like this? He's superstitious and likes to have a certain number."

"They start at fifty-one," she said. "Go to one hundred. We assign them when you join. He'll have to take what's available."

"I understand." I tried to keep the excitement out of my voice.

"Anyway," she said. "You saw the cardio room. Let me show you the yoga studio, and we can finish up in the weight room where you can join your cousin for a complimentary workout."

"Sounds good." But as I followed her around the gym, I hardly listened to her spiel. I nodded a lot and tried to seem interested. Lexie was on autopilot, and it was obvious her pitch was well-rehearsed. She wasn't expecting feedback. All I could think about was how I was going to pull off entering the men's locker room without getting caught.

"Here you go." She led me back to Joy, who was doing deadlifts. My cousin's concentration on the buff man across the room was messing with her form.

As soon as Lexie left us alone, I said. "I'll be right back. I need to pee."

Which was true, but I had no time for that. I strode past the women's locker room until I was just outside the men's. Flashing a glance behind me to make sure it was clear, I pulled up my hood, tucking my hair inside.

Afraid I looked more like the Unabomber than a gym goer, I entered the room. It had that locker room smell, a mixture of sweat and commercial cleaning products. I tried not to gag as a wave of nausea overtook me. Pregnancy was a bitch. As I rounded the corner, a trio of naked guys, deep in conversation, stopped me cold.

I tried to avert my gaze, but I'd already seen enough to need therapy. I turned my attention to the lockers, noticing that number fifty-six was directly behind the hairiest of the group. No way was I asking him to step aside.

I walked past them, hoping to hide in a bathroom stall until they left, but there was only a row of urinals and one stall, which was occupied.

Glancing over my shoulder, I confirmed no one was paying attention to me. Easing the door to a supply closet open, I stepped inside and left the door open a crack. I wanted to track their conversation, so I knew when it was safe to go back into the room.

Now what?

Gripping the key in my hand, I strained to hear. It was hot in the confined space, and I stood nose to nose with a smelly mop. Bile climbed up my throat, and I willed it away. The last thing I wanted was to be found puking in a closet in the men's locker room. It would be hard to explain that away.

The toilet flushed, followed by a door closing. One down. Three to go.

It was hot, and I was worried I'd pass out. Joy had to be wondering what was taking me so long. If she went looking for me in the ladies' room, she wouldn't find me, and that could start all kinds of shenanigans.

Just when I thought I couldn't last another minute, I heard retreating voices and then a door slamming shut.

I chanced a look through the crack in the door. All clear.

CHAPTER FIFTY-NINE

I crept out and headed straight for locker number fifty-six.

My hands were slick with sweat, and I dropped the key on the floor in my first attempt to fit it in the lock. I fumbled for it, stood up, and slid it into the slot. It fit. With a turn of the key, the lock popped open.

I pulled the latch and opened the locker door. Inside was a single envelope. Nothing more. I grabbed it, tucked it into the waistband of my yoga pants, and secured the lock.

Heading for the door, I was almost in the clear when I came face to face with the buff guy Joy had been drooling over in the weight room.

"Ah, this is the men's locker room," he said, pointing to the sign.

"Oops," I offered. And took a beeline down the hall.

###

I found Joy doing bicep curls in front of a mirror, checking her hair more than her form. Seeing me, she racked the weights and, with hands on hips, looked me up and down. "Where have you been?"

I cringed.

"You're all sweaty. And pale. Are you okay?"

Good cover idea. "Actually, I'm not feeling well. Do you mind if we leave?"

"But we just got here. I have to finish my circuit."

"Yeah, but I think I'm coming down with something."

"Oh, sweetie." She touched my arm. "It's probably just sadness. You know, because of Marcus."

Gut punch. I'd stopped thinking about that for the last twenty minutes. Now it was back in my head.

"I can see you're not up to this," she said.

I motioned toward the exit. "Don't worry. I can walk back to Kate's. Finish your workout."

"You sure?"

"Yeah." And I headed for the door. If I didn't get some fresh air soon, I'd need that mop in the closet.

* * *

Outside, I wrestled my way out of my sweatshirt. Because I was so sweaty, the fabric clung to my skin. Once off, I tied it around my waist. My skin was clammy, and for a moment, I feared I *was* getting sick. But Joy was probably right. It was sadness mixed with the fear I'd had of getting caught in the men's room. But as I walked, the cool air revived me.

Key in my pocket, I felt for the envelope in my waistband, making sure it was still there. That it was real. I wouldn't open it until I was alone in a safe place.

The envelope wasn't thick enough to hold money. It was hard in spots, difficult to bend. A card?

But what did it have to do with Hana? Was it worthy of her parents' murder? Of Phillips killing them and living a life on the run?

I picked up my pace to find out.

Chapter Sixty

At Kate's, I slipped inside unnoticed. Grabbing my bag off the side table, I hoped to get out of the house without running into anyone. But in the hallway, I bumped into Hope.

"You're back," she said.

"Not feeling well. Headed home," I said, reinforcing my lie.

She put her hand on my arm. "I've been meaning to ask you…"

I gave her a blank stare.

"The pregnancy," she whispered. "I haven't shared your news with anyone. I figured that was your job, but how are you doing?"

I'd forgotten that I'd told her. "I confirmed it with the doctor. So far, so good."

"Have you told the father?"

A knife to my heart. "Ah, no. Not yet."

"Well, take care of yourself and let me know if there's anything I can do."

Like, bringing me back to reality? Which was the last place I wanted to be. Sticking my nose into Betz's investigation allowed me to pretend things were normal. But no matter how hard I tried to fake it, there was a heaviness in my heart that wouldn't budge.

But Hope had no way of knowing what I was going through. She didn't know about Marcus. She knew he was missing, sure. But she didn't know what he meant to me. Or that he was my baby's father, and I might never be able to tell him.

A rush of emotion flooded through me. I reached out and pulled Hope into a hug. She seemed as shocked by my outpouring of affection as I was, but she recovered quickly and squeezed me back.

When I pulled away, I said, "Thanks for keeping this between us for now. I'm not ready to share this with the rest of the family."

"They'll support you."

"I know. But I need to deal with finding Hana first. Then I'll tell them. Promise."

"Take whatever time you need. And I'm here whenever you want to talk. If the last few months have shown me anything, it's the importance of having a support system. I'm glad you're part of mine, and I want to be there for you, too."

"I appreciate that," I said. "I'll see you later, okay?"

She nodded, pulled me into another hug, and then walked me to my Jeep. Her pep talk left me with a warm feeling as I started toward home.

* * *

Luckily, my father and Millie weren't there when I arrived. I needed some alone time so I could decide what to do about the envelope I'd taken from the locker at the Shred Shed. I let myself in through the garage and rescued Felony from his crate. By now it was past his dinner time, and he let me know it by going to the pantry and barking at the door. He was more reliable at keeping time than my watch. At least at mealtime. I fed him before getting myself a glass of water.

Sliding the envelope out of my waistband, I laid it on the counter in front of me.

It flashed through my mind that I should share my find, whatever it was, with the police. That I should have alerted them to the existence of the Shred Shed before I pretended to be a man and stole something from the locker room. Backing it up even more, I should have told them about my conversation with Jill. I pictured Betz rolling his finger, indicating I should go back yet another step. I probably shouldn't have even gone to the restaurant.

Betz would have said I should have realized my first step was a mistake and to redirect. To make the next right choice. Wasn't that what I told my clients?

I brought out my phone and called him. He and Moody should be involved. But the call went straight to voicemail. "Call me," I said.

I stared at the envelope on the counter. Found a letter opener in the kitchen junk drawer and held it at the seam. I willed my phone to ring, but it was silent.

I blew into the envelope; it bowed open. Inside was a card. I tapped it against the counter, and a debit card fell out.

Attached to it was a sticky note with a four-digit number.

Pay dirt.

These days, people don't cart around and hide a bag full of money. They had their fake earnings deposited into a bank account. It probably didn't go straight into the account. There might have been some money laundering. Probably what the gym was for. But when ready, someone could claim it. The name on the card was Hana Stevens.

Had they always meant for it to be hers?

I sent Betz a text. *Found something. Call me!*

When he didn't respond right away, I made my way to my room. Changing back into jeans and another sweatshirt, I lured Felony back into his crate. "Sorry, buddy. I won't be long."

I drove to the bank and parked in the far corner of the lot, out of sight of the camera on the ATM. With my head down, I walked to the cash machine, something my family called the "ugly teller."

I checked my phone for messages. One last chance for Betz to convince me to turn matters over to him. He hadn't gotten back to me—and I was running out of patience. Hana was running out of time.

My hood was up, my sunglasses on. I wouldn't be identifiable on the security camera.

I slipped the debit card into the slot and typed in the code from the sticky note attached to the card.

A gust of wind swept the paper away, but it didn't matter. I was in.

My finger hovered over the check balance button.

In seconds, the amount of money popped up, and my eyes widened. One-hundred dollars? All this for one-hundred dollars? That just didn't make sense.

I selected the mini statement option and out popped a receipt of the most recent transactions. The last withdrawal, just days before the murders, showed a balance higher than any I'd seen. I pretty much lived paycheck to paycheck and never had more than a few thousand dollars in my account, and that was on payday. My automatic payments usually depleted most of my balance by the end of the day.

But this account had just over 250K in it. A nice start for a young adult. But the money was gone. It wouldn't become Hana's. But did Phillips know that?

I pressed the cancel button, pocketed the card, and hurried back to my Jeep.

Chapter Sixty-One

Betz

The paramedics got to work on the young guy Betz had removed from the trunk. Before they'd arrived, Betz had patted the kid's pockets, hoping to find a driver's license. Some way to identify him. But he found only a Baggie of marijuana and a pipe.

While the ambulance loaded the still unconscious teen inside, Betz walked in circles, deep in thought. Phillips had abandoned the car he'd stolen in Flagstaff. He'd need another means of transportation. Betz would bet his pension that it was where the kid fit in. Phillips took the boy's vehicle and stuffed him in the trunk so he couldn't report the theft, giving Phillips time to get away. Hours could have passed, maybe even a day. Even in the cooler weather, a few hours in a trunk could be a death sentence in Arizona.

The boy wasn't wearing hiking clothes. He probably came to the area so he could smoke some weed in peace. Or maybe score some. They had to identify the kid and figure out what he drove.

Betz snapped a photo of the teen before the ambulance took him away. Then he called the information officer for the department and asked him to get the word out so they could learn his identity. But that would take time. And they were running out of that.

Once the paramedics had left, Betz and Moody got back into the Interceptor. His adrenaline dump had dissolved, and exhaustion wrapped around him like a clingy toddler. "I need coffee," he said.

Moody took the wheel. "Circle K it is."

Betz laid his head against the seat and rubbed tired eyes. What had they missed? What did Hana know or have that Phillips wanted so badly?

At least Casey was safe. Her involvement in this whole mess seemed to boil down to being at the wrong place at the wrong time. He knew she was like a pit bull with a burglar's arm in her mouth. She never let anything go until it was resolved. She felt responsible for the girl. He hoped she was home relaxing, but knowing her, she'd find a way to be part of his investigation.

He was about to text her to see if she was behaving when his cell buzzed in his hand. Savage.

"We got into the phone," she said in greeting.

"And?"

"Phillips' girlfriend was keeping notes. Some of them were about your wife. Thought you'd want to know."

His wife? For a moment, he'd forgotten that Savage had assumed he and Casey were still married. He'd said nothing to challenge that assumption. "What did they say?"

"I'll send you copies, but basically, she suspected that the girl, Hana Stevens, had gotten close to Casey. That she was telling her things. She wanted to let him know Hana wasn't the only one who could lead them to whatever they wanted so badly. She believed Casey also had the information."

The key? Casey had mentioned that Hana had passed her a key before Phillips took her. He should have taken it and logged it as evidence. But with everything going on, he'd forgotten about it.

"There's more," Savage said. "We think we've identified the third member. The one who killed the ranger took his clothes and pretended to be him. The one who kidnapped Hana Stevens."

"I'm listening."

"His name is Donald Jackson. He's got a long record of violent crimes. He makes Phillips look like a Boy Scout."

"Does Jackson know Casey might have the information he's looking for?"

"I don't think he did. Otherwise, he probably wouldn't have left her for dead in the fire tower. He would have thought he could use her."

But Phillips probably told him by now. If they hadn't gotten what they wanted out of Hana, they'd go after Casey. He ended the call and glanced at Moody. "Forget the coffee. Head to Tempe."

Chapter Sixty-Two

Sliding into my Jeep, I sent another message to Betz. *Meet me at my dad's. Have important information.*

I dropped my phone onto the passenger seat, but it bounced and fell between the seat and center console. Shit.

I heard it buzz in reply. Reaching down for it, a cramp in my lower abdomen made me flinch. My first thought? Great time to get my period. Then I remembered I wouldn't get that for a long time. Oh, please, no. I could not lose this baby. I couldn't believe how badly I wanted this. It was the "why" that hit me like a semi-truck. Because I'd lost Marcus. It had been way too long since the floodwaters had taken him. I hadn't checked for information on the search recently. I didn't have to. No news was bad news.

I couldn't even picture him in my mind anymore. I had no photos of him. It was as if he had never existed at all.

But a piece of him did. He was part of the child I carried. I couldn't lose them both. I glanced at the paperwork from the doctor I'd left on the front seat. Diagnosis: Gestation. Medical talk for pregnancy. My stomach cramped again. Was that still the case?

Grabbing the papers, I shoved them into my bag. I'd read them over carefully when I had a moment to catch my breath. That moment wasn't now.

From beneath my seat, the phone buzzed again. Betz calling me back. I couldn't wait to share what I'd found. Even if he'd be mad at me for investigating on my own, he'd know what to do with the information.

If the money had still been in the account, I'd have what Phillips and his friend wanted, and we could make a trade for Hana. He wouldn't have gone through everything… tracking us in the woods, murders, kidnapping…if he didn't think the money was still there and Hana had access to it.

Pulling into my father's driveway, I put the Jeep in park. I had to get on my knees to fish my phone out from under the seat. Sure enough, three missed calls from Betz. Then a text. *On my way.*

Thank God. I dropped my phone into my bag and let myself inside the house, expecting Felony to meet me at the door. It was dusk. My dad and Millie were usually home by now. But no lights were on. No patter of paws on the tile floor. No clanking of dishes in the kitchen as Millie made dinner. No one was home.

Was Felony still in his kennel? But he would have barked when he heard me open the door. Had my dad and Millie taken Felony to the park?

Dumping my bag and car keys on the table by the door, I fumbled for the light switch, then flipped it on. My heart nearly exploded when the light illuminated Phillips sitting in my dad's recliner and the fake ranger standing behind him.

"Welcome home," Phillips said, casually aiming a handgun at my chest. "Shut the door and come inside, Officer Carson."

I glanced around the room, terrified I'd find my dad, Millie, and Felony tied up or worse. But my dad's car wasn't in the driveway. They weren't here.

I followed Phillips' directions, closing the door and standing against it. "Where's Hana?"

"I'll ask the questions," the fake ranger said. "Unholster your weapon, lay it on the ground, and kick it toward me."

Having a gun had never helped me. Not once. I did what he said, knowing he could shoot me before I'd have the chance to draw and fire at him. Cursing myself once again for not getting more comfortable with the thing, I followed his demands.

"Where's Hana?" I said again.

"Where's the money?" Phillips shot back.

"I'll tell you. After you let her go."

He laughed. "You really think you're in charge?"

I shrugged one shoulder, trying to act cool, coy. But my heart thudded so hard my shirt had to be moving. "I can get you the money. But I need to see Hana first."

"Fine." Fake ranger stepped over my gun on the floor. "We'll take you to her. But if you try anything, you're both dead."

I guessed Phillips wasn't looking for a debit card because he didn't make me empty my pockets. When my cell chimed in my bag, he grabbed my shoulder and squeezed it. "Give me the phone."

I took it out and passed it to him, holding it long enough to see it was another call from Betz. He'd arrive any minute.

But I wouldn't be here. And Betz didn't know that we couldn't give them what they wanted. There was nothing left to give. How long did I have until Phillips and the fake ranger figured that out?

Chapter Sixty-Three

Betz and Moody arrived at the house, finding Casey's Jeep parked in the driveway. "You should come in," Betz said. "Casey's hardheaded, and it might take me a while to convince her to go somewhere safe."

Moody snorted as she climbed out of the vehicle. "Good thing you're so easy to get along with."

"Touche." When had he become such a grump? Maybe they deserved each other. Between his beef with Jasmine and Casey trampling all over his heart, his mood had taken a nosedive. He needed a vacation. Take a page from the Casey playbook and indulge in a little self-reflection. Then again, that hadn't worked out so well for her.

The front door was ajar. As soon as he noticed it, tension tightened his body. No way Casey would leave it open and risk Felony getting loose. His hand automatically went to his service weapon. With his other hand, he tapped his palm against the door. "Anybody home?"

Silence.

Shit. They were too late.

Betz and Moody exchanged a knowing look, and both drew their weapons, holding them at the ready. Pushing the door open, they eased inside. Betz headed in one direction while Moody went in the other. They went from room to room until they were sure no one was in the house.

When they reconvened in the living room, Betz holstered his weapon as he spotted a handgun on the floor. Leaning down, he gave the firearm a closer look without touching it. "Looks exactly like the one I gave Casey."

Moody took in the room. "No sign of a struggle."

"Something happened to her." He pulled gloves on and slipped the gun into an evidence bag he'd had in his pocket.

"Looks that way," Moody said. She motioned to the table by the door. "That her bag?"

Betz made his way to the table. "Her car keys are here." He opened her purse and checked inside. Pulling out some paperwork, he peered into the bag at the contents underneath. "Her wallet's here, too." Glancing at the papers in his hand, he noted today's date. Might be important if they needed to retrace her steps.

He scanned the first page. Cigna Healthcare. Casey had been to the doctor. Something she rarely did. Even that time she'd broken her arm, he'd had to force her into the car and drive her to urgent care. She'd complained about getting medical help the whole way, claiming she'd just pulled a muscle. But maybe she wasn't feeling well after her time in the woods.

Her name and date of birth were at the top of the form. Beneath it, a diagnosis. Gestation six-eight weeks.

It took him a minute to figure that one out. When it dawned on him, everything stopped. He forgot to breathe. No wonder she didn't want to get back together. She was pregnant with another man's baby.

The room spun, and for a moment, he held onto the wall. Emotions he didn't know he had crashed down on him like quickly melting snow off a roof. It was one reason they'd ended things. He'd wanted to start a family, and she wasn't ready. That was three years ago, but still.

Marcus had to be the father. And now he was gone. No wonder she was so crushed. She had to be going through hell, yet she hadn't shared it with him.

He didn't know how long he stood there, reliving the past and agonizing over his future, which had just rounded the bend and dropped him off a cliff. But he was suddenly aware of Moody laying her hand on his shoulder. "What is it? Are you okay?"

He shook his head and released the death grip he had on the paperwork, now creased where he'd held it. "Nothing," he said. "But we have to find her. If Phillips got to her…Jackson…"

"I know. I just got a message," Moody said. "The hospital called."

He hadn't even noticed her take the call.

"They identified our boy in the trunk. Name is Lenny Albright. His parents say he drives a green Ford Bronco. The vehicle should have been with him. Since it wasn't, guessing Phillips switched cars. Jasmine had already alerted the media about the car. After that, the tip line received a call. A security cam at a gas station off Interstate 10 in Surprise recorded a video. The manager saw the story about the APB and said he was suspicious when a man matching Phillip's description stopped to fill up. Guess what he was driving?"

"A Bronco."

"And a blond-haired woman sat slumped in the passenger seat."

The blood drained from Betz's head. "How long ago?"

"About ten minutes."

Betz held out his hand. "Keys, please. I'm driving."

Moody pulled the door shut behind her and followed Betz to the Interceptor. Making their way to the Sixty, they headed west.

Chapter Sixty-Four

I fought to open my eyes, struggling to figure out where I was. The side of my head pounded. Pain tensed my stomach. A seat cradled my body, and my head rested against something hard. My face slid down the smooth surface. A window. I was in a car.

I tried to make sense of things as I opened one eye while reaching up to rub my head. Squinting, I looked out the windshield. Traffic whizzed by as we passed a sign. The exit to Buckeye was a mile ahead. That was at least a half-an-hour drive. I'd been out for a while.

Turning, I took in the driver's profile. His name wouldn't come to me, but I knew he was on my caseload. And then I remembered. Martin Phillips. He'd been at my father's house, and he and his buddy had forced me at gunpoint to leave with them. When I refused to get into the vehicle parked on the street, the fake ranger slammed my head against the door.

There was a hole in my memory after that.

Phillips veered to the right, taking the exit onto Route 85. I tried to figure out where he was taking me. Buckeye was on the west side of Maricopa County, past Tolleson and Goodyear. I wasn't all that familiar with this side of the valley. To me, the outlier city was a place to stop for gas on the way to California. But with the valley growing at a breakneck rate, it had become a popular place to live. It was no longer known mostly for its cotton and alfalfa fields. Although as we got closer to town, I could see they were still there.

"Where are we going?" I asked.

Phillips glanced my way with an arrogant smirk on his face. "You'll see soon enough."

"Will Hana be there?"

"You ask too many questions," a voice said from the backseat. "I should have hit you harder on the head."

A glance in the side mirror showed me Fake Ranger sitting in the back seat.

They thought I had information, and as long as they believed that, they'd keep me alive. If they searched me, dug in my pockets, they'd have the bank card with the transaction printout I'd folded around it. They'd know I had nothing to offer, and I wouldn't be useful anymore.

Neither would Hana. I tried to concentrate on her and figure out a way to turn things around. How I might get both of us out of this unharmed. I usually made things up as I went along. But so far, that had mostly led me to the brink of disaster. I couldn't imagine this time would be any different. Except that my luck might run out.

If I survived this, I'd have to give some serious thought to getting my shit together. Like I hadn't promised myself that a million times before. Guess I needed to work on procrastination, too.

But it wasn't just my life on the line. I owed it to Hana to keep her safe. I couldn't dwell on the child I carried. That would paralyze me.

When we slowed for a light, I thought about opening the door and jumping out. Taking my chances. But then I wouldn't find Hana. A fall like that could end my pregnancy. If the cramps in my gut weren't a sign that it had already happened. Even if I didn't have those considerations, my reflexes were off as I tried to get my head right. At the very least, I had a goose egg and a whopper of a headache.

After passing strip malls, we entered an older part of town. A quick right turn brought us onto a residential street with big properties that were encircled with low stucco walls. Several houses down, Phillips pulled into a driveway and drove through a grove of orange trees before coming to a house that was hidden from the road.

It was deep brown stucco in need of a renovation. But it was private. No one would hear my screams.

Phillips got out of the car, along with the fake ranger. I pressed the lock button before they could open the door. Phillips only shook his head and used the key to open it.

It wasn't taking much to outsmart me. I wondered if I had a concussion.

"You're quite a pain in the ass," Phillips said. Grabbing me by the arm, he squeezed hard until I yelped, and then he yanked me out of the vehicle. Loose gravel crunched under my Converse as he pushed me toward the front door.

Inside the house, two rooms came into view. What looked like a living room to my right and a dining area to the left. Both were devoid of furniture or belongings. No one lived here.

An arched doorway led to a hallway. Phillips placed his hand between my shoulders and gave me a shove. "When I came to see you in your office, you always made me walk first. Like you don't trust me. How does it feel?"

I moved forward, passing a dinghy bathroom with a broken mirror hanging over a grimy sink.

"Keep moving," he barked.

The kitchen was at the back of the house. Dark cabinets had missing doors, and a drawer front dangled, about to fall. The Formica countertops had chips, and empty spaces showed where appliances had once stood. At the back, the sliding glass door was so caked with dirt, I couldn't see through it.

Taking hold of my arm, Fake Ranger clicked the latch on the door and slid it open. With another shove, I stumbled outside and into the backyard.

Sparse desert landscaping stretched as far as I could see in the grainy light of night. Off to the side were a firepit and camp chairs. Dormant.

Where was he taking me?

We walked to the middle of the yard. Still holding my arm, he swept at the ground with his boot, brushing away leaves and dirt. Fake Ranger kicked a flattened handle until it popped upright. Grabbing the lever, he pulled the trapdoor up, exposing a gaping hole in the ground. A tornado shelter? That kind of weather wasn't common in Arizona. A bunker?

A dim light flickered deep in the hole. A ladder leaned against a wall made of concrete.

"Climb down," Phillips commanded.

"No fucking way."

"If I push you, you might survive the fall, but your back and legs will probably break. You could even end up paralyzed." Fake Ranger laughed.

And I'd lose the baby. Worsening cramps told me that probably had already happened.

But going down there was a death sentence. Remembering that I'd gotten out of tough situations before, I struggled against Phillips. I kicked and swung my fists at him. Before I could duck out of reach, Fake Ranger grabbed me by the back of my neck and forced me to look into the cavernous space. Instinctively, I reached up and covered his hands with mine, holding on.

"Casey?" a soft voice called.

A shadow moved below me, standing behind a lantern that illuminated her face. Hana.

Phillips shook me. "Climb down or I'll kill you both."

"Okay," I said. "I'm going."

He let go of me, and I turned. Finding the first step with my foot, I started my descent.

Chapter Sixty-Five

Betz

Betz pulled into the gas station parking lot, taking a space near the door. Entering the store with Moody by his side, he found the clerk sitting on a stool at the cash register, her face resting on an open palm while she scrolled through her phone lying on the counter.

Both detectives held up their badges, eager to get to the reason they'd come. "The manager called," Betz said. "You have a video?"

The twenty-something slowly looked up from her phone and blinked at them. She'd shaped her blue hair into a mohawk. "Please tell me that look isn't coming back," Moody uttered under her breath.

Betz didn't care if the girl had just time-traveled from the eighties, as long as she provided a lead that would take him to Casey.

"Oh, yeah," she said. "Chuck said you could view it in the office."

"Which is where?" Betz asked.

With a head nod, she motioned toward the back of the store.

They passed aisles of chips and canned goods. Betz's stomach growled. He couldn't remember the last time he'd eaten. Not that he had much of an appetite, but he knew he needed to keep his strength up. He made a mental note to hit a drive-through when there was a break in the action.

Through the swinging doors, they discovered a storeroom that also served as an office. Someone had shoved a table against a wall. A safe butted up against it. A computer waited for them. A note lay on the keyboard with the login information. *Sorry, my kid had a soccer game. Help yourself.*

Betz pulled out the chair and sat down, bringing the machine to life with a shake of the mouse.

The manager had left the video frozen at the moment they needed to see. The stolen Bronco sat at the pump while a man pumped gas. The image was black and white and blurry. Betz felt like he'd lost his contacts again. Someone needed to clean the lens on the camera. He pushed the play button, and the video started.

The man, who matched the mugshot Betz had brought up of Donald Jackson, wore a ranger uniform.

"Is that Casey or the girl?" Moody asked, watching it over his shoulder.

"I can't find the zoom feature." He paused the film. A head rested against the window of the front passenger seat. He couldn't make out the face, but the hair was blonde. Just like Casey's.

"That's her," he said.

Moody pressed her lips into a thin line. "She's not moving."

Betz swallowed a giant lump of fear as he resumed the video. Phillips put the hose back and got in the vehicle before turning right out of the parking lot. Betz checked the timestamp. Just after eight p.m.

They could have been going to California. Or Mexico for all he knew.

Placing a call to Jasmine seemed like the next logical move, even if he had to eat some crow.

Chapter Sixty-Six

I made it to the bottom of the bunker with Phillips right behind me.

Hana rushed into my arms. "I knew you'd find me."

I didn't have the heart to point out the obvious. This wasn't a rescue. I'd just added to the victim count.

I gave her a hug, patted her on the back, and then pulled back. Looking around the space, I saw concrete walls covered in moss. A single dirty mattress lay shoved against the wall. A folding table was the only furniture in the room. On it sat a small kerosene lamp. It provided little light and cast ominous shadows onto the dirt floor. A bucket sat in the corner. I didn't want to think about what it was for, nor imagine using it.

Phillips stepped between us, backing Hana until she was against the wall. From above, I caught the fake ranger pointing a rifle our way. "Tell us where the money is, Hana. Or my friend blows your probation officer's head off."

She hugged herself, bringing my attention to the damp cold of the bunker. With wayward strands escaping her pigtails, she looked young, scared, and vulnerable. But she'd obviously put them off, not telling them about the bank card. I wondered if she even knew.

She struggled to breathe. If she didn't have access to an inhaler soon, they might not need a gun to kill her.

I had to think of something. If we told them there was no money, there was no reason for them to keep us alive. I had to offer them something.

"I...I..." Hana said. "I told you. The money is in a bank account. But I don't have access to it. I don't even know what bank they used."

From above, a sharp metallic clack sounded as Fake Ranger racked the slide of his weapon. I ducked as a single shot rang out, the bullet burrowing into the dirt floor. "Next time I won't miss," Fake Ranger called from above.

My ears felt like they were bleeding. "Okay," I said. "I know which bank. But I have bad news."

"Spill it, blondie," Phillips said.

"I found the bank card. I went to the ATM. Someone recently made a large withdrawal. There's nothing left."

"You're lying."

"No," I said. "I have the receipt."

I took the card out of my pocket and offered it to Phillips. He ripped it out of my hand, unfolded the transaction record, and sucked in a deep breath.

"She's telling the truth," he said to the fake ranger.

"Probably my mom," Hana said. "She had a gambling problem."

Phillips wadded the receipt into a ball and threw it on the ground. "Then we have no reason not to kill you both."

He pushed his gun against Hana's forehead.

"Wait," I said. "I have a plan."

Chapter Sixty-Seven

Betz

Jasmine made several calls. The police took every step to find the stolen Bronco. But the Valley of the Sun was huge with countless places to hide.

After leaving the gas station, Phillips could have traveled in any direction. Their best bet was that a red light or traffic camera would capture the vehicle and at least give them somewhere to start.

But so far, nothing.

"We're driving around in circles," Moody said. "We need to get something to eat. You're no good to anybody if you pass out from low blood sugar."

Food didn't appeal to him. But maybe he'd think clearer if he got some protein in his belly.

Seated across from each other in a booth at the nearest diner, Betz ordered a cup of black coffee, bacon, and eggs. He could hardly taste the food.

"You want to talk about it?" Moody said, scooping up a forkful of hash browns.

Betz pushed his plate away, the food mostly untouched. But he'd finished three cups of weak coffee. Leaning back, he rubbed the back of his neck. "About what?"

"Casey. You've still got it bad for her."

He groaned. "Doesn't matter how I feel. We aren't going to happen. Not again."

"Then you need to get over her. Move on."

"And how am I supposed to do that?" She was in the hands of madmen. He could lick his wounds later. He'd move mountains to find her if he only knew where to start.

Moody shrugged one shoulder. "I have to admit, looking at you now, it's hard to imagine. But around the department, you're considered quite the catch."

He ran a hand over the stubble on his chin and barked a laugh. "Your girlfriend tell you that?"

Moody rolled her eyes. "You're not her type. Mine either. But word on the street is that you're hot."

"People you deal with on the street are criminals, drug dealers. I'll take that compliment with a grain of salt."

"There's a new hire on patrol. She's pretty cool. Used to be a model."

Betz tapped his chest. "Not ready."

"I get it." Her cell buzzed, dancing across the table. She scooped it up. "Moody."

As she listened, her eyebrows shot up. "On it." She ended the call. Grabbing the bill the server had left on the table, she stood. "Jacob Stevens' sister Jill wants to talk."

Betz jumped to his feet. "Let's go."

* * *

Betz was out of the car before Moody could put it in park. He found Jill on a bench outside the restaurant. A cloud of smoke engulfed her, and she bounced her leg furiously.

She took a drag of her cigarette before reaching for a bag that sat between her feet. "My sister-in-law stayed with me the night before her death. She and my brother were having problems. Marilynn was drunk when she came over. She was a mess. She told me she'd ruined everything and that Jacob would kill her when he found out.

"I was sick of their drama, so I didn't ask questions. Anyway, she left some things in my guest room I was cleaning this morning, and I came across this bag. Thought it might be important."

She held it out, and Moody took it, slipping her arm through the handles so she could peer inside. She pulled out a well-worn day planner and flipped through it. "Have you looked at this?"

Jill nodded, took one last puff, and tossed her cigarette butt into the industrial ashtray at her side. "I'll save you the trouble. There's a bank transaction receipt in there. A few days before her death, Marilynn withdrew two-hundred-and-fifty thousand dollars from an account."

"That's a lot of money."

"Yeah. And there's a gas receipt from the casino that same day. I'm guessing she blew it all. I remember she asked me for a loan. Like I had that kind of money. Probably thought she could win it back.

"There's a journal in there, too. Her last entry talks about how they planned to stiff the guys she owed a gambling debt to. And that since she no longer had the down payment for the place in Mexico they were supposed to close on, Jacob would kill her."

Jill took a crinkled pack of cigarettes from her pocket and fished out another smoke. With shaking hands, she lit the end. "There's more. I noticed cross streets in Buckeye that she'd jotted down on the inside cover of her calendar. She took me to Buckeye once. Marilynn said she had an errand to run. She didn't feel safe going alone. I waited in the car. I remember being mad because she took so long. A few men came and went from the property. I knew she had a gambling problem, so it was pretty easy to figure out what they were up to.

"When she came out, I flat-out asked her if she was gambling again. She gave me a sob story about getting in over her head. She begged me not to tell Jacob. She was afraid he'd take Hana and leave her. Said she was one big win away from making things right.

"I thought I'd talked her into coming clean with my brother. That he would help her sort things out. But then, two days later, they were both dead. I didn't want to sully her memory. But with Hana missing...there's no reason to protect her anymore. She had an addiction and got involved with the wrong people."

Moody opened the planner and found the Buckeye coordinates. "This what you're talking about?"

Jill nodded. "I know the house was close to there."

Betz clung to this shot at good news. "If we take you to the area, do you think you'll recognize the house?"

"Maybe," Jill said, getting to her feet. "Let me tell my manager I have to leave."

Chapter Sixty-Eight

"You're of no use to us," Phillips said. "I'm not lugging your dead bodies out of here. Climb the ladder."

So his friend could shoot us at the top? "There's another way for you to get your money. Maybe not as much, but enough for you to make a fresh start somewhere else."

"And you have a suggestion?" He sounded bored.

Even though he had his gun pointed at my face, I stood strong. "I do. You let Hana go to show good faith. She needs her inhaler, or she won't make it much longer. Then you ask my husband for ransom money."

He cocked his head to the side. I could see the dollar signs clicking in his eyes. "Your husband has that kind of money?"

"He can get his hands on it."

At least I hoped so.

Phillips thought for a moment. He looked up at his partner, who kept his rifle aimed our way. Hana took a step closer to me, took my hand, and squeezed it. A silent thank you. I thought they wouldn't go for it, but I could see them calculating their choices. Kill us and get nothing, or take a chance and maybe line their pockets with enough money to get out of Dodge

He reached into his pocket and pulled out the phone he'd taken from me. He started to hand it to me, then pulled back. "If I suspect you're pulling bullshit, you're both dead."

"You're in the driver's seat," I said. "You have the guns."

He thought for a moment, then waved his weapon toward the ladder. "Climb up."

I looked at Hana. I didn't want to leave her.

"If your plan's going to work," Phillips said. "We can't call from here. They can ping your phone. Climb up."

I gave Hana's hand one last squeeze and scaled the ladder. Once we gathered at the top, they locked the trapdoor. Phillips took me roughly by the arm and led me through the house and outside to the Bronco. We drove out of the neighborhood and further into the desert. Once we were parked, Phillips took my phone out of his pocket and handed it to me. "Put it on speaker and make the call. If you try anything, my friend will make sure Hana joins her parents at the graveyard."

Chapter Sixty-Nine

Betz

With Jill Stevens buckled in the passenger seat, Moody drove up and down the residential streets in the older section of Buckeye Marilynn had recorded in her planner. "Anything look familiar? Anything at all?"

"I remember the area," Jill said. "But I was here months ago, and I don't see the house."

Betz's phone jingled in his pocket. Casey's ringtone. Hope filled his heart, but then turned to dread. Shit was about to get real.

He had a hard time pulling the device from the back pocket of his jeans in the cramped space, but he extracted it by the fourth ring. "Casey?" he asked, hopeful. Maybe, just maybe, she'd managed to escape.

"Betz?" Her voice was strained, fading his hope. "I've got a situation."

He snapped his fingers to silence the women in the car. When they looked back at him, he put his finger to his lips. "Are you hurt? Are you safe?"

"I'm not hurt," she said. "But I need you to do something."

"Are you with Phillips and Donald Jackson?"

"Phillips is here, and you're on speakerphone. He's agreed to let Hana go if you pay a ransom. Then he'll release me, too." Her voice caught at the last part, and he knew she feared that might not happen.

There was a rustling, and a deeper voice came on the line. "Listen up," Phillips said. "I want fifty K. Small bills. You have until noon to deliver, or your wife takes a bullet to her forehead. Understand?"

"Where?" Betz said. "Where do I drop the money?"

"You'll get a call," Phillips said. "Get the money together. That's all you have to worry about for now."

Before Betz could ask about Hana's release, the line went dead.

***

Betz slowly lowered the phone to his lap. Casey knew he wasn't flush with cash. He had a cushion, sure, but not fifty grand sitting in the bank. She was buying them time. Time for him to figure out some way to end this with no loss of life. Until he figured that out, he needed to gather as much cash as he could. He didn't have that kind of money, but his sister did.

"Pull over," he said to Moody.

She stopped in front of a ranch set far back from the road.

Betz filled them in on Phillips' demands, then placed a call to his sister. When she answered, her voice was thick with sleep.

"I heard from her," he said.

"Who? Casey?"

"And Phillips."

"Is she okay?"

"Seems to be. He's demanding a ransom. I need money."

"The department doesn't—"

"I'm not asking the department; I'm asking my sister."

She was silent for a moment, and then said, "How much?"

"Thirty K. I can come up with the rest."

"How long do we have?"

Betz checked his watch, which had died a long time ago. "Till noon."

"It was her cell they called from?"

"Yes."

"I'll see if I can get it pinged. I'll get back to you ASAP."

"Thanks."

A moment of silence stretched between them. "Betz, I'm sorry. I really hope this ends well."

The crack in her voice had him believing she actually meant it.

Chapter Seventy

Back at the house, Phillips shoved me roughly across the backyard. "You need to let Hana go," I said. "That was the deal."

As long as Hana couldn't lead police to the property, she was no threat to him. Identifying him didn't matter. Everyone knew he was the one responsible for the plethora of crimes he'd committed. He and Donald Jackson, the fake ranger. They didn't need to kill us. That didn't mean they wouldn't. Seemed like it was sport to them.

Jackson waited in a camp chair in the yard. When he saw us, he got to his feet. "I hope you asked for enough money," he said.

"Fifty grand," Phillips said.

Jackson snorted. "That's not enough. That's twenty-five K each. You're a stupid fuck."

Phillips lifted his gun and pointed it Jackson's way. He pulled the trigger so casually, I almost thought I'd imagined it. But my ringing ears confirmed the truth. Jackson took the bullet in the chest and went down before he knew what hit him. "You're right," Phillips said. "Not enough to share."

"Keep walking," he said to me, shoving me forward.

At the trapdoor, he pulled it open and pointed to the ladder. "Go."

"Not until you release Hana."

He sighed. "Have I told you that you're a pain in the ass?"

"You have."

"Climb down. I'll throw you a blindfold. Put it on her and make her climb up."

Once she was out of my sight, I'd have no way of knowing if he kept our deal. And if he'd so easily killed his partner, the slightest irritation would make him go off again. But if he wanted Betz to deliver the money, he'd have to give him Hana. I didn't see any way I could ensure things would go as planned. I had to have a little faith. I turned around and felt for the first step of the ladder with my foot. "Betz will want confirmation Hana is safe before he turns over the money. Then you'll need to release me, too."

"I know how ransom works. Get your ass down there."

It felt like I was getting into my own grave, but I climbed down the ladder. Phillips tossed me a bandana. I caught it and turned to face Hana. "I'm sorry, but I have to put this on you. He's going to release you."

"What…about…you?" she asked, barely able to talk, her breathing was so labored. She'd gotten worse since I'd left. "What's gonna happen to you?"

"I'll be fine," I said. But the lie rang hollow in my ears.

She pulled me into a hug. "Thank you for helping me."

How could I not? She needed medicine. She didn't have much time. I gave her a squeeze.

"I don't have all day," Phillips called from above.

Folding the bandana into a blindfold, I tied it around Hana's head, blocking her vision. Then I led her to the ladder, placed her hands on it, and nudged her to make the climb.

I watched Phillips pull her onto the ground, and then the trapdoor fell shut, and the lock clicked into place.

A minute later, the lamp went out, plunging me into darkness, and I wondered if anyone would ever come back for me.

Chapter Seventy-One

Betz

Betz's phone chimed in his pocket. He pulled it out, and his favorite photo of Casey popped onto the screen. They'd been at the beach in Coronado, her face sun-kissed and her bikini strap falling off her shoulder as she flashed a beaming smile at the camera. Happier times.

It was ten a.m. They'd spent all night looking for the house Jill had been to with her sister-in-law, with no luck. Then he got the money. Now it was time to get instructions.

"Casey?"

"She can't come to the phone right now," a male voice said with a chuckle. "You got the money?"

Betz patted the bag between his feet. "I do."

"There's a neighborhood where construction was started, but then the builder went under." He gave Betz the cross streets. "There's an old playground there. Leave the money by the slide."

"Gotta release the girl first."

"You'll find her there. My partner will be with your wife. After I get the money, ensure I haven't been followed, and count it, I'll give him the okay to release her. Anything goes wrong, she dies. Be there at noon. Not a minute before, not a minute after. And come alone. If I smell cops, they both die." Before Betz could respond, Phillips ended the call.

"Shit." Betz lowered his phone onto his lap and rubbed the back of his neck. "I'm gonna have to drop you ladies off. I need to find this place or at least get close to it."

"Leave us at the Buckeye police station," Moody said. "While you do the drop, we'll keep looking for the house."

Chapter Seventy-Two

Betz

After dropping Moody and Jill Stevens at the Buckeye police station, Betz drove as close to the deserted playground as he dared, keeping in mind Phillips' order not to be there a minute before noon, not a minute after.

He parked in a neighborhood down the road from the abandoned master-planned community. From his position, he could see the development and the mountains in the distance beyond it. Homes in various stages of completion made up what had become a ghost town. His life savings, mixed with a good portion of his sister's, sat in a bag on the passenger's seat.

The houses were enormous, some collapsing in on themselves, victims of weather, time, and vandals.

It gave off a dystopian vibe, which added to his unsettled mood.

Betz checked the time on his phone. 11:45. Too soon to make the drop.

Phillips didn't need to keep his end of the bargain. Betz tried not to think about that. Casey was their ticket to getting enough money to go on the run. He didn't know if they also got whatever caused them to go after Hana in the first place. What started this whole domino game?

They had already killed several people. The death penalty would be on the table. Committing more crime wouldn't change that. They had nothing left to lose. If Phillips didn't make it back with the money, what would Jackson do to Casey? He didn't want to think about that.

They had Betz by the balls. There was a tracker hidden, sewn into the bag that Phillips shouldn't be able to find. Agents stationed nearby monitored the device. That would hopefully lead them to Casey.

11:47

It would only take a minute, maybe two, to drive to the chosen place. He had to wait at least ten more minutes. Enough time to lose his mind.

He couldn't imagine life without Casey. Even if they'd never be a couple again, he needed to know she was out there. Safe. Happy. Even if they didn't spend time together. Even if she was going to become a mother to another man's child. A man he could never compete with. Especially since he was probably dead.

11:50

When this was over. Once Casey was safe. He needed to find a path forward. He'd been stuck for three years. Hope came and went, but the possibility that things could work out between them was always there. Dangling. Now it was gone. He didn't want to be a bitter old man who lived with his sister. Whose job was his whole life.

Things needed to change.

11:56

He started the Interceptor and messaged Moody. *I'm going in.*

Slowly, he rolled toward the deserted neighborhood.

Once inside the community, the abandoned houses became even more ghostly. Shattered windows and missing doors marked each weathered structure he passed. Most of the homes were near completion when, for whatever reason, the builder pulled the plug on the project. Betz imagined looters had taken whatever they could, even punching through walls for the copper wiring. The area was a thieves' paradise.

He turned down the next street. In the distance, he spotted an overgrown golf course and the shell of an unfinished community center. To the right sat a playground, almost indistinguishable, buried in the vegetation that grew wild. A row of swings had a plastic slide attached.

12:00 p.m.

Betz pulled into the lot and put the SUV into park.

Stepping out of his vehicle, he grabbed the duffel bag and listened for a moment.

In the distance, a coyote howled. Wind rustled the leaves on the overgrown bushes. Nothing else.

On high alert and constantly scanning the horizon, he took careful steps toward the slide. Next to it was a sandbox. In it lay a young girl. Betz tossed the money bag so that it landed against the slide, then ran to the sandbox.

The girl was curled up in a ball. Gray smudges marred her puffy white coat. Dirty blonde hair was a tangled mess. Betz recognized her from the Amber Alert. Hana Stevens.

He leaned over her, brushed strands of hair away from her neck, and felt for a pulse. There was one, although it was weak.

Knowing Phillips was watching him, most likely from one of the houses, he scooped Hana into his arms and ran for the Interceptor. Lying her on the backseat, he put the vehicle in drive and asked his GPS to guide him to the nearest hospital.

Chapter Seventy-Three

Betz

Moody was pacing the hall when Betz emerged from the room where hospital staff tended to Hana. "We found it," she said. "Jill remembered the house sat far back from the road. She knew there were citrus trees, but didn't remember that they blocked the view of the house from the street. We didn't want to mess with Phillip's demands, so we didn't approach, but undercovers are surveilling the property. No one has come or gone."

Betz checked his phone. No messages, no incoming calls. How long was he supposed to wait to hear from Phillips?

"And the tracker on the money bag?"

"Hasn't moved."

Betz felt sick. "He didn't pick it up?"

Then his phone rang, and Casey's smiling face popped up on the screen. Was Phillips going to keep his word?

He answered. "Betz."

"Thanks for the moola," Phillips said with a chuckle.

"Where's my wife?"

"Oh yeah, about that," he said in a sinister tone. "I know you must have traps. I took the money and left the bag because I suspected a tracker was attached. I didn't want to take the time to linger in town. And I'm not gonna bring her to you. She's already as good as dead and buried. You'll never find her. Wouldn't waste my time if I were you."

He ended the call.

Betz threw his phone at the wall. Pounding both fists against his forehead, he paced. Phillips had played him. Had taken the money and skipped town. He never intended to keep his promise. What was one more death?

But maybe, just maybe, there was a chance. "Take me there. Take me to the house," he said to Moody.

Moody scooped Betz's phone off the floor and followed him out the door.

* * *

On the way, he received a call from Jasmine.

"We pinged Casey's phone outside Tonopah. Have officers responding."

Phillips had used it to call him, to taunt him. That didn't mean she was with him. She was no longer a pawn in their game.

Betz fought to keep it together when they arrived at the house. Just like Jill said, the house sat far back from the road, hidden behind rows of unkempt citrus trees. Rotten fruit lay on the ground.

Stopping in the driveway, Betz jumped out of the Interceptor before Moody could shut the engine off. Gun drawn, he entered the house and went from room to room, clearing it. Since it was empty, it didn't take long. Moody met him in the backyard.

Next to the firepit was an overturned camp chair. Beside that, a body.

"Donald Jackson," Moody said. "Looks like there was trouble in paradise."

"But where the fuck is Casey?" he said.

Moody holstered her gun. "I'm sorry."

Betz kicked a deflated soccer ball lying on the ground. "Fuck, fuck, double fuck." He walked in circles, rubbing the back of his neck. "Okay, let's think. Phillips had me make the drop at an abandoned residential development. This house is vacant. He has a thing for deserted properties."

He patted his pockets, took out his phone, and placed another call to Jasmine.

"We found her phone," she said in greeting. "Smashed on the side of I-10."

"Never mind that," he said. "I need a team out here. We need to search that abandoned neighborhood inch by inch."

"On it," she said. "I'll meet you there."

***

With the Buckeye police handling Donald Jackson's body, Betz and Moody headed to the derelict master-planned community. "Any word on Hana's condition? She might be able to tell us something."

"She's still unconscious. Apparently, she had a severe asthma attack, and it has affected her heart."

"Jesus," he said. "She's so young."

"They'll call me if there's a change," Moody assured him.

"We'll start with the clubhouse," he said.

Chapter Seventy-Four

Alone in a dark hole in the ground, I felt claustrophobic, and a tightness squeezed my chest. I had to get out of here. Feeling my way across the room, I walked like Frankenstein so I wouldn't crash into a wall and knock myself out.

Feeling the cool concrete, I moved to the right, where I thought the ladder would be. When I hit another wall, I realized it was in the other direction. I reversed, running my fingers over the moss-covered cement.

Finding the ladder, I carefully climbed it, stopping when my head hit the trap door. Shoving it with both hands, and then my shoulder, did nothing to budge the thing. Someone had latched the door from the outside. Phillips wouldn't have been so stupid as to leave it open for me. But I had to try.

Now, I was out of ideas.

I took the climb back down slowly, relieved when my foot hit the dirt floor. Damp and cold, I wondered if I'd freeze to death before I withered away from starvation. Both scenarios ended the same way. Death.

Feeling each careful step, by swooping my foot in front of me, I slowly made my way across the space to the mattress on the floor. I sat down and crossed my legs. I felt so scared, so alone, all I could do was cry.

Laying my hands on my stomach, I closed my eyes and said, "I'm sorry, little one. I've already let you down. I'm so sorry."

A sob caught in my throat, choking me as I thought about a future I'd never know. I imagined what life might look like as a single mother. I was probably romanticizing it, picturing an episode of The Gilmore Girls—a daughter who'd become my best friend. More likely, I'd be sleep-deprived and clueless about all things parenting. How could I even afford daycare on a government salary?

As dark as those thoughts were, they kept me from panicking about my current situation. But then I opened my eyes and realized I couldn't see a damn thing, and reality slapped me in the face.

Something moved across my shoe. I screamed, jumping to my feet. The noise I'd made echoed back at me as if a laughing psychopath had entered the room.

A rat? A snake? *Please don't let it be a snake.*

I moved across the room until I collided with the table. The useless kerosene lamp fell to the floor with a thud. I climbed onto the table, pulling my legs up and hugging my knees to my chest.

I missed Marcus. He'd been my sidekick when I was in tight spots before. The thought that I'd never see him again gripped my heart so tightly, I could barely breathe. His mother and sister must have been told he was missing by now. I didn't know them, but they were special to him. He'd selflessly put his life in danger for his sister once. And then, for me.

He'd seemed invincible. He got knocked down a lot, sure, but he always got back up. But this time was different. Mother Nature had done to him what no man could.

Resting my head on my knees, I tried to insert Marcus into my dream of what my future might have been. I wanted to have those memories, even if they were false.

But I couldn't even picture him.

A thump on the trapdoor startled me, dragging me from my dark thoughts. I sat up straighter, straining to hear. Two more bangs, then nothing.

"Help!" I jumped off the table. "Help down here!"

I found the ladder, climbed it again, and banged on the trapdoor. Yelling. But there were no more sounds. If they'd come looking for me, somehow found the house, they'd never think to look in the ground.

Chapter Seventy-Five

Betz

Hours passed, and they had nothing to show for it. Maybe he'd been wrong. Maybe Casey was nowhere near the abandoned neighborhood. Officers from several jurisdictions combed the area. All coming up empty. Betz knew he had to think outside the box, but his thoughts were a jumbled mess. He could barely focus.

He'd started the search like a madman, running from building to building, even checking inside the damaged walls of the vacant structures. Ripping away sheetrock with his bare hands. But as time passed, the enthusiasm from the search party waned. Even Betz was losing steam.

Jasmine had arrived hours ago and managed the operation. He'd pretty much avoided her. Still mad, sure, but mostly he couldn't stand the look of pity on her face.

Eventually, Moody came to him, laying a caring hand on his shoulder. "She's not here. I'm sorry."

He clicked off the flashlight he was holding. "What are we missing?"

"I don't know. But we're not doing any good here. Lieutenant Faulk is sending people away. She thinks we'll do more good checking cameras around town. Boots on the ground."

She was right. This was a waste of resources. A waste of time.

But if he didn't have something to do, he'd fall apart.

Shoulders sagging, head down, he followed Moody out of the clubhouse.

The place he'd started and ended the search.

Jasmine stood by her car. She waved him over.

With a deep breath, he went to face the music. But he knew one thing. If she was going to throw in the towel, he'd lose his shit.

"I've got some news," she said. "They've got Phillips in a standoff."

"Where?"

"The Walmart parking lot. I—"

But Betz didn't wait for her to finish her thought.

* * *

Betz pulled up behind five police vehicles surrounding a parked Tacoma pickup. Jumping out of the Interceptor, he ran toward the group of his colleagues, who had their guns aimed at the truck.

A middle-aged man wearing a Buckeye Police uniform with sergeant stripes on his sleeve held up a hand to stop him. "He has a hostage."

His heart soared. "Casey?"

"Don't have an ID. But it's a twenty-something guy."

Hope shriveled and died. "We need to keep Phillips alive. He knows where my...where Casey is."

The sergeant nodded. "I'm aware. We're trying to get him to surrender."

But then, out of his peripheral vision, Betz saw Phillips step out of the truck, turn, and point his weapon at the posse of officers aiming back at him. "No!" Betz yelled. But he knew even before the shots rang out that the only outcome of pointing a weapon at a bunch of police officers was suicide by cop.

The explosion of five Glocks being emptied had Betz ducking and covering his ears. As soon as the last shot sounded, he rushed forward, ignoring the calls for him to stop. Dropping to his knees in front of Phillips, Betz stared down into soulless eyes.

"Where is she?"

A smirk spread on the dying man's face. It stayed there even as blood bubbled out of his mouth. As the life drained from his eyes, he took the details of his last dreadful deed with him.

Chapter Seventy-Six

Betz

Betz staggered back to the Interceptor, climbed into the driver's seat, tilted his head back and blew out a long breath. There had to be something he could do. Somewhere else to look. But his best hope of finding Casey was lying on the ground, being declared dead by the paramedics who had been cleared to enter the scene.

"I hope he rots in hell," Betz said when Moody climbed into the seat beside him.

"He will," she said. "Hell was designed for guys like him. But get your head back in the game. I've got some news. Hana Stevens is awake."

Betz opened his eyes and turned to look at her. "Has anyone questioned her?" He was almost afraid to ask. She really was his last hope.

"Jasmine is with her. She wants you to FaceTime her."

Betz reached into his pocket for his phone. His sister looked distorted on his fractured screen, but he could still make out her spiky blonde hair and the hospital bed behind her. "Please tell me you have good news," he said.

"That's what I have," she said. "Hana said Phillips held them in an underground bunker. We haven't thought to look under the ground."

"The first vacant house," he said, with a breath of relief.

They blindfolded her, but she remembers walking through a house to the backyard after they took her. And she remembers the scent of oranges."

"Oh, thank God," Betz said.

"Remember, a few months ago, we used ground penetrating radar to find those weapons Diablo had buried in the desert? It should work here. I'll swing by and pick up the equipment and meet you at the house."

Betz started the SUV. "I'm headed there now. And Jasmine, this has to work."

"It will, brother. I can feel it." And she actually seemed to mean it. He wasn't sure if she just wanted to put an end to his suffering or if she had a soft spot for Casey after all.

Chapter Seventy-Seven

I was giving in to the dark, cold space. My throat ached from screaming. First for help, and then at my impossible situation. I would die down here.

The life inside me was giving up, too. I could feel it. Cramps had me doubled over, wincing in pain. First, I'd lose the baby, and then myself. My thoughts drifted to my father, to Kate, then Hope and Joy. To Betz. They'd never know what happened to me. No closure. My spirit would float between two worlds. Just like Marcus.

It would destroy them all.

So much destruction, all because of two greedy, heartless men.

And the child inside me never had a chance. Doomed. Just like my relationships with Marcus and Betz.

I lay on the table in the fetal position. My cheek flat against the hard surface.

I had no idea how long I'd been in the hole. It could have been hours or days.

When a sound pierced the quiet, I thought I was hallucinating. I had to quiet my sobs so I could hear.

A scraping sound, then footsteps against the trapdoor.

Pushing myself up on my elbows, I strained to hear. "Help," I croaked.

Silence.

It **was** a hallucination. I lowered my head back onto the table.

But then the bolt turned, the door lifted, and I was bathed in light. I rolled onto my back and looked up at the entrance. Betz's face appeared. "She's here," he yelled.

The next thing I knew, I was in his arms being carried across the room.

255

Chapter Seventy-Eight

I woke in a strange place, with a heated blanket draped over me. A machine next to me beeped, and tape secured a needle to my forearm. Betz sat at my bedside, head bowed as he held my hand. He let go and jumped to his feet when I cleared my throat.

"Casey." He lovingly brushed the hair from my brow. "Thank God you're awake."

"Where am I?"

"The ED," he said. "You're safe."

My hand settled on my belly. "Did I? Did I lose—"

"The baby," he said. "No. The baby is fine. Just a little spotting, according to the nurse. Nothing to worry about."

"You knew?"

He patted my hand. "I saw the discharge summary from your doctor. Didn't mean to invade your privacy, but I was looking for anything that might help me find you."

I wiggled up into a sitting position, and he helped me by adjusting the bed. "It's okay," I said. "I didn't know how to break the news to you."

He shoved his hands in his pockets and looked at the floor. "Marcus, he the father?"

I bit my lip, then nodded.

"So, there's no chance for us," he said, not meeting my eyes.

The forlorn look on his face nearly broke me. "I'm sorry. Sorry about how confused I've been. It hasn't been fair to anyone. But if Marcus is…well, if he's really gone…I can't just carry on like he was never here."

Betz blew out a long breath. "I know. I thought I'd lost you, and that would have killed me. I understand how hard not knowing must be. I'm just glad that physically, you're going to be okay. When I was searching for you, that was all I'd ask for. I made a deal with the guy upstairs. If you came out of this alive, I'd accept whatever happened. Even if there is no us. Kind of puts things in perspective."

We fell silent as his words sank in. There was nothing left to say. Not about us. But there was still something I needed to know. "Hana. Is she okay?"

He nodded. "She's down the hall in her own room. She's the one who let us know about the bunker. She's the reason we found you."

"I'll have to thank her."

"There will be plenty of time for that."

"And Phillips?"

Betz crossed his arms. "Dead. He was a bookie. Seems he went after Hana's parents when her mom didn't fulfill a gambling debt. Her husband, Jacob, did everything he could to set things right. He embezzled money from the restaurant and laundered it through a gym he started. But his wife found the money and lost it all. We have a video of her at the casino. Phillips went after them when he learned they had no intention of paying him back. He killed them, thinking the money was safe. He thought Hana could lead him to it."

"But the money was gone," I said. "That's why I convinced him to ask for a ransom. I thought that was our only chance of making it out of this alive. I hoped it would give you a trail to follow."

"If you hadn't thought of that," Betz said. "I think he would have killed you and Hana. He knew he was on borrowed time, since he was already on the run for several murders. Your quick thinking saved Hana's life."

So why did I still feel like crap?

"Anyway," Betz said, squeezing my hand and then letting go. "The gang's all here. Your dad, Kate, Hope, and Joy. They're in the waiting room, champing at the bit to see you. I begged for a few minutes alone with you, but they deserve to know you're awake."

I smoothed my blanket and ran a hand over my hair. "Okay, send them in."

He started for the door.

"Betz," I called after him.

He stopped and turned to face me.

"Thank you. You never gave up on me. I know I'm not easy to love."

He gave a little laugh. "Loving you is easy. Moving on will be the trick." With a wink, he left the room. Maybe we'd never be a couple again, but I knew I could always depend on him just the same.

Chapter Seventy-Nine

Betz

With Casey in the company of her family, Betz felt like a fifth wheel. He no longer belonged there. The doctor had signed the discharge papers, and her family waited for a wheelchair so they could take her home.

Walking out to the Interceptor, he found Moody and Jasmine in animated conversation. There was excitement in the air. They turned to look at him with questions in their eyes.

"She's going to be okay," he said.

He wanted to go home, eat something, shower, and collapse into bed. He planned to sleep for a week. But Jasmine had a request that would derail that plan. "There's one last thing you need to do," she said.

"Whatever it is, find somebody else."

"I think you'll want to handle it," Jasmine said. "Moody will drive you. Just get in and enjoy the ride. You can catch a nap if you want. We're headed to the other side of town."

* * *

Moody wouldn't elaborate as she followed Jasmine across the county. Betz was able to nod off. When she pulled into a parking spot, his chin hit his chest. He struggled to come around. "Where are we?"

"Tempe Medical Center. There's a surprise for you in the lobby." She handed him the keys. "You can take the car after. Figured you should be the one to share the good news."

Bewildered, he got out and stood outside the door.

Jasmine pulled up, and Moody headed toward her car.

"Where are you going?" he called out to her.

"Home," she said, not breaking her stride. "I'm going to spend the weekend with my girlfriend. I'll see you on Monday. They'll be other cases waiting for us, but for now, somebody else can handle them."

He gave her a mock salute and watched her get in the car with Jasmine. Both women waved at him as they pulled away.

Betz looked to the hospital, wondering what loose end he needed to tie up. Inside, he scanned the lobby. It was full of people waiting to be seen. Confusion moved to clarity as he spotted what he now understood he'd come there for. Clapping his hands in front of him. He threw back his head and laughed.

Chapter Eighty

Back at my dad's house, I showered and then devoured the pancakes and bacon Millie had prepared for me. Mindful of the child inside me, I passed on the Diet Coke and opted for a glass of juice. It was going to be a long pregnancy.

My family sat at the table with me, their love spilling out in words, hugs, and laughter. They were ecstatic about the news of growing our family. They offered support, promising to be there for me every step of the way.

Eventually, I excused myself. Yawning, I shuffled out of the room. A rap on the door startled me as I walked past the entryway.

"I'll get it." I pulled Felony back by the collar as I opened the door.

He stood on the front porch. The light behind him glowed, making him seem like an apparition. Did I even dare to imagine he was real?

I let go of Felony's collar and brought my hands to my face. Tears splashed down my cheeks.

"Hey, Sunshine," he said, his voice hoarse.

He was dirty, bearded, and his hair was wild and loose. But it was him. That was all that mattered.

"Marcus," I whispered, stepping into his arms.

I squeezed him against me, breathing him in. "But how?"

He pulled me tighter. "The river spat me out. It took me a few days, but I found my way to the road. I heard that they found you. I wasn't going to give up—"

I stroked his back. "I know."

From over Marcus' shoulder, I caught sight of Betz sitting in the driver's seat of the Interceptor. He gave a little wave and a smile.

I rested my head on Marcus's shoulder and mouthed "thank you" to Betz as he pulled away. He'd given me the greatest gift. Selflessly.

As he drove off, I held onto Marcus a little tighter. Maybe I could have it all.

Acknowledgments

There are many who encouraged me and offered critiques and advice on my journey to publication. First off, I'd like to thank Mary Keliikoa, Harriette Sackler and Dawn Ius for being early readers of this book and providing valuable feedback. And to my writer's group, Laurie Cutter, Keli Esser, and Rod Langer, for keeping me on task, and also my women's fiction group. Good friends Deneen Bertucci and Jennifer Vaughan have also offered feedback, reading an early draft. And to Judy Pearson, who always has my back. Special thanks to my daughter, Brittany Goyette, for pointing out the lines that made Casey sound old like me so I wouldn't embarrass myself and for brainstorming plot problems. And to all the other people who have supported me on this incredible journey, even if it was just listening to me talk endlessly about writing and my dream of seeing Casey's story in print. You know who you are!

To Harriette Sackler, who believed in this series and signed me with Level Best Books, and to Gwyn Jordan, Shawn Reilly Simmons and the people behind the scenes for helping me elevate this series to its best version.

Bravo to Michael Verdun for designing another fabulous cover.

The support I've received for *Obey All Laws* and *Early Termination*, from coworkers, friends—old and new, and book clubs continues to be one of the best outcomes to being published. The writing community and local bookstores have also been fabulous. And my readers! Thank you for all the wonderful reviews and feedback. You are what it's all about!

Without the support of my family, especially my husband Paul Hummel, daughter Brittany Goyette, son-in-law, Michael Verdun, and my mother, Beverly Schmidt, and Carole and Larry Willson, I never would have seen Casey's adventures in print. You have always had faith in me, even when I didn't have it in myself. I love you all. Thank you for understanding why I'm always on my laptop and for riding this wild wave with me.

About the Author

Cindy Goyette is a former probation officer who had a front-row seat to the criminal justice system. She kept her sanity by finding humor in most situations. A mix of these things helped her create The Probation Case Files Mystery Series. Book one, *Obey All Laws,* won a Public Safety Writer's Association award, and it has been a finalist for Lefty and Silver Falchion Awards. Book two: *Early Termination* released in 2025. She also authors The Wiggle Butt Manor Mystery series. *Diamond In the Ruff* is book one, with book two, *Dashing Through the Show*, releasing summer of 2026. After spending over twenty years in Arizona, Cindy lives in Washington state with her husband and two Cocker Spaniels.

AUTHOR WEBSITE:

https://ccgoyette.com

SOCIAL MEDIA HANDLES:

https://www.instagram.com/cindy.goyette/

https://www.facebook.com/profile.php?id=100077005287995, https://x.com/cindy_ccgoyette

https://bsky.app/profile/cindygoyetteauthor.bsky.social

Also by Cindy Goyette

Obey All Laws

Early Termination

Diamond In the Ruff